W9-BZV-166

Island Odyssey

Cheryl Blaydon

North
Country
Press

Copyright © 2012 by Cheryl Blaydon

All rights reserved. No part of this book may be reproduced or transmitted in any form or by any means without written permission of the author.

Cover art by Cheryl Blaydon

Author photo by Melanie Howe

ISBN 978-0-945980-01-8

Library of Congress Control Number: 2012944808

The characters, incidents, and dialogue are drawn mostly from the author's imagination, with one exception—the major hurricanes that do occur.

North Country Press

Unity, Maine

For Denise

ACKNOWLEDGEMENTS

I am grateful to many people for the creation of this book: My wonderful friends, some who lived the experiences and some who dream it. To those who were given chapters to read as the novel grew and returned graceful and accurate critiques. To Patricia Newell and Jeanne Hunter Lachance, my North Country Press family, for their guidance and enthusiasm during the entire process.

PROLOGUE

A small void still exists within my soul, an emptiness that draws me back to the water's edge, much like an addict seeking a fix, even here in this coastal corner of Maine. It is more than loneliness—it is a bond I've always sought, strong and unbreakable like these solid forms I now take refuge upon.

I, Lily Harmon, boldly attest that I've become the consummate witness to an ever-changing sea; have been repeatedly pulled by its powerful magnetic force. I can say this to myself with renewed confidence, because it has again taken a firm grip on my soul. It too has daily patterns: it swirls and spouts beneath the huge granite showing off its might and lies peacefully beside the submerged black bulk that looks ominous until the early angles of light cause the glint of sun on stone, a sparkle of diamonds in the rough. There are no reminders here of growing up inland without so much as a glimpse of the sea, only whispers of another time. It is in these whispers that I find the most comfort and not just a little dose of mystery nudging at the periphery of thought. I've also come to appreciate all the sounds and how they connect me to the water, and I've learned there has been a price to pay.

The blanket of warmth that wraps St. Margeaux, a small isle set in a long chain known as the Antilles, remains in distinct contrast because of these cool mornings even though it is the beginning of summer. The weather here changes often and while only a small thing, I'm glad I remembered the hooded sweater before leaving the rental cottage this morning, not only to ward off the chill for my short walk to the sea but to temper my curls from spring boarding in the last of the foggy dampness. The little cottage clumsily adorned with green painted shutters, aging shingles and pretty window boxes, gave me the first whiff of ocean the moment I opened the door—a heady bouquet no matter the weather. All of this would become a more natural fit than once imagined, and softened the walk on this new path in a strange place.

When I sit out here my heart lightens and again I am a child of the universe, and as always, I ponder the vast dimension of the undersea world, believing fervently the way it must have been envisioned by the magnificent sperm whale, its oversized head casing orienting its natural migration through the oceans of the planet. Together in our dream-like place, Eddie and I shared rare and incredible opportunities during our voyages, sighting the many creatures that roam there, and they have guided my spirit in much the way they would guide our boat in the blue depth, dark as night.

I remember with childish glee falling in love with dolphins for the first time, but the greatest passion was for the whales that made their appearances along the route to the Anegada Passage, surprise escorts for the easy journey. I was eager to know more about them all and their soundings and echoes that bounced off the cavernous valley below creating a song of their making, and all that I discovered reinforced my belief in this cetacean world through every breath of salty air floating on the atmosphere. Even here, it again touches my skin, finds its way into my nostrils, and blankets my hair like a blessing from above.

And while always aware of my aloneness, today brings an overwhelming sense of it that surpasses all else. I never believed that I would again cross the expanse of time and distance to be a silent voyeur to yet another changing seascape, but this special place lifts some of that residual sadness. Admittedly, I've tried to conjure up a friendship with these northern waves that also tug at my heart, as a salve to soften that aloneness, and find myself questioning aloud their origins as though meeting someone from a foreign land. Then, of course, I chide myself at an imagined response in their sighing presence, as they peacefully tumble pell-mell, gently closing in. Some days they have a boldness and louder threatening gesture as their foamy might hurls toward the rocks that I might take as warning I've gotten too close to the edge and possibly their deepest secrets.

The ocean, either roaring in tumultuous activity or softly gliding forth like a virginal bride in white lace, had me in its grasp from the beginning and I treat it with reverence, respect, a healthy dose of fear, even a balm to soothe and heal. Perhaps that is why this morning, in need of more healing, my mind has wandered farther back to another time, and I'm reminded of the pearls. They represent another attachment between Eddie and me and the sea. They were his gift, and often lay in the folds of my clothing, circling my neck, their radiating warmth against the soft flesh ministering my thoughts.

This free association that also reminds of another pearl, Pearl Buck, and the strength and wisdom of my childhood heroine, Peony, all discovered in the pages of her books. Crazy, convoluted thoughts...peonies of my childhood...nose pressed to the flowers taking in the sweet perfume. There are peonies here, planted outside the back door of the cottage. I cut two of the soft pillows of light pink and placed them in a slim vase to rest atop my Pearl Buck novels that rest atop the stories of the sea that are all watched over by the photo of Eddie standing at the bow of the *Wanderer*.

It all seems a lifetime ago, but today, the 23rd of June, early in the statistical hurricane tracking charts, is meant solely for this type of contemplation. This earmarked anniversary, this burdensome season, exists here too in this colder climate but lacks the enticing warm water required to build their optimal strength. However, each warning of a named storm still brings reminders of what the wrath of winds building over the African coast could do to anything that challenged its path. It might be as fickle and without substance as a flirtatious lover, falling apart before it reaches the heated borders of the Caribbean Sea. Or it could turn into an angry raging wind that pummels forward with all its might, building strength and momentum, invading those rising temperatures until it finds something tangible to slake its thirst.

Instinctively I rub the pearls between my fingertips as a talisman, guarding the tears against those remembered winds and everything that happened because of them. The onshore breeze is picking up and I feel the nipping spray as if on cue. Grabbing for the complicated binoculars adjusted as best I can before it forces my retreat, I'm automatically steeling myself for the return of that now most intimate feeling—hope.

Chapter One

Eddie's hammer is clashing against the intermittent gusts of wind now begun in earnest as if doing battle but without much hope of winning. This sound has been resonating loudly everywhere, a clattering of anything that needs fastening. Even at my office on the other side of the island that normally exudes serenity, there was no escape.

I had forgotten some important documents and gone to collect them before it was too late and was nearly sorry I'd done so because it was no ordinary day. I walked through the empty lobby and I immediately longed for the scene normally witnessed. The one with tourists idling their way to the many offerings presented at check-in, ones shown in the glossy brochures I knew they'd run their fingers over again and again in planning their trip. Then, having shed the hustle and bustle of their stateside existence in exchange for bikinis and swim trunks and slathered in suntan oil, been anxious to match the island pace for as long as possible.

It had always been pure pleasure to watch them enjoying their newfound freedom, whether from a distance through my office window or whenever we crossed paths as I moved around the grounds of my workday habitat. And my ability to share in their freedom through these interactions has made being on this island so very special.

But instead of the pounding echoing throughout, there should have been the softer sounds, absent for a while now, of flip-flops and sandals against the cool tile floors, their owners always anxious to trade pleasantries about the resort, allowing me a temporary break from the myriad duties of the day. The more outgoing tourists were openly inquisitive and plied me with the typical questions about what it's like to live here year round and work in a place so surrounded constantly by beauty. And after happily and honestly replying, I never failed to recognize that slight yearning that comes with discovery, the small twinge of envy, especially when I threw in a short but tantalizing story. It was the same way I had looked when I first arrived.

But that look of envy may never show up again and there may be nothing left to brag about in our island way of life that I succumbed to many years ago. There is a major storm of vast proportions bearing down on us that we have been forewarned may be nothing less than life altering. Our home aboard our large sailboat *Wanderer*, aptly named by Eddie, her captain and keeper of my heart, is in jeopardy as well as this house we are care-taking while its owners are in Europe on another of their long buying trips. I could not imagine which country would tantalize their multi-cultural tastes this time, but they were well away from this new fear.

And the visitors now shaken from their holiday reverie have fled in unison like the proverbial geese, having been advised to be out ahead of the storm. The burden of it all is now quite palpable.

But like so many before me when first discovering this small island, I had found it impossible not to be drawn in by the pristine beauty, peaceful lifestyle and glorious temperatures offered year round. I never, however, anticipated hurricane season. But the enormity of destruction and cleanup after the major tropical events that I've so far witnessed since making this my home, will apparently pale in comparison and become record breaking, and the odds are that we will all be unceremoniously introduced to the very worst very soon.

I am not naïve, nor had I been living under a rock prior to moving to this one protruding from the ocean floor. Obviously I was well aware of hurricanes before this, but back then only in the context of excitement as documented on the news from some quarters where they were awaited with glee, a little like Mardi Gras, as the revelers geared up for a proper 'hurricane party' replete with music, beer and a few candles, often held in a popular pub. Then it seems when I wasn't looking the planet shifted and storms grew larger, louder and more destructive and the very thought of a party to celebrate this event would not only seem foolhardy but life threatening. And as proof, we're working at fever pitch, filled with dread as we await this new breed like an uninvited guest at a somber party for two.

Whichever type previously showed up at the door, whether simply tropical depression or hurricane, I had little to lose in those early days. My possessions and emotional baggage had already been pared down to the bare necessities for a hurried departure from the cold northeast, long before Eddie entered my life. And looking back now, I remember he did so with little fanfare on a day he chose to take a lunch break on that same little north shore cove I'd chosen in my quest for answers.

It had instantly become the perfect sheltering curvature of solitude for soul searching and on that fortuitous morning, the tease of a light tropical shower, the type that cleanse and clear the air, seemed to be waiting for me to complete my task. Some mornings I would be deeply mired in the many self-imposed questions, weighing what I knew were thoughts of a purely romantic nature against those of logic, seeking a balance somewhere in between. It seemed I was in a constant struggle and hoping with each visit for some kind of evidence to let me know that I had what it took to call St. Margeaux home.

To complicate matters even more, I was newly arrived from San Juan, my first stop in the Caribbean, and already sensitive to some unexpected force that had begun its slow transfusion through my body, offering the unimaginable. It was a deliciousness to be savored after everything I'd been through. And I can remember feeling freshly minted and even a little like a 'phoenix risen', though a brief unexpected love affair in Puerto Rico might not qualify for that lofty a sentiment. But that had, however, set the tone for what grew into my adventuresome spirit that might otherwise have remained buried or simply gone unchallenged. I was glad, even then with all that uncertainty that I had paid attention.

And I recall, the only constant on that very auspicious morning was the sound of incoming surf gently snuggling the shore, gracefully pushing delicate lacy nettings of foam ahead, patterning the sand and leaving behind only a wet, coffee colored stain as the bubbles of light disappeared back into the sea. It had taken only a few visits before recognizing the power of that steady ebb and flow and its mesmerizing effect, slowing my breathing like a meditation.

Those placid first days with nothing more than the atmospheric sounds of surf pounding and flushing itself accompanied by the instrumentation of wind and bird call did much to put the pieces together. And every one of them brought another barrage of questions regarding my future. On top of that there was the daily struggle that time was quickly slipping by, requiring the decision to return to New York and a life that no longer held enthusiasm.

Before Eddie, my only companions were the small hermit crabs that curled into their protective shells whenever I wiggled my toes nearby. Or if I was particularly lucky and extremely quiet, I could watch in amazement the preferential exchange of habitat as the tiny creature peeking out of the outgrown shell began groping and grasping for the newer abode. There was barely a sound other than a clicking of shell on shell as it turned itself into and over, rolling its entire body, filling its new home with practiced ease.

Occasionally, the endearing semi-translucent ghost crabs joined in and darted past, flashing their large headlight eyes that I thought could be interpreted as either flirtatious or suspicious, but certainly recognizing me as alien to their excavation needs before dropping their golden bodies into their sand cave.

And what helped so much during those early struggles was that spit of cove, so utterly comforting in its uniqueness. Unlike most of the well-known sandy beaches, it is distinguished more by its predominant layer of rocks mixed in with an abundance of shells and pebbles. The highly pungent tanginess hanging in the air came from the ever-present seaweed ripening in the sun, carelessly deposited over everything nearest the water. This predominance also kept it free from sunbathers, allowing me daily claim.

I know, as I look back now how much I actually loved the rewarding monotony in my self-imposed chore of picking up the plastic and Styrofoam debris. It often washed up from offshore ships passing on their cargo routes or those multi-level structures ferrying party-going throngs on holiday throughout the Caribbean. The task was calming and accepting, the tone I was striving for. Once in a while I would even sit there in the evenings and watch the cruise ships on the horizon ablaze with lights as they made their night passages between ports, envying their knowledge of their destination while I floundered daily about mine.

And now, with what is going on outside our door, how seemingly carefree life was even in my perpetual state of confusion. And how wonderful it would seem to again be that quiet collector of colorful shells that once graced my path on that very contemplative journey, eventually becoming prized possessions, or at the very least, enjoyed through books while tucked into a shady spot to read.

There were many: the very delicate sand dollars; striped tritons, ribbed cones, gold-veined cowries, and one extremely fragile intricately beaded urchin shell kept as a cautionary reminder of pain that could be inflicted even from something so pretty.

I had my particular favorite though, a wonderfully large, nearly white from age conch shell with still visible splotches of pink and gold that I occasionally put to my ear expecting the roar of the ocean. That one lives in a space carved out of a shelf filled with nautical books opposite the galley on the *Wanderer* where I cannot protect it from this new behemoth breathing down our necks. The rest are cradled inside boxes in a closet at Eddie's old apartment, used now only for storage as well as the odd overflow when too many visitors arrive at once.

But no matter what happens, they will always represent a part of something bigger that not only began with wanting one of each of the fascinating array left for my scavenging, and my need to understand these islands, but also my strong inexplicable affinity to the sea that expelled them for my viewing.

At one point, tiring of my chatter about all things sea related, and being a great believer in the fates predicted by the stars, a good friend convinced me to visit a local shop run by an aging West Indian lady known for her uncanny predictions. My worries as I climbed the narrow staircase, over the possibility that I might be entering into a world of voodoo rituals, were quickly put to rest when I stepped into what looked more like a spa with an engaging Zen atmosphere, filled with incense and the sound of soothing water bubbling in a small fountain.

After being introduced to tarot cards, rune stones and charts that looked both impressive and complicated, drawn with an expert hand by this delicate woman with dark eyes expressive and yet quite at peace, it was hinted at that my being here was no accident after all. She not so much walked as floated across the room in greeting, wearing the softest of cotton sarongs and buttery leather sandals. It was nearly impossible to place her in any one local culture, her skin a mix of many and the more beautiful for it.

Mariah had the uncanny knack of looking directly into my soul or so it seemed then. And as she spread the great circle drawn on parchment paper out in front of me, placing her long fingernail in each quarter of it before writing and naming those that apparently pertained to me, I began to believe her. I had already become more aware of the ocean's force on me since leaving Puerto Rico, so I felt strongly that there would be many more visits to this magical kingdom of her domain to learn more.

And while I know there are still so many things beyond my grasp even after so many years and much as I'd like, for the moment it is impossible to give these things their due. Our world has narrowed with fear in these last days and there is still much to deal with and more than the shells at stake, there are many lives as well. Therefore, looking upward as one tends to, believing that He is watching, I offer up another promise beginning with 'if we make it through this', as I've done before. And I wonder how many times have others exchanged promises big or small when placed before that altar of fear? And how many times had I reached out in a similar manner during those lonely visits to the cove?

I more than likely was doing just that on that fateful day I heard Eddie's voice filling the air around me. I would have been prospecting for the many treasures the island held but also carefully tending to the fear licking at my dreams, grateful for the ability to do so in quiet seclusion. I know that as I waited for my mind to offer the proper responses, thoughts seemed nothing more than a large jigsaw puzzle and I had yet to figure out how the pieces fit.

"Looks like a late morning shower brewing out there."

I had straightened slightly, taking cautionary glimpses from behind my sunglasses, not at all pleased by the intrusion on either my thoughts or my space. So I had replied at first with little enthusiasm. But then without pretension or invitation, I noted the smiling stranger came closer and dropped his lean, well-tanned frame onto the largest boulder near me.

"Mind if I join you?"

"Looks like you already have."

Ignoring my somewhat curt response with a very self-confident manner, he pulled out a pair of rather important looking binoculars and began scanning the horizon as if to prove his own purpose there.

He didn't know that I had caught him sizing up my plastic bag full to the top with the day's revenue of 'beach junk' and sensed his delight at my conscientious habit. Then I noticed a softer smile yet when glimpsing my tote with shells carefully stacked inside, thinking perhaps I'd touched a kindred soul.

But as he continued to scan, I unwittingly found myself following his unhurried motion only to see he had discovered a large schooner out beyond the headland. Then I got caught up watching and laughing at the gulls and frigate birds swooping about fighting for territory with the brown pelicans, all out on their morning fishing expedition as if this were something we did together daily. They would swoop, dive, and then bob for a while on a small cresting wave, and begin all over again while the rain stayed locked behind stiff clouds.

Noticing this softening, he smiled over at me though I still hadn't encouraged him, *"I'm Eddie Tremain."*

I continued to assess him from behind dark lenses. Interesting features, yes. Well built, yes. Flirtatious... probably.

"Lily, Lily Harmon. So tell me Eddie Tremain, are you a visitor too, or do you actually live in this paradise?"

"Well, Ms. Harmon, right at this moment I'm pretending to be on vacation, but I've lived here for a little over six years now. I'm a landscape designer by trade and am taking advantage of a late delivery to take a lunch break with my favorite birds. And in my line of work I do think of it as paradise, especially when everything is lush and blooming. How about you? I'm guessing a visitor since I haven't seen you before and because you've got that look."

"What look?"

"The first time seeing everything look. The one that says I don't want to leave yet look."

"At the moment that is exactly what I'm trying to figure out. It seems I've run away from New York and a pretty good nine to five job, only to find myself here with no answers to the million questions running rampant in my head."

"Well, since I know those looks, maybe I could help by showing you around, if you have time that is; it might help sort things out. This really is a terrific place. Better still, you might let me take you to dinner. I feel positive you'll never want to leave after that!"

That last remark, while flirtatiously said through a wink and a grin, obviously enjoying his ability to capture a woman's attention, also hinted at his genuine love for the island. And having finally captured mine, I sized him up a bit more thoughtfully. Thick reddish hair, the type I knew would gray attractively when he aged, differing in shade from my own auburn curls already filling in with sun-tinted highlights. His eyes, a bit mysterious, appearing neither brown nor blue because of the angle of light, still added to a genuinely easy smile.

With the ice broken, I had gone on to explain that I'd just visited Puerto Rico and only been on St. Margeaux a little over a week but was already totally caught up in the dream of permanent residency. Furthermore, I had no idea what I would do for work. That seemed to set the wheels in motion and he quickly took it upon himself right there and then to become my personal advisor. Intriguing, I thought. With that confidence and ready smile, he was, I had surmised, used to getting his way. The more we talked, the more he seemed anxious to reinforce how quickly the island gets under one's skin, gently urging me to take a chance.

Big flirt, I told myself. And with little encouragement from me he continued on, comfortably relaxing into his new position as instructor of all things tropical that he presumed I had no awareness of. He then opened his backpack causing fragrant steam to burst forth its spicy scent of cumin and curry revealing the hot chicken 'roti' inside and with a mock flourish of serving me, offered to share. I knew he'd purchased the delectable smelling bundle from one of the vendors I'd quickly become used to seeing in the marketplace where everything food related still seemed foreign to me. Slipping off his boat shoes noticeably softened by wear and putting his feet up to rest on the rocks, he then began to amuse me with stories of his earliest days on the island.

"What a sad tale I weave, Lily. Life was looking a bit bleak back then; minimal number of clients and times were tough. I was so broke that I took up free diving, the kind without scuba gear, for lobsters with a couple of my native pals. They'd been doing it all their lives and it was hard work, but it paid the bills."

"It seems like your life has changed quite a bit since those days," I had offered, in answer to his humorous 'woe is me' tale and the brief litany of his work schedule, beginning to enjoy the easy give and take.

I had already read about the West Indian langouste, the Caribbean spiny lobster that thrive in these waters and around reefs, and really couldn't picture that as a means to an end. But the conversation became easier than expected and I remember thinking I didn't want to appear rude and I certainly needed help, so we just continued there on the rocks talking about life in general, his many friends and all the nearby islands, until he had to get back to work.

A great deal of time has passed since then and he's been rewarded with a growing business for the work he loves to perform in his outdoor office. We are continually discovered by those with time to enjoy the fruits of their own labors and wish to possess a piece of their own paradise. And he is all about transforming their properties in just such a place.

And because of Eddie on that fateful day, I found my wonderful job at the small Starfish Bay Resort nestled in that amazing profusion of wild exotic growth on the most verdant side of the island, which all in turn created countless memories. It is inevitable with what is now about to happen that my mind is harboring so much since memories exist everywhere. But I am also acutely aware that if I dwell too hard or too long, I will surely break down completely.

Right now, however, like all island residents, all that matters is our safety and the strength to cope with whatever gets thrown at us in the coming hours and even days. We are on this promontory in someone else's house awaiting the many unknowns. And while the house is simple, it is not unremarkable. But like many island houses it's invested with a carefree spirit and open concept living that I've come to love, normally inviting less threatening winds and offering magnificent views richly colored in with wide ranging tropical growth. Eddie and I spend so much time on the water enjoying a lifestyle that suits our requirements, owning a house like this would be foolishness. All the regular upkeep and lovely objects obtained over time, would be a form of entrapment and completely unnecessary for our present needs and leave little time for play.

Not that we are lacking anything either since becoming live-aboard boaters and have discovered just how many pleasures can be had with careful crafting to the interiors by the creative use of space, even a piano if that's your pleasure. All of this was thanks to an energetic couple named Eli and Sally. They introduced us to that ingenious idea when they arrived from Texas for a short stay at Long Point Cay. Sally said she got the idea from one of Sloan Wilson's novels and decided to adapt that for their boat. After that, I knew anything was possible for the *Wanderer*. There were many parties held aboard their sailboat at anchor under a watchful moon while a very perky Sally kept up with the non-stop requests for music, filling the bay with song before moving on to their next harborage.

The live-aboard lifestyle had captivated me from the earliest stages of sailing, offering up many challenges and even more gratification. It is thrilling and adventuresome and a place where love can thrive, perhaps because of the closeness and dependability required. Or perhaps because of the romantic novels that build on that, which I found myself reading at every opportunity.

And a special treat is the easy access into that sanctuary of calm that exists beneath the boat and that particular world of the green turtles that tease me into joining them when I return home from work. I don mask and flippers, and occasionally a swimsuit if others were nearby, shedding the office concerns from my skin, and slip into the shallows, the day's problems quickly melting as they fall into the water around me while the tiny faces almost in recognition, beckon me to follow. The filtered light shining down on their wide patterned shells as they play and feed in the long grasses of the green water, bounces off everything below the distorted water line, creating a halo from above. It also quite naturally encourages me to perform a little necessary 'housekeeping' on the hull, brushing off the fuzzy growth much too difficult to ignore once in the water and far less a chore because of the heads bobbing up to watch me, not ready to end their playtime.

I count my blessings often for the lifestyle we've chosen and they never fail to reinforce my love for this place that is already imbedded deeply, but now absolutely everything we love and care about is being threatened and we are helpless to prevent it. Angrily, adjusting to this unwanted insight, I'm forced to push the happier thoughts aside, simultaneously pushing the homely floral curtain back judgmentally, wondering why anyone would choose them for such a pretty room.

I can see that the sky has already changed from its earlier rainy day gray to deepening ribbons of pewter tinged with green and an unexpected shiver runs down my spine. Even though it is nearer to the end of the charted hurricane season when the probability and intensity of storms normally increase, this particular season has been unusually quiet, that is until now.

Everyone's nerves are frayed, and tempers are showing and there is still more to come. The bulky portable radio that Eddie located earlier amongst the owners' emergency items, always necessary due to frequent power outages, is now propped on top of the extra box of candles and blaring loudly just as I imagine is happening in homes all over the island, warning residents to batten down and prepare. This is a full out disaster preparedness speech repeated often in these past days, and is doing little to make me feel equipped for what lay ahead.

"Yell if you need me, Eddie, I'm going to try Russ again," I said, grabbing the phone, remembering my earlier promise to keep in hourly contact with our friend for as long as possible.

"Hi, Lily. You caught me in between outages. How're you guys doing?"

"Oh, Russ, I don't know. We've been going non-stop trying to get everything tightened up. Have you heard that latest update?—not what we've been hoping for. We're both pretty exhausted and I'm even beginning to run out of cheery uplifting thoughts. How about you?"

"I've finally got most of the great room closed off, and the rest, well, we'll have to see if the design works. This will be the real test, but I can't stand being shut in and my power's gone out twice, so you're lucky you even got through. The next big gust could take it all again and probably for good."

My first impression of Russell Longforth III when introduced at the Sea Crest bar was not kind, thinking him probably intoxicated as he leaned toward us and nearly toppled his drink onto the shiny countertop. It was then he picked up on the vibes between Eddie and me and voiced them irreverently. A thin-boned man of medium height, he was nearly molded into an old beat up director's chair, his rumpled shorts showing through a tear in the fabric seat that threatened to empty him onto the ground.

Of course all of that changed when I discovered the bond between them and realized how he not only championed our budding relationship, but could always be counted on in a crisis as well. He is being put to the test today as we all are, but the house he built has a ribbed structure set over the great room that exposes the sky for stargazing with a superb telescope. This will be the first major storm to test that theory of openness against battering winds that supposedly left unimpeded cannot destroy.

"The sky looks outrageous up here, but I'm guessing it's even worse with the ocean so close to your door."

"It's like a dark tunnel and getting darker by the minute, so I better get going before it all opens up. Nessa's busy putting last minute items away, and sends love. I know she's scared and trying not to show it. We all are."

"I know, Russ, and unfortunately, by the looks of it, this is probably going to be the last call before we lose lines up here too. So stay safe, okay? Don't do anything foolish. We'll catch up to you somehow when this is over," I replied, though unable to envision the days ahead.

"Thanks, Lily. Tell Eddie I'll be down to help with the boat as soon as it's possible to get through. My guess is we're in for the worst ever and I don't kid myself, it's going to be rough. You guys be safe also."

The frenzy of the last few days has nearly blurred all time lines. Eddie and I have been going back and forth between the boat and the house, joining forces with our many friends and neighbors, all marching to that same drummer, exchanging thoughts and ideas filled with watchfulness and worry exceeding the norm, securing as much as possible everywhere. I have also made the necessary numerous trips for non-perishables, noting the controlled chaos that happens when people are trying to figure out what they will need and for how long at times like these. No one is ever prepared totally with so much uncertainty, but we try anyway.

After much consideration, Eddie, with Russ's help, sailed our beloved *Wanderer* from the town harbor to the marina at Long Point Cay where he felt she would be less compromised if all hell broke loose. The added bonus, of course, was the ability to catch a glimpse of her from this house.

So many difficult decisions have had to be made in quick time while we all hoped for a reprieve that had occasionally been known to happen if the fickle wind changed in any pertinent way. The placement of the boat during the storm was one of those decisions. Waiting till the last as if for some miracle, Eddie then wisely opted out of the group heading to Sweet Bottom, the island's only protected lagoon and 'hurricane hole' created naturally by the shallow water surrounded by heavy mangroves.

His wealth of knowledge due to the nature of his work had already made me aware of the importance of mangrove trees. They grew well there, and built up land by sending their roots deep into the water to trap sand and silt. But now the probability of damage caused by a broken anchor line that under great pressure might snap as easily as string, leaving it at the mercy of the wind, brews in the mind. No matter how many anchors placed, with the many boats expected to take refuge in that spot, the risk is too high with so much at stake, so the *Wanderer* is mightily tied down with double and even triple lines threaded like a giant spider web crisscrossing bow and stern, all leading to the concrete portion of the pier. This one is going to be bad, really bad; and with the rapidly dropping barometer, I can already feel it in my bones and on my skin.

In the meantime, not only out of necessity but trying to calm the continuing attack on my nerves by 'busy work', I've commandeered a nearly empty closet for our personal items and any extras in case we're detained here longer than anticipated and that includes the emergency supply of bottled water too since the cistern pump won't work without power. The likelihood of no power in this fragile environment after Mother Nature has her way, is always a given, even during heavy rainstorms so I can well imagine what havoc will now be created.

Added to the stores is a hefty supply of Malta India, my favorite carbonated drink. Not only did I love the taste, but the sugar provided a terrific power boost when needed. And I even took a bit of time to bake off some chocolate chip cookies from dough found in the freezer—no point in letting it defrost and spoil. What perishables we have are packed tightly in our large cooler taken from the boat. I also left an enormous supply of dry goods not only in her storage compartments but stuffed into any available space, in the hopes we will be able to draw upon it when this is over. This could prove invaluable in the days to come.

Fortunately, our vantage point here on the hill overlooks the entire bay, normally a hub of noisy activity that in this past week especially, has lost all its sparkle with all concentration on the impending storm. It is lacking the all too familiar sound, that 'smack' from air filling sails, beckoning exploration to other destinations. Or the noisy chatter as they're readied for the rewards of a refreshing swim or cocktails on deck while witnessing the sun setting over a new harbor. There is no purring and sputtering of outboard motors or powerboat engines in need of repair or tuning. They have taken refuge elsewhere. It is only a few miles away and though I can just barely make out the masts of the few other boats tucked in there to brave it out with ours, I can see the combers building up beyond the breakwater, but only just, as the swaying trees keep obscuring my view.

The danger looms over everything and is now completely unavoidable and while it is no small gift to be ensconced up here far away from the roiling water, the morning light alone will reveal whether the *Wanderer* has been spared. I know we've done the best we could and now the rest is left to the gods and the mighty spirit of the wind. That is not enough for Eddie whose anxiety is becoming more noticeable as another hour ticks by; the obvious giveaways, the set of his jaw, the sweat beading on his tightlipped expression and his quick movements, all telltale signs. How that face has always intrigued me. From the beginning, given to an easy smile and huge laugh, making worry so evident now as it always had when something major was about to occur. Our relationship hadn't always been easy and we took a few breaks from each other when things moved too quickly. But we always found our way back and now we find ourselves racing against time as we face our most difficult challenge so far.

Here in the islands, the beautiful days that remain a constant throughout much of the year, the ones highly touted and giving the tourism coffers a boost, ritually fill with added moisture and a well-tolerated humidity during the late summer months that feed the tropical storms. But now, at the mercy of such a major hurricane, there is nothing but the nearly tangible oppressiveness living inside these walls. Even the freedom of our standard issue shorts and tees and bare feet do little to assuage this feeling of clamminess. And in the last couple of hours I've noticed that our conversation has become almost a form of shorthand, treading about the house as though in fear of waking the monster with our louder movements, hastening its arrival.

Securing everything by utilizing the shutters and wood left for these occasions by the owners has heightened the growing weight of our responsibility, and caused us to add to the stockpile purchased at the lumber yard just in case. They have entrusted us with so much as the situation did not allow for their return to St. Margeaux in time. I only hope we are up to the task.

Eddie has done what he could at Long Point but as he pointed out when we first came up here to survey our needs, we could have a major problem in the back of the house if the large roof overhang covering the rear patio is breached in any way. The wind could then pull the entire roof off. Much of our safety will depend on its course throughout the night. Even if this is our necessary and only alternative shelter, I don't feel much relief with this new knowledge.

A few days earlier, after completing all the other items on our individual checklists, Nessa and I joined forces to tackle all outdoor furniture at both locations. She is one of my closest friends and to my amazement has sustained a rather unusual on and off relationship with Russ ever since I've known her. Presently it's 'on' but her independent streak was showing anyway. At least I know she'll be with him during the crucial overnight hours when no one should be alone. But I can still see her expression when she saw why I needed her help up here.

"Good god, Lily, this is really a lot of stuff, don't you think?" She said, her dark eyes critically surveying everything. "What on earth do people do with all of this, especially given the type of storms we get? I don't care what Russ says, I like the sparseness of my apartment just the way it is."

"I agree, Ms. Barnes, my rebellious friend, but that's why I've got you to help me move it all since we had so little to do at your place. I'm inclined to think more like you regarding all of this and am happier still that Eddie and I are on the same page about living aboard, enjoying the freedom it gives us. Perhaps that's what finally brought us closer together." Mocking a feeble throw of an imaginary rope, "But who knows, maybe in time when we're very old and can't toss a line anymore, we'll think more seriously about this."

I could hardly imagine that time and what might be left of our comfort after all of this, and admittedly there really was a lot of *stuff* to deal with. But the owners were counting on us, so sizing it all up and forfeiting our usual give and take of conversation and laughter, we started hauling. There was much to store away: the exceptionally oversized hammock, the outdoor lighting apparently used to create an oasis amidst the plentiful ferns, a multitude of garden ornaments and birdbaths and lastly the beautifully glazed and extremely heavy decorative pots that are part of the overall grouping of collectibles from foreign ports so prized by the owners. It truly was a magnificent garden and patio, before we took it all apart.

After leaving me alone with my *useless* objects, Nessa, unable to resist the tease, headed off to Russ's and the last of her own chores. I watched from the doorway of the shed as she walked down the hill to her car, moving as always with determination in her self-assured manner, her thick shoulder-length hair held back with a scarf that accented her soft print calf-length skirt. She preferred the flowing fabrics in the tropical heat, creating an odd mix of her California days and island ease. The picture leaving behind a happy feeling about a friendship built on compassion and humor and always at the ready. She and Russ really were well suited even if they had difficulty seeing it.

But I'm still questioning the placement of all those things, realizing their value, no matter what she called it. Everything has now been tucked into the substantial work shed alongside the house and the car parked in the lee of that. Then, after much mental debate, I brought in many of the fragile potted plants, whispering words of encouragement more for my own comfort than theirs. Even with all of that, each new storm update fuels more concerns about the placement of everything all over again.

Everyone on this island that spans little more than seventy-five square miles is by now well aware as the deadline approaches, that all decisions made will have to be lived with since there is no going back; it's too late. As Eddie and I are in charge of unfamiliar property, our efforts have already been quadrupled. The number of possibilities that could occur in such an unusual situation is completely unknown, and the darkness will, if it can be believed, be even more ominous very soon, especially with that noticeable change in the color of the sky. We have made every possible effort to protect this house and the *Wanderer*, but in a very short time we will be forced to manage solely by candle or flashlight as we shut ourselves in with nothing more to hold onto than hope, and for the first time in the long day, I taste fear.

There is such a physical awareness of danger compounded by fatigue that I know the barometric pressure is changing again. It's as though a heavy curtain is being dropped over the entire structure like the seaweed that suffocates the rocks. I tuck my long hair up out of the way craving the coolness on my neck, hoping to toss away some of the needles of fear lying beneath its weight.

I don't want to think of food right now, but as if by rote, I've made room on the little kitchen table for a meal that was prepared earlier and will need to be consumed very soon. I can only pray that this small habit performed every day in all our lives to provide nourishment for our bodies will also provide even a small amount for our souls as the night wears on. There is little else for comfort.

"I can tell by looking at you, you're pretty exhausted. We'll get a break soon." Eddies says, noting the plates.

"I am exhausted, but once you've closed it all up, that break won't be a very pleasant one even though we have no choice. I did manage to get everything of importance into the bathroom that I could think of—the emergency bag with medical supplies and valuable papers, and of course, the sleeping bags. And I took a couple of the smaller glass hurricanes from the master bedroom just in case, even though I'm not sure I'll feel any safer there."

The hard flooring I know will be only slightly more comfortable with the mats that had been stowed on the boat for sleeping on deck occasionally during the cooler Christmas winds. But islanders who'd ever experienced these things had learned the hard way when walls have only hinted at falling away, that a bathroom shower stall or preferably a cast iron tub, were the very few spaces considered able to withstand heavy wind damage. Something to do with their placement within the houses, I seem to remember being told in preparation for one of my first storm experiences. But with the unusual size of this one, even that premise may turn out to be a fallacy.

The cold radio momentarily springs to life with more force as the voice, reaching a higher pitch, exclaims the new update on the storm's breadth that is now tightening its widely cast net and closing in on us. It is more massive and powerful than any of us have ever seen and appears to be chewing up the map. It is already inching up to predicted category four proportions beating up on other islands in the way, with the probability high for a direct hit, the worse possible scenario. I saw the alarm register on Eddie's face when he heard the first reports days ago that were beyond cautionary even then, and can tell how worried he is about my reactions with each new update. We've been through a lot together but no one is trained for what is about to take place. This has been wearing hard on him too, so the best I can do right now is stay focused and alert.

And yet, I have this terrifying desire to laugh right now, laugh out loud at the futility of all our hard work, exhorting to all this effort, because the predictions being blasted in our ears are so utterly frightening that I know they can only be true. I keep busy, knowing I must not give in to such madness. It is cloying and claustrophobic but I don't dare quit. Instead I've taken to compensating each time I feel the fear building, by using my memories, flooding my thoughts about the days when I first set my feet and heart on this lovely island. This time, and without warning, I feel a tear running down my cheek. Just the mere thought now of what it might all be like in the morning is unbearable. I know that if I allow myself the luxury, that one tear could open the floodgates of emotions I've held in check through all these prolonged days of waiting.

Chapter Two

The ear-splitting cacophony of strange sounds is now increasing to a monumental level just beyond our walls, steadily reinforcing the impending danger within and without, and I feel my already shaky composure breaking down bit by bit as it changes. Time is moving in the same slow motion as the hurricane but the storm is building in volume and it leads to my feeble attempts at resisting all the dark thoughts that come forth and the need to recoil within them. I fear they are winning. I can hear Eddie again pounding away at something nearby, perhaps something's come loose, but I'm afraid to ask what that might be.

Switching back and forth between stations for the best reception, I catch the announcer from the neighboring island projecting that wind speeds might reach as high as 180 mph which is unheard of, and I no longer doubt this as I hear the higher decibel of the already fierce sounds outside trying to penetrate even the tightest barriers. Again and again he throws out the coordinates necessary for anyone paying close attention and wanting to visibly watch the track on a chart placed on a table much like ours, that reinforces the storm's intensity spreading and reaching out with giant circular tentacles, not yet veering as everyone had hoped—one sharp turn off either quadrant to avoid the direct hit. I can no longer fathom these numbers nor relate to the possible consequences they represent, and must force myself not to try.

Racing across the room to tell Eddie what I've just heard, knowing he will want to fix the numbers onto his mental map much memorized from his years of experience on the water, I catch him struggling with a weighty wooden table that I'd paid no attention to earlier. He's apparently decided at the last minute to use this as extra protection to reinforce the long shuttered windows and I now see what the pounding was about. One of the shutters needed shoring up and the table placement means he too is already expecting more from this alien wind. This is not the picture I was hoping for.

The house is solidly built and obviously safer than riding the storm out on a boat, but whether it will withstand these new more violent conditions remains to be seen. After all we had no part in its construction, automatically eliminating any expectations. I would, however, be hard pressed to find anywhere at the moment, after hearing those blaring reports, where I think we would be safe, and I realize with each tick of the clock how hard we have both been striving against what could easily become overreaction. And overreaction means doing stupid things or forgetting to do the necessary or obvious ones. We cannot afford either. It's getting even harder to concentrate as it is, without falling into some kind of fear-heightened trap.

"That's it, sweetheart. The entire house is now closed up with the exception of this one small window and I'll have to do that very soon. The ocean is riveting—come look."

Reaching for the glasses, I note that outside noise is now competing and Eddie's voice is louder than usual.

"I really can't see anything out there except that mass of greenish-black that was there the last time I looked, and even that is a blur with the wind swirling the trees so badly. I'm just glad we're up here well away from the water. Why don't we try and eat something before you're forced to shut that last little bit; we could use that break."

"Let me do that first, Lily, I don't like what I'm hearing. Then I'll be able to relax at least a little easier."

I'm almost sorry I suggested eating, especially as I look around now at all the solidly covered spaces that really do have us boxed in. I feel it's nearly impossible to swallow, let alone taste the food. Anxiety is high and more to the point, I'm finding it extremely difficult to ignore what should have been and what I'm desperately missing now that we're totally enclosed—fragrant air wafting through open windows and across terraces or boat deck, giving each one of our senses a chance to take in all of the satisfying pleasures natural in a tropical existence and what we've come to expect here. But it is going to be a very long night and we'll need all our strength to get through it.

The radio was nearly silenced when power went out momentarily just before we sat down, but the food is still warm. The overhead light flickers tenuously while the wind plays with the power lines, as if announcing the end of a theatre intermission, so I made sure before sitting down, to place the many candles strategically throughout the house. There are long impossible hours ahead, and they will flicker against any frail air movement in the now very stuffy rooms, alerting us to possible breaches. Unfortunately, that makes trying to eat more difficult because it sends us instantly scurrying, immediately creating more tension. Oddly, at the same time, this timid glowing of flame also illuminates some old memories for me.

"I'd give anything if those cast shadows could take us back in time; when soft candlelight washed over everything, gracing tables as it bounced off all the crystal and silver. We've shared some pretty romantic moments together over the years in exactly that type of setting."

"I know we have and I'm certain many more are waiting for us no matter what happens tonight. But it is really hard to think about that while we're locked in the house like this. It's funny, it seems so much more natural to expect something powerful to come up out of the blue when I'm on the boat; hard for me to accept we're at its mercy up here.

"But then you always manage to remember the best, don't you? I don't think I tell you enough how much I need you." Eddie said tenderly.

"Well, maybe you don't, but I'll be sure to remind you when this is over and you can say it all over again."

There have been so many wonderful parties attended or given over the years, but for some reason watching these shadows, a particular favorite springs to mind like an old painting that's become an old friend. It was a touching party hosted by Clarice and Jeremy

Carrington, a rather posh party but set with simplicity. Their villa is high on a mountaintop with a 360-degree view of the sea, exposed to the elements and framed by wide columned openings. And small outbuildings used as bedrooms casually flanked the main house.

I had loved that house from the very first time I laid eyes on it. Its inviting use of space captured the breeze as well as a vista that never lacked for something to grab the attention through its wide windows: sea birds soaring, small birds feeding, goats roaming and people sailing to other island destinations.

It sits so high that the wide expanse of the ocean caught the eye before glimpsing the coloring from the tops of the flamboyant and African tulip trees standing out brightly below in the hot sun and everything out at sea appeared like small toys in a bathtub. Even the color of the water from that height enhanced and glorified the shades normally seen at sea level, greatly defining the depths of the blues and greens. And, it was the perfect party house.

Coming to life now was that special evening planned in recognition of a knighting for Jeremy by the British government that included among their island friends a couple of visiting ambassadors. I was so proud because the newly designated 'Lady' Carrington invited us. Eddie had been responsible for creating the magnificent gardens and meandering paths surrounding the house that had struck just the right chord to match their new status.

I would occasionally pick him up after work to find her doting and fussing over everything, including Eddie. She was not a young woman, but when he was around she seemed to take on an air of girlishness that actually made him blush.

He had really outdone himself on that project using plants he'd nurtured from seedlings just waiting for the right place to be featured. The stone walks were stamped in unique places with the family crest, small and tasteful; and more stone was used for short walls creating borders to outline the best views. They in turn led to a centerpiece for iron seating placed in the shade to await the viewer. And he'd put in two magnificent palms at the entry in welcome, all of this endearing him to her ladyship. I noticed it also gave her a proprietary slip of her arm through his when we were introduced to the many guests.

Not that I blamed her; he looked terrific. He had borrowed a white tuxedo jacket used for a friend's wedding that he wore with a pair of dark trousers, striking a new tone to his personality that I thought I already knew well. I realized then Eddie was full of surprises and like Christmas I just wanted to keep opening the presents.

That had also been an unusually starless night making everything stand out against the darkness. The tables inside and out in an overflowing pattern onto the terrace were all lit with white tapers and pillars that softened the starkness of the linens. All the candles were encircled with small garlands of white native gardenias whose delicate perfume competed with the heady fragrance of the night blooming jasmine. They even had white paper lanterns of different sizes fancifully hung, adding to the drama and everyone's pleasure.

Sadly, tonight's candlelight so necessary for our safety provides none of the warmth and ambiance created then and on so many other occasions with less pomp over the years. And someone else will be worrying about that house tonight since the Carrington's moved back to England a few years ago to spend the rest of their years surrounded by the country gardens of the family estate. I'm happy they are not having to encounter what I know will be a devastating blow to that mountaintop as well as to my memories.

A more immediate problem, however, is the lowering barometric pressure recorded on the wall-mounted unit registering at 924mb and dropping, and again reinforced by the radio's high-strung weatherman, causing me to feel eerily lightheaded.

"Oh, for those sun-filled days out on the *Wanderer*."

Eddie looked over, catching the phrase I'd whispered without thinking, and offered a reassuring hug, "I know it's not easy, Lily; I know you're upset. But I promise when it's all over, we'll somehow manage to get down to the boat. We will find our friends and use the single sideband as planned to make the necessary emergency calls."

Increasingly, we had both taken to reflecting silently, but those are no longer strangers to be pushed to the recesses of the mind. Because of my own terrors they've taken ownership, and more often than not find their way, sometimes audibly into the forefront like now. Perhaps it is a normal way of coping, but then I don't know what normal means in circumstances so dire.

Though I've expressed just about everything else, I'm still very reluctant to verbalize my biggest concern. He sounds strong and in charge, but this, after all, is new territory even for him. I, on the other hand, have no problem worrying for both of us and am terrified we might not even have a boat left in the morning to return to, let alone a radio. Trying to push that thought aside with a few more bites of food, I can't even pretend enjoyment.

"It seems like things are picking up even more," Eddie says, grabbing his last piece of bread and nearly overturning his chair as he heads to the rear patio.

I know he's not oblivious to my thoughts—he most of all knows how deeply I feel and that I'm scared beyond reference in a place that, if the reports are correct, will be virtually cut off by morning from the rest of the world. And we both realize that it is only early evening with many more hours to go.

"You're excused," I replied to the air around me. "I might just as well clear up the table."

I'm not proud hearing such peevishness come out of my mouth, and I know it's because I'm afraid. Eddie doesn't respond, letting me off the hook. He knows me well. Suddenly I hear a loud shout from behind the door, stopping me in my tracks. The dish falls out of my hands, crashing at my feet, and the large pillar candle I was taking into the corner of the kitchen for better light, rolls away in protest bearing a large dent on one edge. Eddie's braced against the small opening in the doorway letting me know the wind is now beyond a howl and taking on the sound of jet engines. This is real... everything dreaded... much too fast even though we've been expecting it. Grabbing my flashlight I start re-checking the walls for movement the way he has shown me during our preparations, placing a palm flat against and moving across and around the room to each one. Any signs of shaking will alert us of possible loosening roof ties and even though it might not happen this quickly, I feel the need to move, to be useful, anything to stave off more fear.

Fortunately, all of the artwork and personal photos had been removed days ago when time was less panic filled, and stored in a solid lower level closet built like a safe to protect them from just such an occurrence. As we tucked them away I thought of the talented and shy watercolorist that could often be seen painting the aging boats dotting the small harbors of these islands, using his characteristic palette of soft blues and greens. What will he have to preserve on paper when this is over? The owners had collected many of his pieces and have entrusted us with a great deal and those works at least for the moment are one less thing to fret over.

Just as I finish, Eddie forces the door with all his strength. He is totally drenched, his old clothes looking rougher still, and it is obvious that the heavy downpour is making it even more difficult to see let alone track all the new sounds. Then, what seems to be a foolish attempt at security, he locks the door. Simultaneously we comprehend the finality of that one act and the realization through the incredible sound enveloping us that this ordinary, normally efficient lock cannot possibly keep the demon wind out if it chooses to break through.

I'm brought up short by this mundane performance, my breath catching in my throat before I hear a moan escape my lips. The fear so real it's now become physical and like a gong, is striking against my ribs. This fear that I've thwarted at every opportunity, using everything in my mental arsenal has continued to build throughout the day. It has also, with only slight success, been countered by foolish wishing that we could simply go back in time in order to escape the endless hours predicted by the stranger through the airwaves. But the villain outside, outsmarting us, has been evilly teasing with its slow movement crawling rather than rampaging, taking its energy from the decimation of those islands before us like an appetizer. And then even stalling for a while in order to build its appetite, readying for that havoc and mayhem we've been dreading, forces us to at last accept the reality of what is to come. Now I just want to hide.

I've already expended more time in the preceding days than has ever before been needed, in trying to fool that demon into thinking I'm unafraid, willing my mind artfully to play out lovelier images of this island, and there are many—the grand old trees that dot the healthy, lush landscape along my daily route to work and all the vibrant flowers giving bees a will to thrive and the wonderful honey from their keeper who is almost as colorful as the flowers. In my mind she is always attired in a printed dress that blends beautifully with her own works of art, the many beds of tropical plants, where she will consult with Eddie. I see their heads together over a sickly stem refusing to grow, her gloves and a trowel at the ready, wearing squishing rubber plimsolls, sharing their secret recipes concocted and proven over time.

I am free to peruse the many plots carefully marked and laid in pretty patterns, but am always more interested in the honey and take my time poking around for myself while they're busy, waiting to select one of these delectable items lined up and labeled in her cursive writing. It is a small thing, but seems such a special event since she stores the abundant dark amber filled jars inside the ruins of an exaggerated upside down thimble. This was once an active sugar mill, now at rest on her property and put to good use. And though crumbling at the top from years of decay, the cool interior walls come alive with aging moss all accentuated by the essence of sweetness.

And now what will become of all of that as well as those iconic palms that I had been advised early on to beware since dropping coconuts could land with disastrous results on a passerby? Their long gnarly trunks always reminding me of elders within a society flexibly bending but rarely breaking under stress. Would their usual heartiness withstand this or would they be brought to the breaking point after all? And how I loved the many stalwart mahogany trees prominently pointing up the landscape everywhere, surviving and thriving from importation to these islands, standing like sentinels, guarding.

I've let my thoughts jump around haphazardly and touch upon things without continuity in the suspended moments within each rush of new fears and there have been many occasions to do so. Maybe it's simply the pressure causing these great mental leaps that come without warning, but now I also find myself fretting about all the many animals that will be out there in their natural landscape forced to protect themselves. Especially, for some odd reason, the ubiquitous chickens sharing their patches of sustenance and many a dooryard, and those I would nearly trip over when walking around the town market where they seem to know no fear. They have all taken a foothold in layering my unrelenting worry and now I pray for even the simplicity of the rooster crow in the morning.

Where would they all go and what will be left? Unimaginable consequences to a storm of this magnitude have been speculated about daily, ever since the winds invaded warmer water giving islanders reason to be concerned. Could anything survive a slow moving storm with this much force?

Without question, the lives of thousands of people are at stake tonight, no matter their color, financial status or place in the community. Vulnerability is the common thread as fear takes up residence within each beating heart waiting in the wide dark void of the unknown. Maybe, just maybe, the blessing of that sheer darkness will prevent life from being lost by people leaving their shelter. It is not unusual in these islands subjected to brutal storm winds that people will venture out during the crucial and dangerous quiet of the passing eye thinking the storm to be done with, only to be caught in the changing wind pattern unsheltered and falling prey to the many hidden dangers—perhaps even being hit or speared by a flying object. A broken off two by four piece of wood framing flown directly into the trunk of a palm tree by a raging wind could and did make a necessary road sign when all else was gone. I shudder at the thought of it flying into soft human tissue.

Startling me out of my tangential travels, "Listen, the storm is now officially announcing its arrival!" Eddie exclaimed, looking up as though the swirling mass would be visible on the ceiling.

Wondering if this is truly the beginning or possibly the end, I can't answer. But I can feel the building momentum, hating every second of it. We are quite suddenly thrust in the thick of it. Then, between gusts, sharp sounding objects are crashing against the overhang as others go zinging past like arrows flung from a bow. Every sound now jarring teeth and bone, causing my fear to lay like a coiled cat ready to spring for safety.

My thoughts shift; instinctively I know that the long hours of this continual harangue from the wind will be beating on the nerves of every resident just as it pounds away at our shelter. I wonder of the whereabouts of all of our close friends all over the island. Are these conditions forcing memories of easier times to push forward in some form of prayer for them as well? All we can do now is to mentally share in their helplessness.

"Listen," Eddie says, pointing toward the radio. "This is bad!"

It is becoming surreal in the semi-darkness, having no say whatsoever, to be awaiting our fate just as all the other islands mentioned throughout the day during the storm's track, pinpointing each stop en route to us. It had been another form of cruelty to identify each of them on the map with frightening numbers next to the line that shows it slowly inching toward our place in this building turmoil. I'd give anything to be anywhere else.

As we listen more intently, hanging onto each key word, there is suddenly dead air. That station has now been silenced and we have no connection to anyone. Waiting to see if it will come back on, I look down to document the time and realize that the face of my watch is filled with moisture, blurring the numbers, and at first I think it's my eyes that are filled because I'm so frightened. But it is obvious that the seal burst from the drastically dropping pressure. I'm certain it is now imperative we retreat to the tiny bathroom.

Eddie checks the dive watch I'd given him for his birthday. It's still fine, meant to withstand underwater pressure. "I'm not sure right now if it's better or worse knowing the time, but we have to get away from these open spaces."

Once inside the smaller room, conversation becomes more difficult, not only because the noise is definitely louder at this side of the house, but also this air or lack of it, is already making us listless with a great need to become prone on the sleeping bags. We're now left with only our thoughts and our few important possessions to which we've added one working watch, the hurricane lamps throwing off eerie shadows, and the now silent radio that I've stopped trying to will back to life. And we are both totally spent from days and days of physical activity that surrounds any hurricane warning, as well as the strain caused by the extremes from this one.

It continues until there is no sense of time, especially because we're so tired. No wonder once finally encased inside the smallest room, clinging to each other for comfort, trying to stay awake in the event that something rips open needing immediate attention, our conversation is diminished and muted. We are accompanied by the consistent sound of the droning wind overhead, forcing us against our will in and out of sleep.

୭ ୭ ୭

"What just happened?" I ask, shaking him awake, realizing Eddie's watch isn't visible to me from this direction. I'm now oddly uncomfortable.

"What do you mean? I don't hear anything," Eddie says, still groggy as he instinctively checks the glowing hands on his wrist.

"That's exactly what I mean, no sound."

"Then that can only mean one thing, a small miracle. The quiet I mean. According to this, it's been almost six hours and given the predictions, we must finally be in eye. We have to be fast; we've got maybe fifteen minutes and probably our last chance to take a good look around, make sure everything is holding. Then it'll hit from the opposite direction. But I have to stretch, my back is killing me."

It is shocking to me that we've slept at all and that we're still unharmed, but I too am stiff and disheveled and the thought of stretching out on the sofa or in a soft chair seems like such a small gift. Eddie somehow pulls on deep reserves of strength while pulling me to my feet and once again goes to check on the places of most concern, waving his flashlight toward the beams to see if there is any thus far unnoticed problem.

"I'll be damned. It seems like the hurricane clips are still holding. And I don't see any signs of water, which is astonishing with all that force. They really built themselves a sound house; but I hate to get my hopes up, it's not over yet." He is shouting and his voice sounds hollow from the next room.

Grateful seems too small a word in response to having made it to the halfway mark, but everything internally is condensed like a time capsule. Sore and stiff and feeling more like a somnambulist, I wander past him and out to the living room, headed for the sofa. He will be better able to assess it all more quickly than I would anyway. Knowing there isn't much time, all I can think of is a ten-minute catnap on anything more comfortable than the floor. I pick my target and quickly put my head down as I feel the power of sleep again tugging at me. As if in a trance, perhaps alerted to a sound, I turn my head to the left and see the sliding doors beginning to bow, and then I notice a slight pulsing of the glass. I'm certain an angel was watching out for me through my drugged senses because I couldn't have been asleep for even those ten longed-for minutes. Screaming for Eddie, I race into the adjoining room before the throbbing glass comes to life and splinters fly across my coveted space.

"My God, Lily, what the hell just happened? Are you okay? I heard your scream and thought maybe you'd fallen, but I never expected this. You could have been seriously hurt from that blowout. Look, the outside boards are fastened and other than a little seepage at the bottom, still holding tight. It's the pressure; unbelievable and the glass is toast. Thank God you're all right. I'm fast realizing I've never known what to expect from this storm or this house, but I do think we've just been baptized. What a mess. "

"That was such a close call."

"It's okay, don't cry; come here. I know you're frightened and I don't mean to sound insensitive but I need your help with this spare wood for just a minute so I can quickly cover this opening. Are you okay? I don't know if it will hold against the new direction, but we have to at least try. We don't have that much time."

Now I'm fully awake and unspeakable horrors are roaming freely through my mind as I hold up the wood for him to secure, some of those conjuring up the owners and not knowing what we'll be able to tell them when this is over. Will everything continue to hold against this onslaught of wind and pressure or will they come back to total destruction? Eddie's doing his best for my sake to make light of each situation as it occurs, feeling I think, that if he doesn't I will fall apart and that's too much to handle on a night like this. Now I'm certain our friends are going through the same horrific if not worse experiences. It is all beyond the imagination and I picture everyone hovering in bathrooms all over the island, quaking in fear, waiting without knowing.

"I'm sure some of our luck so far, with the exception of that window, is because of the way this house is positioned. I looked at that heavily planted embankment behind us just last week, and hoped it would do the job as intended because we're so neatly nestled in against it. But I'm not so sure anymore about all the neighbors along the slope of the hill who are far more exposed," Eddie says while tightening things up—as if that understanding will comfort me.

As if in answer, something with weight tears through the black space overhead.

"Back to the bathroom, quickly," Eddie says as I look upward waiting for the sky to fall. It's obvious to me the shattered glass was just a precursor to what will be thrown at us from a new direction.

"I'm terribly worried about everyone now, and what about Essie and her baby, and all her neighbors near the market. I'm so upset I didn't get a chance to get back there again during all the confusion."

"I knew you would be, so I checked on her before I came out here yesterday and she said they were all planning on going over to the mission. Don't worry, we'll go find her as soon as this is over."

A stone mission, built in the twenties near an abandoned sugar mill and run by a couple of Franciscan monks I affectionately nicknamed Friar John and Friar Tuck, though they bore no resemblance, had withstood many bad storms, so I have to believe that she and her friends will be safe there.

Essie Caldwell and I have a special bond from my earliest days on this island, and she, taking all my doubt in stride, took in my whole story and has become like family. I have to have faith that they will make it through this, too.

Lying on my side to be able to fit my length closer to Eddie's curled form as we struggle in the limited floor space and wanting to weep from sheer terror, all I can do is silently chant my prayer-like mantras, digging deeper still to squash my anxiety before it takes control. The mind plays funny tricks when pushed with extreme stress and my salve tonight is to curl up in retreat. It is a waiting game now, waiting for the rage that will be spewed upon us from this new direction and I again want to fall into this now customary woolgathering, to be allowed to drift off perhaps to another island a long time ago, anywhere simply to be away from this.

The sight of Eddie, his eyes closed resting beside me, hair in disarray and still wet in spots from all his hard work, causes a familiar tug at my heart as I watch him in repose, his exhaustion so evident. My eyes fill just thinking of the sequence of events that directed me to this magical place allowing us to meet. And even through this marginal moment of serenity in a horror-filled night, I am convinced I arrived 'riding on the wings of prayer', just where I belonged.

"I love you," I whispered as the heavy weight of sleep closed in.

Chapter Three

The propellers slice through the cotton-candy cloud blanketing the coast, at first exposing just enough to get a glimpse of the island before revealing a sliver of blue water that surrounds Puerto Rico. Watching wide-eyed as we drop below the clouds hovering over the landing strip of the Luis Munoz Marin Airport, it openly hints at the many dreamed-of delights. And then sheer relief brings on the applause of the twenty-three very rumpled and highly disgruntled people on board. The overbooked jetliner that departed New York was forced to land elsewhere due to mechanical difficulties that caused an unpleasant chain of events for the disappointed passengers waiting their turn on the smaller much older aircraft.

As I stepped out from the wheezing twin-engine prop plane, my first impression is the unexpected mirage effect created by waves of shimmering heat high off the tarmac. Their appearance, as I shade my eyes against the glare, is so intense I'm half expecting a camel caravan will come forth in welcome, but instead it is the handsome gate attendant who has come out to shepherd us into the terminal ahead of our luggage.

I am grateful the frigid December air is behind me and yet the pain of the divorce seems to have taken up permanent residence in my breastbone. I slowly begin to acclimate to the powerful tropical warmth taking hold and sense it already doing its best to penetrate my skin and melt away that persistent knot. I can only hope it will succeed. After doing a little research and talking with my co-workers and friends, my get-away location nearly became a coin toss with all the suggestions before I submitted my leave of absence request, but what could be better than the healing waters of San Juan?

It had been a horrible divorce, made more so because he fought so hard against it. But no matter how hard it was a cheating husband who apparently had wanted to be caught is now a fact of life, and I am now signed forever on the rolls of divorce court documents where my name will reside with others in a cold, unfamiliar place. I'll never forget returning home from a short business trip and sensing a shift in him, imperceptible to anyone not as close, but it was more than that. My sister Carrie was there with him, not at first unusual since she was the type who would show up uninvited. Little Carrie, smart, eager and a little too greedy for her own good.

I came out of our bedroom where I had removed my travel clothes and heard whispers instead of words just as I reached the landing. Something primal was alerted and I allowed myself to stay perfectly still until I was able to decipher the sounds. Then I walked softly down the stairs, stopping mid-way too shocked to move further as I caught the hurried end of an embrace and flushed faces turning away. Unable to move or speak, I felt my world shift. My own sister and the man in whom I'd placed my trust.

Grateful to be on solid ground once again after the nerve-wracking experience of bouncing through giant cumulous clouds all the while watching a large bolt on the wing trying to unscrew itself with every changing rev of the engines, I take a moment to release the months of built-up tension and drink in my surroundings. Already in this one spot there is much to notice.

I had used all of the in-flight hours well away from him, to reflect upon Rob's infidelity, the humiliation, and the agonizing months that followed and unraveled our lives. The still vivid scenes replaying in my mind of all the wailing out loud as though a participant in an Italian wake, throwing myself across the bed like a widow over a coffin. And those ugly moments from the past months that didn't just end when the signatures dried and my stomach carried the perpetual feeling of a baseball having made a direct hit, leaving me feeling vulnerable and sick and out of breath—feelings frozen in time. Grabbing my large Hartman duffle from the moving ramp and heading outside, an unexpected breeze kisses my skin as soon as I exit the doors, as though in response to all the past ugliness. It was indeed time for a change!

Hailing a cab from the many lined up outside the terminal, I instruct the mustached driver in my hastily studied guidebook Spanish, to take me to the Amparo Seaside Inn near the Coral Bay section of Punta Las Marias beach. The Travel section of the Times has promised it to be 'an ambrosia for the senses'. The brochure stated with its picturesque photographs, "delightfully welcoming, family run and muy tranquilo"— more than enough to entice me to bask in the warm embrace of the sun.

"Si, Senorita," he replied tossing my duffle into the trunk. I can see he is trying hard not to chuckle at my poor pronunciation and promise myself to work on that while I'm here.

The light in the sky and the effect it has on the world I've just entered hits like a force in contrast to the midwinter grays and even more fortunate, a short ride later the 'posada' is exactly as advertised—quaint, charming and very inviting with its beachfront backyard. It's topped by a burnished red tile roof and is entirely engulfed by lush tropical foliage.

Entering, I let my eyes adjust to the lack of light before walking deeper into the cool interior that is both lobby and sitting room and partially closed against the heat of the day. This is so stunning that I can tell already from the use of mahogany stained shutters that adorn the long windows and the overstuffed brightly colored furniture resting on the twelve by twelve eggshell white floor tiles that it has been lovingly put together. These are the kinds of details I coveted and enjoyed reading about in design magazines because of the small ordinariness of our New York apartment, now my apartment, that harbors nothing but stagnant air for my return.

My enchanted expression must have been obvious to the fascinating woman standing before me with a gracious smile. I had been so deeply engrossed in the inviting use of color I hadn't seen her heading toward *me. Patting some unruly strands of her glossy black hair into place, offering me a warm knowing smile and introduction, Rosa Amparo de Garcia (I'd read the inn was named for her family) gathers me up in the soft folds of her flowing caftan as if sensing I need more than the guest register to sign. The range of emotions that had turned me toward this island had already begun to flee with the mere touchdown of tires on tarmac, and this kind, welcoming embrace did much to chase them further from my mind.*

"Such dark circles, my dear Lily. Please, go change into your swimsuit and sit by the pool for a small siesta before we meet the others for dinner. There is the one couple at the moment, and an elderly gentleman who will be leaving tomorrow, so for a few days at least, dining will be more intimate before the other guests arrive. I may even get a chance to sit down and visit over coffee and dessert, which by the way is a beautiful flan of my own recipe. Let me get Jorge to take your bag and open your room."

After being shown to my room by young Jorge, who tells me in blushing English how happy he is to welcome me to Puerto Rico, I immediately rid myself of the impossibly high Charles Jordan sandals I had changed into the moment I boarded the plane, and quickly rummage my duffle for my bikini, nearly the color of key lime pie, loosely tying a gauzy sarong around my waist. Feeling immediately at ease, I'm positive I've made the perfect choice with this inn and from Rosa's kindhearted greeting, I know I made the right decision to personally call and book the space, hinting at my need for change.

Taking the shortcut through the veranda outside my room to the pool, I can feel my muscles loosening with each step. I'm on autopilot as I head for the far end so that I can more easily hear the unfamiliar and highly anticipated sounds of the surf, and without a moment's hesitation, softly collapse into the cushy chaise that beckons; sleep coming quickly behind my lids.

"Rumor has it that it's very good luck to make friends with iguanas." A male voice penetrates the stillness.

Shielding my eyes against the sun and forcing thoughts through a sleepy haze with no sense of time, I try and take in the image before me—a deeply tanned man with thick, dark-brown curly hair, wearing aviator glasses. He is dressed in a white short-sleeved shirt with what appears to be a small logo over the breast pocket and khaki shorts, both accentuating his ability to lift weighty objects.

"I beg your pardon," I snap before noticing that in fact a miniature storybook version of a dinosaur is resting quite peacefully at the foot of my chair. There he is, sagging jowls, eyes contentedly at half-mast and completely uninhibited by my presence while sharing in the warm sun.

Rising up on my elbows just about to scream, the stranger immediately puts a finger to his lips to hush me while ever so slowly inching closer to the chair as I stare open-mouthed at this otherworldly creature. With my senses clearing, I can see that its body looks textured because of the greenish-blue skin coloring that so obviously camouflaged its appearance. Still trying not to move, I watch as the stranger's long shadow stretches across the odd little body, causing it to slither away under the clump of ferns nearby where it could blend in with ease once again.

"I never saw that one coming," I said as I expelled my held-in breath.

"They're not at all uncommon around here, but usually not as bold as this little guy. Can't say I blame him, though, being attracted to pretty colors and long legs myself."

Blushing terribly since I've been startled and embarrassed at the same time, I simply stare.

Leaning over with his outstretched arm, "I'm Carlos."

"Lily," I said shakily accepting his hand but still wondering about lucky iguanas.

"When I'm not rescuing ladies from the local wildlife, my real job is running a small charter flight operation providing tours for small groups or hauling small cargo. I'm here to get the week's roster from Rosa, but I'm glad I decided to come in on the beach side today...possibly you are on the schedule for tomorrow?"

"*I wasn't even aware of its existence since I only arrived this afternoon.*"

"*Then maybe you'll want to sign up for one in a few days after you get settled. It's easy. Just fill out the short form at the desk. See, Palm Coast Charters,*" he says, handing me a business card showing him, Carlos Fernando, to be the owner.

"*Thanks, but right now the only thing I'm really interested in catching are the sun's rays.*"

He had taken off his Ray-Bans, revealing eyes the color of sage flecked with gold and framed by small lines etched into their corners when responding to his wide smile. I watched from behind the obscurity of my sunglasses while he confidently sauntered into the inn, and am left feeling slightly jarred but at the same time marveling at this unique encounter with both man and creature.

Later, on my way into dinner, admitting to myself how unexpectedly that very good-looking guy had piqued my curiosity and after all, I justified so easily, I had come all this way seeking change and perhaps a little adventure, it seems a perfect opportunity to tell Rosa about Carlos' heroics by the pool and see what happens. After a miserable separation and continuing arguments prior to the divorce decree, I'm due for more than a little change.

Stationed at the front desk enjoying a cup of café con leche, awaiting the night clerk's arrival, Rosa looks over the rim inquisitively with her gentle expressive dark eyes. I feel a slight blush coming on again as I describe the earlier events.

"*You know, Lily, Carlos is a good boy. I've known him a long time and he has a good head on his shoulders. I also knew his father, and he too loved the pretty women. You would enjoy the flying; all my guests do.*"

It is easy to sense Rosa's natural exuberance and to be drawn to her soft accent, loving the sound as she rolls the letters in a rich, dusky trill that I will have to master, and I listen attentively while she gladly gives me the full scoop on Carlos' background, as well as that of some of his friends. Then, not leaving any chance for further apprehension

*about this whole charter thing, she takes some of the company
brochures from the corner of the desk and stuffs them into my hand.*

*"Is there anything else I should know?" I ask, looking pitifully at
my handful of printed material.*

*It's obvious that she is very fond of him in the way a proud mother
would be, and according to her, he is a well-known local who began his
business career by taking over his late father's small six-room hotel
and bar near Luquillo beach. Since his true passion had always been
flying, he saved all his money to buy the first plane and began taking
small charters, booking mostly through the smaller inns like this one in
order to log the flying time he craved. Apparently, he has turned his
passion into a very successful and highly flexible business venture now,
but continues his close tie with Rosa and her clientele. The pleasure on
her face lighting her eyes made me secretly wonder if Rosa and Carlos'
father had at one time been more than good friends.*

*That is how only a few days after our meeting, and with the help of
this same motherly encouragement, I find myself once again in the air.
Hearing that there were no other bookings for the day, Carlos resorted
to using his favorite plane, the older Piper 250 from his small company
fleet; and to my surprise and delight, invited his best friends Jonas and
Carmen to round out the seating.*

*They arrived just in time for Carlos' scheduled take off from the
Dominicci Airport in Isle Grande, their arms waving frantically as they
see us approaching the plane. They are wearing matching white tee
shirts that display a small company logo in the upper right corner: a
line of palm trees against a wisp of blue water with the name lettered in
deeper blue all encircled inside an orange border, just like the one he
presented me with when picking me up. It was a delightful gesture on
his part as I'm sure other guests would have been required to pay for
them as souvenirs, although I did notice mine said a size small on the
tag and wondered how Carlos pictured me in it, and I felt my face go
red.*

*So here I am, unimaginably, in this unexpected, free-spirited union
already embellished for me by their boisterous and natural ease of*

friendship, being indoctrinated into their view of island life. The casual plan he pointed out, since his old friends would be aboard, was to spend the entire day roaming the nearly cloudless sky in this weathered orange and white capsule with its well worn upholstery, touching upon as much of interest as time allows.

Perhaps he is taking no chances that this experience will be easily forgotten, having already forewarned him that my stay on Puerto Rico will most likely be short-lived, or just perhaps his interest in me has been urged along with a little prodding from Rosa. Obviously, working at what he loved and running a business the island way suited his gregarious personality and need for freedom and flexibility that gave it all a tantalizing quality.

Looking out of the windows of the tiny plane, I have a strange sensation that it will tilt if I lean too far over and trying not to show my fear, I cannot help but openly marvel at this new experience, feeling such a rush of happiness and independence that it momentarily startles me.

As Jonas points out the dolphins at play crisscrossing bow waves of the boats below, my quiet shyness over this new adventure begins to dissipate, and when Carlos tips the wings a bit for effect, Carmen and I squeal like schoolgirls. Then as we approach the southern shore of one of the islands, the beguiling light, the likes of which I've never seen seems to be playing tricks with my vision. Ripples appear nearer the shoreline and the water that is a sparkling glass green slowly turns into yellow ribbons where it meets the white sand beach. And in that yellow light, the sharks feeding close to shore shockingly appear like dark torpedoes.

Conversation is uncomplicated in this suspended atmosphere and some of my earlier trepidation as well as the shyness are fast melting away and the soft hum of the engine thankfully never skips a beat. It is a beautiful day and Carlos' personal, joyful and obviously untiring view of a small chain of mountains varied in size and volcanic in origin that he has witnessed many times over becomes contagious. Looking with fresh eyes, their forms either rounded or peaked appear to me to have either unruly looking scrub flourishing with cactus and wildflowers or are covered in soft drapery folds of green hues, lain carefully and with seamless precision by an imaginary gardener. I've never witnessed the world in such color as land and sea spread out beneath.

The water is particularly calm and each and every one of these forms also appears to have a beach kissed by the tender lap of wave. Most are either ringed completely by the soft white sand, half-mooned or even, the very few, showing the tiniest hint of white powdery pebbles. Depending on the angle I sought, I thought they resembled either a smile or a frown much like the often-viewed painting of Mona Lisa, and all were nudging up to various sized rock outcroppings. And all of it beckons further exploration.

The midday sun is changing the effect of the scenery, letting Carlos know the time, so spotting a particular favorite among the many shapes closest to home, and without fuss, he makes an instantaneous decision that it's the perfect place for lunch and drops down smoothly onto a small, unpaved runway while my stomach tries to comply. Hailing a handy 'publico', Carlos' word for a small taxi-van, it is just a quick ride to the nearby beachfront restaurant that is no more than an open-air structure with three sides and an overhang for the tables. I'm assimilating it all as fast as I can.

Over a soothing lunch of rice and beans and icy cold beer that I immediately note is referred to as 'cerveza', I decide I will always refer to this amber liquid by that more exotic sounding title. With shoes off and toes tucked into the soft sand, the mood is light and I feel as though we've been friends forever. It doesn't hurt to notice Carlos' eyes on me intimating more than I expected. The heat of the sand easily flows upward causing a slight quiver before another blush sets in.

At least on land it is much easier to talk without the engine noise and prompts a grand discourse that encourages individuality and a peek into our personalities at a more pleasant decibel. Carmen, much less introverted than Jonas, is someone I'm instantly drawn to, and I know Carlos couldn't possibly have known the commonalities related to art that would help the day unfold so easily. I had after all just walked away, even though temporarily, from a job that connects me often with artwork, handling a bevy of duties at the Metropolitan. It is not lost on the men that we've instantly bonded.

All through lunch, this trio of longtime companions continues to astound and fascinate me with their tales of pirates and the many treasures sunken and lost off Drake's Passage where the Atlantic meets the Caribbean Sea, all of it required learning as far as they were concerned. The importance of it all stirred my interest as well—this was an area I'd never researched.

They let me know almost proprietarily that Sir Francis Drake himself had taken up his post on the very hills we're about to fly over in order to keep his eye on the Spanish fleet, which made me really anxious to get back in the air. Had anyone suggested that I'd want to spend this much time on an airplane of any size, they would have been met with an expletive or two, but I'm learning quickly, this is not just 'any' flight.

Carlos began tossing out other brief snippets of island history, some of it relating to Columbus' arrival in 1493, and his naming of certain islands "Las Once Mil Virgenes" in honor of St. Ursula. Plus, he said there were many countries claiming a hold on the various islands throughout the centuries, making it sound a bit like they've been in foster care until now, but that's probably just my imagination gone wild.

There are islands owned by the English, the French, the Spanish and the United States and I'm struggling to remember them all as well as the many not looking large enough to have names longer than their spot on the map I'm holding. They are being tossed at me like properties on a monopoly board.

Thankfully, because Carmen is a high school art teacher, the topic is turned to our mutual interest in art and antiques making it easier for me to contribute a bit more to the conversation sharing some of the events of my own life stateside and the many weekends spent browsing the art museums and antique shops of Manhattan.

She had a particular feel for the work of Camille Pissaro whose background was an island mix. I knew he had attended school in Paris and that Corot was one of his most important influences. My interest in Corot matched hers as it cross-referenced the two artists. I had always favored Corot's landscapes and knew he was one of the leading painters of the Barbizon School of France, making for a far more enjoyable give and take while the men discussed sports.

I noticed Jonas paying closer attention and sense his pride in her as he picks up a bit of our conversation. He is obviously aware of her passion for art. But I must admit, all the while I gaze out on the spectacular length of beach lined with high coconut palms swaying gracefully in their own private dance, that other life is beginning to fade away. It is as though it is of another time, or else I'm simply in a dream. They've now completely enfolded me with their warmth and camaraderie and I don't want to wake up.

There's more talk of the sea but it is beginning to be drowned out by loud holiday music played by a scratchy band coming from the kitchen, providing an upbeat backdrop to our conversation.

"Go check it out Lily. JoJo, the owner, is a real gem and I know he'd love the visit," Carlos offers, noticing my glances since he seems to be watching me again.

I excuse myself and find him flouring fresh chicken parts next to a bubbling pot of oil, flour up to his elbows. He points out not only the importance of the temperature of the oil and the secret blend of spices in the flour, but that the music is part of the upcoming Three Kings' Day (Epiphany) celebrations. I am somewhat baffled but he says unabashedly that I should stay here in the islands not only for his popular chicken but the holiday fun celebrated on many islands. That fun, he says expansively, would include a parade of colorful floats, lots of steel pan music, a food fair and the treat of 'Mocko Jumbies' walking around on tall stilts wearing masks to ward off evil spirits, the latter sounding like just what I need. There is so much to absorb and I've only touched the surface. And now that I've shown an interest, I get to sample his chicken for good measure.

*Time is passing too quickly with so much yet to discover, but well
sated and relaxed, we are once again back in the air flying low over a
similar grouping of islands, all ringed with the ubiquitous white
beaches that lay flush with the dazzling blue water. The clear weather
has held, and I'm even able to see swimmers from a large Catamaran
anchored in the pale aqua calm casting deep purple shadows beneath
them onto the sandy bottom.*

*Carlos has by now primed my interest with his version of the
history of the "Baths" on Virgin Gorda, not only because of its
Stonehenge-by-the-sea appearance but also the legend of St. Ursula
and her eleven thousand sacrificed virgins during the Middle Ages. The
'fat virgin', supposedly Columbus' name upon first viewing the plump
looking island, immediately puts me in mind of a circus lady in a
traveling carnival, nothing akin to the rounded forms seen from the sky.*

"Down there to your right, Lily, you can see Prickly Pear and
Pelican Island. And as we swing around, you'll see the Baths. You can't
miss them. It's those huge boulders over there that come right down to
the water's edge," *Jonas pipes in, taking Carlos' lead.*

"I never imagined anything like this. It's extraordinary; they're
nearly as big as houses!"

"The story about the Baths has long held a fascination for visitors,
mostly due to their size, but also that legend. I hope you get a chance to
get inside those caves and see for yourself one day. It's like a rock maze
with interesting color striations and boulders toppled together forming
a 'grotto' large enough to swim through, and the beach is
spectacular."

*Grabbing thoughts from Carlos, perhaps having noticed him
watching me earlier, Jonas teasingly adds while winking at Carmen,*
"Very romantic too as long as there are no jellyfish."

*My guess is they have had some very satisfying explorations into
that grotto.* "Believe it or not, I remember coming across something
about that legend when I was doing some research on porphyrite stones
used in the healing arts."

"What's porphyrite?" Jonas asks and I can see I've awakened a new interest.

"I've read many definitions about igneous rock crystals, but my instincts always led me back to the Chinese letter stone, 'Stone of Trust' used to impart trustworthiness in the holder as well as intuit trust in others. At least that's my recollection from material located in some dusty storeroom a long time ago.

"And strangely, a bit of research turned up porphyrite tiles in Roman ruins that were used as portable altar slabs in the 11th century and stirred up quite a bit of interest about relics and St. Ursula and those 11,000 virgins. But it seems there have been many interpretations through the various translations as to whether it was eleven, eleven hundred or eleven thousand women. Now I can see I'll have to do some more digging into these connections."

"There's a ton of history around here as well as lots of strong myths, Lily; I hope you'll at least have time to delve into some of it," Carmen says, knowing we both love the search as much as the discoveries.

"I hope so, too, Carmen and if that happens, I'd love to have your help to direct me."

There it was. Remembered articles; some fanciful travel fluff about islands with names like Blessing, Parasol, and Prospect and some in-depth library and museum-related material that I read by chance before choosing Puerto Rico, also richly steeped in history.

Columbus, as is known, had been a very busy man during 1493, naming the many Caribbean discoveries and he called it 'San Juan Bautista' in honor of John the Baptist. The impressive six-level Fortress El Morro with its tunnels and dungeons below managed to hold off Sir Francis Drake but succumbed to a land assault by the forces of the Earl of Cumberland. Like the Baths, I yearn to discover more about this important sounding fort and this island also. As much mystery and magic as one woman trying to break out of her cocoon of heartbreak could hope for. I wondered silently where it all might lead. Maybe I can figure out a way to take a little extra time to explore on my own and see for myself.

Tucking these thoughts away as the waning light forces us to make our final approach to Isle Grande, I'm surprised at my reluctance to say goodbye. Even though I've never been fond of flying, and had no high expectations for the day, it had been storybook from the beginning; perfect weather, grand scenery, tall tales, and a delightful mix of warm and generous personalities.

While Carlos takes a little time with his plane and necessary paperwork, Carmen and I exchange information and promises to stay in touch. She has given me many things to think about with her warm-hearted openness emanating through extremely dark eyes, so much like Rosa's. Possibly the warmth comes from this Spanish heritage that I'm being introduced to but it is a strong draw to this land I'd like to know better.

Her willowy body topped by black thick wavy hair braided down her back, glides lightly when she walks, reminding me of a ballerina, pairing nicely with Jonas' trim frame as their steps become synchronous. It is easy to mentally intrude and imagine them frolicking inside the grotto and I have to force my mind away before Carlos returns.

"Sorry to rush off like this, Lily, but I've got to get back for the night shift at the hotel. It was great meeting you. Have him bring you by for a drink before you leave the island," Jonas says, taking Carmen's hand with a glance over my shoulder toward Carlos as he exits the Piper.

Carlos had told me that Jonas was the manager at a highly popular new beachfront hotel and his shifts were irregular. I was hoping that visit might happen when I heard his approach.

"Why don't we have dinner and talk more about your new discoveries?" he suggests as we wave them off, coming toward me with those interesting green eyes that I've now learned were a legacy of his European mother who left when he was only twelve.

Since I'm feeling both relaxed and exhilarated and still filled with questions, it does seem the only natural thing to do. I also had to admit he does make me smile!

After a quick change of clothes at the Inn, we head into the Condado area for dinner. It becomes obvious very quickly that his attention to detail in the sky extends also to other aspects of his life. His charm is not wasted on me either, and I realize how much it plays into the success of his tour business as well.

Over a meal of baked sea bass richly bathed in fresh citrus and accompanied by a crisp French white wine, he opened up freely about growing up on the island and his dreams, expounding on events with flair. He almost made me yearn for similar experiences though I haven't a clue how to obtain them. But as I listen, I find I'm doing so with intent as if I can feel something intangible tugging at that thought.

It didn't take me long as I listened to his version of island living and his funny stories to realize the captivating hold a place like this would have because of its nearly exotic nature. I'm already convinced I've made the right decision in coming here and the days ahead will be very exciting. But my intuition tells me that this land that seems both foreign and ancient and simultaneously modern in its facilities is teeming with an underlying primitive heartbeat and that beat might unearth a woman who has been trapped in a world without joy far too long.

THUNDERSTRUCK....the only word I can think of as I write in my journal this morning, grateful I remembered to toss the new leather-bound notebook into my bag as I packed for the airport. Someone had told me during my divorce proceedings that journaling was a wonderful tool for healing and I'm now making good use of it.

The flight and the dinner with Carlos proved to be medicine from the gods. As if by magic, the days have grown into weeks, and I've officially lengthened my stay. I'm besotted with this island and without intention, have willingly allowed him to become the emotional fulcrum needed to balance all that had been destroyed by the divorce.

Staying far longer than planned and gladly giving over time I'd hoped to use in another direction, and with happy anticipation, I've let him open up new doors into his universe and my imagination. It has already softened the gnarled edges of that previous hurt as he amazingly deemed it his personal duty to introduce me to the 'rhythm' of the island and its many pleasures, many more than referenced in all the travel articles and novels, and urge my spirit back to life by somehow sensing my every need before they even cross my lips.

His manner while coaxing my smiles and dampening my fears as we share new experiences and daily ventures into the 'island way' through his eyes is almost childlike and yet somewhat like a heat-seeking missile. He guides me with great flourish through the streets and countryside of his native home with obvious pride reflected in everything we do together.

Hours and days now pass smoothly as we've become comfortable together, and happily under Rosa's watchful eyes since she has taken a personal and motherly interest in our new friendship. During the day, under his tutelage, I've been able to experience my first taste of foods till now completely foreign to my lips. Things like stewed goat and lechon asado (barbecued pig) done on a spit over an outdoor fire in one or another of the backyards of his youth as he has already introduced me to many of his longtime friends: Emilio, Juan, Mimi, and Graciela joining with Jonas and Carmen as standing out among many in his wide sphere of acquaintances. I've surprised them and myself with the enjoyment of these dishes and begged for more.

In spare moments, I write about it all in my no longer empty journal, already beginning to see its value as I release thoughts onto page after page, ensuring that they will live on. Especially those at the end of those hours when evening comes and we dance softly out on the moonlit sands of his childhood beach at Luquillo to the hypnotic beat always streaming from the portable radio resting on our blanket. This we usually enjoyed after hastily donning previously shed clothing for a refreshing dip in the sea.

Or the times we simply stargaze the vast sky with no particular plans for the future. I feel I'm absorbing it all like a sponge and I'm reveling in my good fortune with rarely a thought of the past. I'm bent on preserving every moment, but again I feel that unfamiliar tug pulling me into the written words as if I'm missing the real message. I look for it on the periphery of my vision, half expecting it to leap forward, that thing I can't describe.

Carlos takes me everywhere with him as if he senses my internal longing to again feel something akin to real happiness that is lying somewhere quietly below the surface of my carefully presented personality, the one others see when we are not alone. It doesn't matter where; something as unexpected and unfamiliar as a seedy neighborhood pool parlor to sip icy cervezas and listen to a famous guitarist happy to be back in his neighborhood playing in the off hours just for his friends, or colorful back-street open air haunts occupied by more locals than tourists and always humming with activity. He seems determined to shake things up in my emotional repertoire.

To balance that, he has now introduced me to many culinary delights with names like paella and ceviche, both made with the freshest seafood in intimate restaurants at the hands of renowned local chefs or the simplicity of asopao (gumbo) and arroz con pollo (chicken with rice) all accompanied by my now favorite tostones made from fried plantains served in restaurants with stars next to their names and at many tables in the different neighborhoods all over Puerto Rico...delicioso.

Often when there is no plan to the day, our sustenance is made up of simply a Cubano sandwich washed down with thick espresso sips of Puerto Rican coffee grabbed hastily at small street side vendors along our casual walks near the Inn. And feeling the occasional need for a change from the bright sun and sand, we head into the country and find ourselves driving into the lush green of the rain forest, and I pinch myself as though in a dream as we wile away hours under the spell of bird song hidden in the dripping leaves of El Yunque, stopping only to hold each other with thoughts of the next event.

And many a night, choosing a more upscale environment, already aware I will put on that favored dress to accentuate my silky tanned legs showing off newly learned steps, he lures me onto the dance floor of a romantic hotel in old San Juan or if the mood strikes, to the lively and very noisy beachfront setting to share a drink with Jonas, slipping amongst the tourists, dancing with a closeness between us that is physically enticing and by now expected in our behavior.

In my journal I've recorded with a highlighted passage that one evening having danced the night away to the sassy steps of the ever popular merengue and those hauntingly romantic tangos improvised without concern, and with only the wait staff left to witness, a look passed between us that gave us both only momentary pause. My heart was beating as wildly as the fanciful music, and the underlying island rhythm I'd perceived in the very first days now exists within me and all the barriers have dropped away. I'm becoming physically alive again, now awakened to it all as placed before me by a man who makes no demands.

I found myself opening to him as a flower to springtime rain followed by sunshine. My deepest thoughts no more complicated nor intense than trying a new Latin dish, learning a new step or a new word, and basking in the tropical sun that leaves me golden and sensual while the daytime heat flows into the night and our bodies. And all the while, he uses those soft green eyes and his strong body in the ways of a confident lover.

In the magical days and nights that have somehow melded together, with me as student and Carlos my teacher, along with a few more flights exploring in that sweet plane, he has given me the heartfelt gift of freedom. Freedom from my fresh personal pain, and the freedom to enjoy with uncensored judgment our limited time, always with the knowledge that I would leave him by mutual consent. He has asked nothing more of me than the honesty to be fully and completely at one with myself—the greatest gift anyone can give.

Time has comfortably slipped by as witnessed by the penned-in dates at the top of each page but now with inevitable thoughts of 'what next' beginning to appear among the recorded lines. I noted the last time we flew there was a new restlessness between us and knowing he's sacrificed willingly many working hours on my behalf, I had to admit that new thoughts are peeking through my haze of happiness—the need to concentrate on my future once again. We both recognize the time has come to say goodbye.

"Don't forget, Lily, you can always come back here for a little shopping or some good old fashioned ' r and r' especially if you end up back in the states, and, of course, more flying." This last remark he brought forth with such a suggestive wink that it caused us both to collapse in laughter.

"Your friendship means the world to me, Carlos. Without these weeks, I don't know what would have happened. But I realize now that I can either go back to the mainland and city life with a straighter spine taking my place among my career-minded friends, or stay and create new memories for myself here in the islands. Either way, I'm stronger and hopefully wiser than when I first arrived and a whole lot more optimistic about the future.

"But to be honest, I really don't think I'm quite ready to give up this new playground where land always meets the sea. And since your suggestion that I visit St. Margeaux sounded very appealing and really worthy of a look, that's where I'm headed before my leave is up. Then I'll decide."

Silently I understood that this newfound experience could never be duplicated no matter how many times I might return. This wonderful unexpected love affair with Carlos was a goodbye gift to the old Lily. While giving so freely of himself, Carlos had wrapped that gift for me in ribbons of delight to be unwrapped in memories on special occasions and tucked safely under a pillow to dream upon. It is now up to me to make a new reality for myself.

I hated saying goodbye to Rosa who tried not to cry as she held me even more dearly than her first welcome, gifting me with a few of the recipes she'd written down for foods I'd grown so fond of. And even more because of not knowing what would be waiting when I unpack my duffle once again, though it proudly displays the bright orange sticker of Palm Coast Charters' logo as a constant reminder of what is possible.

Importantly, now as I'm boarding the newer Cessna for this shorter leg headed to St. Margeaux, I'm flushed with a different anxiety and anticipation because I can now openly admit I crave a life like this, deeply, in my bones, gnawing at my insides. Perhaps it began the moment I saw the expanse of it all from the air, but I know I can't turn my back on it, not yet, not without trying.

There it is; I've voiced it. That is the knotted end to that intangible cord that has been tugging at my heart since meeting Carlos. Everything that has happened from the moment I stepped off the plane from New York was drawing me closer to this truth and yet he cannot be the outcome of this new fact. He was the catalyst, and responsible for removing the heavy stone from my heart. With that weight gone, I know if I'm prepared to take a chance, I must pursue what comes next.

But decision time is slipping by quickly even in a climate of mañanas and piña coladas and my money will soon run out along with my employer's patience. I know that the old Lily might have simply licked her wounds and returned, but somehow that seems nearly impossible after having digested this visual smorgasbord of beauty and excitement round every turn.

Chapter Four

While thinking myself still on the noisy plane, my connection to Puerto Rico is instantly cut off by a horrible cracking sound magnified tenfold in these very real, almost unearthly, conditions. The steady roar of the wind that has now backtracked since the eye passed has dulled my body and my mind's capability to switch gears. I must have drifted into that other place again as escape.

The noise might well have been the very large mahogany tree opposite the retaining wall that's possibly crashed down on the corner of the roof or worse, and that probability has me shaking all over again. Eddie has already gone to investigate after an all too short nap. I feel paralyzed with fear, something I've never experienced and I can't move to help him.

The rain is pounding and lashing everything and even the toilet just startlingly flushed itself from the horrendous pressure. My ears ache. I've moved inside the shower stall that is even more uncomfortable and stifling, and I'm positive the storm is far worse in this direction. Oh God, will it never end and what if the roof goes now?

Coming back in and finding me crouched on the tile, "It's still holding Lily, I don't see any breaks, not anywhere obvious anyway. You're trembling so; what is it?"

"I'm just so scared, and I didn't think it could be worse than the past six hours. How much more of this can there be?"

He quickly runs into the nearby bedroom to grab a cotton throw from the end of the bed. Ignoring the heat, he gently wraps me like a child, pulling me down next to him on our makeshift bedding.

"Look at me. Do you remember how we met?" he asks, tenderly cupping my chin, offering me a light kiss.

"What an odd question—of course I do. What made you think of that at a time like this?"

"It's a good thought and I'm just trying to take your mind off this for a few minutes. I'm worried about you."

"I'm worried about both of us right now, and to be honest I've been quietly doing that same thing, not only tonight but for the last couple of days, just mentally rehashing the past or dreaming about it in one form or another, praying that by doing so some of this horribleness will just magically disappear. This noise is making me crazy; it almost hurts."

Gentled by his concern, "Meeting you is something I will always remember and part of that is because I was so close to throwing in the towel and heading back to New York. I was feeling disheartened about my newfound bravado. You couldn't have known in that brief couple of hours how badly I wanted what you had, an island life and everything that came with it, except 'this' of course. My money had nearly run out along with any hope of finding something I'd enjoy working at that could support me, and that place was my temporary sanctuary."

"You were pretty annoyed, if I remember correctly, at my appearance on 'your' turf."

"True, but at least you stuck around. You could've just walked away, and I'm obviously glad you didn't."

"You're not sorry are you, about any of it?"

"You know I'm not. If I say anything crazy at all tonight, it's because I'm afraid and exhausted. I don't expect to make a lot of sense at the moment and I have to believe somehow we'll make it through this. But since you started this conversation, admit it, you really were such a big flirt. It's no wonder I doubted!"

"Not that you minded at all my girl…since the rest, as they say, is history."

"Unbeknownst to you, because you were so busy coming on to me, you actually held out a lifeline even in the guise of trying to get a date. I was feeling a bit sorry for myself at the thought of going back, and a little out of my element with left side driving; and even though it crossed my mind that you might just have been blowing smoke simply to charm me, your suggestions got me a reprieve."

The noise overhead thundered on, but his voice steadied me, and the roof kept holding. And as he talked my body began to surrender some of the tightness holding me in like enormous rubber bands. This was helped by his reassurances that it would soon be over, as well as the diversionary tactic regarding the place that had become such a favorite of ours over the years.

We still periodically picnic there, reaffirming our feelings for each other as we patrol for shells. Once in a while the gulls swoop in to pick at the leftover lunch, somehow still the warm West Indian flatbread filled with chicken curry I love, or barbecue of some type, rituals not easily broken. This bad habit alerts their keen honing senses and they flock around instantly, squawking at their competitors over any food captured, holding tightly and leaving without a wink or a nod before they're off again. All of my favored creatures must also be in jeopardy tonight.

"You know, Lily, you're not alone in these feelings. I'm far more scared than I care to admit. While I was checking everything, I even found myself repeating one of those idiotic jingles adapted from one of our cruises, just over and over trying to drown out the noise in my head."

His gentling had settled me, easing the tension that's been so pervasive and his voice began to drift a little, as I relaxed and sensed his turn to relax into the past. As it faded it was replaced by other images, those from better times and how we all first met...

∾∾∾

Eddie's hand, warm on the small of my back, guided me toward the lovely island house in a sweetly protective manner, as if he were intuiting my concerns. I'd taken longer to dress for this debut knowing that his friends would all be waiting to meet the new girlfriend and while that tardiness hadn't bothered him, I knew he would be anxious for it to go well. After all, the closeness among his pals was already well known to me in part because it is such a small island but also because their camaraderie was infamous.

I felt a moment's hesitation hearing the first bouts of laughter pouring out through open windows signaling a party already well underway. But before it could matter, we were crossing the small walkway dividing a vivid blue pool, and standing in front of a blue door of the same color opening as if by magic to welcome us in. One of the guests was heading out, passing us by with a grin so impishly mischievous as to enlist a matching one from me. I relaxed my shoulders and tried to remember what Eddie had said on the way over about seeing most of his friends for the first time. I didn't completely understand but the way he and Russ talked, a stranger might think of alien beings and now the first person I confront appears to be quite normal. Perhaps swimming with ones clothes on wasn't actually an everyday occurrence, but so what?

The room inside was awash with color as people dressed in bright flora and fauna prints, interrupted in a staccato pattern by the flow of cooling white fabrics, moved about in animated conversation. I'd found it necessary very soon after my arrival to imitate the dress code since not only did color and material play into the very fabric of island life and the heat, but my drab though necessary monochromatic tailoring of the past could not be my exterior expression of my new tropical adventure.

Eddie took stock of the entire room and seeing a waving hand out on the deck, veered me in that direction. I scanned the crowd and saw small clusters of people laughing, gesturing and using body language to its fullest potential. There was a man over in a corner by a large potted palm who looked like he was on a surfboard, arms waving and knees bending to avoid a spill. He was at least nearing middle age, showing off to two pretty young women trying to urge him on. This audience happened to be the teenage daughters of our hosts, obviously enjoying their own joke as well as his antics.

He had longish hair tied with a print headband that told me right away that it was the man known for early morning swims in the raw before beginning his surf classes. I could not imagine either the notorious Speedo or the nakedness no matter how hard I tried, but have assured Eddie no matter how nice or helpful he appeared to be I would not be requiring any of the beachfront services he offered.

Whichever direction I turned brought out a different interest or acquired fashion statement, particularly for the women. I would not have to concern myself; there would be no New York uniform of the 'little black dress' here.

I then spotted a beautiful woman standing with a middle-aged man that Eddie referred to by a name that just kept turning into an Abbott and Costello routine each time it was said. Benny Who was a retired harbor pilot and on the wagon because of his recent outrageous behavior on the dance floor. I wanted to hear more about him, but I found I couldn't keep from staring at his girlfriend. I had never seen a woman who could look so much like a genie from a lamp that had been shined to perfection, beginning with her hair worn up with a silky band twining the heavy curls.

It could be said she was adorned rather than simply clothed, in the perfect outfit…a golden halter exposing a very flat midriff indicating strong dedication to exercise, a pair of snow-white bellbottoms gracing her curvy figure, ending with a pair of golden sandals. I didn't even bother to waste time thinking whether I could pull off that look; she owned it.

It was hard to believe the number of faces I was expected to match with the many names offered, creating even more confusion for me than those he had already mentioned. These were his friends, no matter how quirky a name or offbeat an appearance and since we'd been hoarding our hours together learning as new lovers do, my only hint at what to expect came from meeting Russ, which hadn't at first been the best impression. I sensed a lot depended on this communal response.

"I told you that you had to see for yourself, I couldn't just make this stuff up, but wait till you meet Mick and Natasha. They are part of the group I regularly sail with and really two of my closest friends."

Eddie had told me of the sea trials with Mick and that his very young girlfriend Natasha was from Eastern Europe; Hungary I think, and that she also loved delving into island history. I immediately began to look forward to sailing together and perhaps doing a bit of underwater exploring while we were at it.

Mick O'Malley, a hearty Irishman from the Bronx, was decked out in what I had begun to call yachting casual...navy polo, white shorts and well-worn topsiders, and I noted how simply Natasha fit the picture, even though I would never learn to pronounce her last name. Her glistening dark hair kept sweeping across her cheek as she looked up into his adoring expression.

Admittedly, he was a mix of dashing and daredevil, with a trim goatee and silver hair and I found myself nearly swooning. This was all becoming the stuff of novels and I began to sense a little jealous envy wanting my place in the story like everyone else. The dismantling of my former life had really begun in earnest.

As we moved in on them, Eddie mentioned that Mick was a freelance 'stringer' for a stateside paper and 'Tasha', Mick's pet name for her, a teacher's aide hoping for a full-time position as soon as she completed a few more courses.

Greeting us with warm hugs, "Don't worry, Eddie, we won't tell her everything!" Mick baited by way of introduction while still making me feel welcome.

Eddie's discomfort and my wanting to know all were but a small part of the evening full of relentless but harmless bantering at our expense. I would expect nothing less of the men and women that made up his world but also began to be aware of his need for me to like them just as much. It wasn't difficult since they were amazing in all ways.

Russ was in the crowd too, but not Nessa. It was apparently their time off from each other that by now I was used to. I was already well aware of Russ's inability to connect permanently with the woman who was perfect for him and was talked about whenever we spent time with him alone. His friendship with Eddie and Mick had been solidified when he first arrived on the island, angry from a failed marriage, and they had circled the wagons as he told it, to protect him from all the beauties that might have preyed on him while vacationing here. All of that seemed a bit absurd until I'd gotten a taste of their lifestyle. By now, however, they felt he was overlooking the one great thing in his life, Nessa.

I knew that while neither was crazy about sailing, he could be relied on in a pinch if Eddie was shorthanded, and hoped that one day maybe we would all be sailing together. For the moment, however, he was in the middle of a small group standing near a large impressive saltwater fish tank while a tall, ginger-haired man seemed to be holding court, all the while the two orange clownfish looked wide-eyed through the glass, puckering in feigned response.

There was also a rather interesting looking woman standing just a little to one side, keeping her eye on the group, sipping a glass of wine, listening to her mate without much response on her part. The image conjured up boredom within a Manhattan drawing room, her presence both chic and toned down, quite opposite the cast of characters in tonight's theatrical improv, and yet something oddly familiar. And apparently, though world travelers, they never missed a good island party when opportunity struck.

It was then inevitable, with Eddie prodding me on, that I came full stop in front of a couple of men occupying a corner of the terrace where complete introduction was not necessary. The man who appeared to be holding up a pedestal topped by a heavy piece of sculpture was called 'Crash', and it took a few well-rehearsed lines from his brother-in-law 'Boomer' anxious to get past what was becoming old hat for me to find out why. Boomer, whose saltwater-abused blonde hair bespoke of his profession as an underwater explosives expert, had him in his care for the weekend but he seemed to take little pleasure explaining the origin of the man's name.

"He's a poor drinker with a penchant for rum and cokes and after too many, if you're anywhere sharing a meal, you can watch in amazement his head slowly falling to the plate in front of him. He never makes a fuss and doesn't wake up until someone tries to remove the plate."

Once told, Boomer seemed to relax as if a taxing burden was again lifted and took us both on with full exuberance, passing no chance to make Eddie squirm for all the past taunts made to him in similar situations. I found myself enjoying the attention and teasing even with Eddie's reddening face.

And while I sensed there were hundreds of stories to be found in the kinship of those gathered, at least for the moment, I seemed to be holding my own. Or so I thought until without warning, I felt a strong arm encircle my waist from behind and was immediately spun around to come face to face with a very handsome man...tall, bald and wearing a mysterious dark eye patch.

"So Eddie, who is this beauty and where have you been hiding her?"

"I know what you're up to, so take it easy."

Bowing extravagantly, ignoring Eddie's warning, one hand removing the eye patch as he straightened, only to reveal a tiny pirate flag.

Falling backward slightly, feeling Eddie's hands grip my shoulders, "Whoa girl, I've got you."

The eye under the patch startled the hell out of me, and all I could do was huff and puff at Eddie for not warning me in time.

"Okay, now that you've had your fun, tell me, do you have one that actually matches that beautiful blue one?"

"I do, absolutely, but since my accident, I find that humor goes a long way toward breaking the ice. And just for future reference, the giveaway is when you see me wearing the patch. I look pretty much like everyone else otherwise...well, almost."

"You're forgiven, but I have a feeling you're not the least like everyone else!"

"Are you flirting with him?"

"You left me out there on that limb, but I'm not blind; he's gorgeous with or without that patch."

"Just remember, I'll be watching you two."

Eddie needn't have worried—he had my heart, but Vic was truly an amazing specimen of mankind. The shaved head and the patch only seemed to add importance to his rugged six-four frame. This was indeed becoming a night to remember.

The party was moving around, changing scenes as the cast milled between groups, creating new audiences for their conversation. It had already begun taking on a new tenor as the drinks flowed and the time flew by.

At one point, I noticed Natasha appeared to be cornered by a man possessively holding her elbow as she leaned closer to Russ. I hadn't seen him come in, but he was definitely intent on her presence next to him. Dressed out in something of a safari outfit, right down to the pith helmet clutched under his arm, I found myself picturing his arrival for tea with Karin von Blixen after a long day's travel to Nairobi. But for the moment he seemed quite content, leaning in as though telling her of the tale, shaking out the dust of the day. He had apparently arrived without his formidable wife and enjoyed playing up his rough British accent and he certainly had plenty of audience tonight.

The night wore on boisterously and while taking it all in, listening to Eddie and the various exchanges of stories, it was obvious that all of it, the jokes, quips, famous routines and impressions, was generously offered up with more reverence than any ill humor. It spoke of a trust and strong bond I had yet to experience and of his deep affection and attachment to a place that I was steadily beginning to call home.

As if reading my thoughts and smiling with obvious pride, "I have to say, all of this is what makes this island so uniquely qualified to be the best damned place to live, just like I told you when we first met. There is an unspoken code that originality is admired and even encouraged, and loyalties take precedence over everything."

Throughout the rest of the evening introductions were made with many more twists to names or some sort of specialty admired, and with my brain on overload, most of it gone almost as fast as it was given. I knew I would more than likely see each of them again in due course and they would all soon fall into their own setting without effort. But there was a particular couple that stood out because of Eddie's genuine affection for them, our hosts, Renaldo and Maxine Vincent. Reno loved fast boats and brightly colored cars and could fix absolutely anything; that is, if the funny braggadocio spouted by all, accounted for skill.

Max, his bride of many years welcomed me with open arms, a bright smile and a very outgoing personality, helping me to fit in immediately. I noted throughout the evening she never seemed far from his side and, after talking with them, probably insuring that his story lines were accurate. They owned an auto leasing business located halfway between town and the airport and had successfully carved out lots of free time for their enjoyment. I was not only beginning to learn about the art of storytelling from the masters, but that there also seemed to be the fine art of play that was *de rigueur* on this small wonderful island.

"Lily, one thing you have to know about these two is that they can always be counted on for a great party, a helping hand, and if necessary, even a shoulder to cry on; and importantly an innovative touch to any special event," Eddie said, interrupting my conversation with Max.

"They are solely responsible for the creation of an extremely large wooden birthday cake built to hide a cross-dresser as the surprise ending to one of Russ's birthday parties."

"I found him through a friend of a friend and had to import him from a nearby island which, between the building materials, air fare and costume, turned out to be quite an expensive cake!" Maxine said, and then looking at me with a cunning smile, she whispered, "I pulled the wool over everyone's eyes for Reno's 40th and believe it or not, he still doesn't know who the belly dancer was."

"I think I've found a new friend," I said to Maxine with genuine appreciation of her talents. "Can't wait till Eddie's birthday rolls around and we can cook up something for him that tops even that."

Everything was told with such prideful sincerity you'd have thought the accomplishments held a rating somewhere in the Guinness Book of Records. I simply smiled while thoughts of trying to top any of it roamed in my brain. But it wasn't long before my own place among them was acknowledged with a new nickname specifically created because of my generous height of five-ten. I was dubbed 'Lilliputian', solidified with a toast in my honor. It was enough.

᠔᠔᠔

"Wake up, it's too quiet. "You don't suppose it's actually over?"

The incessant mind-numbing noise had been doing battle with us all night, but the fierce wind had died, leaving us a more tolerable pitch.

Eddie pulled me up and into his arms in grateful relief. "We've made it... unbelievable!"

It was true, though our bodies had been nearly vibrating from the percussion of noise, and since the eye had passed earlier, the storm was over at last. It is very early in the morning, but not yet full light with twelve hours endured and we are sticky with heat and exhausted and still dreading what we will uncover but he is impatient to take everything apart again and look for our boat.

"It's still way too dark to see that far even with these babies, we'll have to go outside for a better look," he says, waving the binoculars at me, angry at their momentary uselessness.

"I need a change of air but I'm not going out there yet," I said, ignoring his plea while sweeping up the broken glass. "I'm not anxious to see what my imagination was picturing all night."

Patience is not one of his virtues but he's far more worried about losing the *Wanderer* than he is letting on. She might be our only home now if Eddie's small apartment has been destroyed. The *Wanderer* was his first major acquisition when his business began to grow and he has spent many loving hours on her care and maintenance. He's also made many changes below as he believed that one day he would live aboard permanently, a dream since his youth sailing on the lakes near his home in Ohio. A dream come true and one I'd come to share.

Finally, I can see lighter gray peeking through a small opening, but Eddie's already noticed it and is heading for the front door. I follow timidly, ill prepared for the after effects of such a violent night. I can see him shaking his head as he walks away from the doorway as if he had been blocking my view intentionally.

I'm sure he knew what my reaction would be, but startled by the sound, he turns to hear me shrieking like a demented soul. It is as though the island had become prey to some evil monster far worse than predictions given, and that being had taken out its maniacal revenge by pulling everything into its vortex. Then the predator, having filled itself up at last, disgorged it all haphazardly and cruelly to be witnessed in the light of day—nothing appeared recognizable or in any sort of natural order.

The earth in front of us once lush and infused with color is all completely barren. The once white stucco façade of the house now mimics a disgusting shade of green from the dirt and foliage that is plastered against and totally embedded into the paint as though it had always been that color. And the darker wood trim of the door is stripped away, gouged by sharp objects.

Where there used to be great varieties of trees patterning the hillside, or groupings of hibiscus and great huge expanses of flowering bougainvillea that nearly devoured the entrance wall...nothing. The few large solid trees that were left are as disabled by the wind's mutilation as soldiers on a battlefield, their leafless limbs torn and mangled. The difficult tan tans are gone as well as the more delicate lime trees and tougher grasses and cacti. Gone also are the graceful tropical fronds that had spilled over, raining down their soft feathery tips everywhere. The landscape is nude of color and form and totally void of the sounds of birds or insects to remind us where we are.

The source of the earlier sounding crash is also made obvious with the light. The tree has toppled the shed, splitting open the roof, leaving it exposed to the rain and tearing apart its contents. Who knows what property would now hold the favorite hammock or the many items stored that had no doubt gone flying in the night? Or for that matter, I thought, any of the remnants from any household likely laid open by the wind, exposing the destruction that is now so evident here.

Then as I look up from the shed, something of color catches my eye. Some of the shards from the beautiful glazed pottery that had made their long journey from another part of the world, have been catapulted across the yard and are impressed into the side of the house nearest the drive giving it the look of a hastily created mosaic…the only spot of color in our now drab environment.

As we walk around the house in a near state of shock, I see a fallen shade tree that has come within inches of splitting open the roof of the extended terrace which would have taken out the windows on that side of the house. Had that happened, I've no doubt everything inside would have been sucked through as easily as money in a pneumatic tube. As it is, it broke apart some of the railings, splitting and tearing up tiles while those left are greasy with soil. How were we able to survive what I'm convinced was near to impossible? How many guardian angels are we allowed in one lifetime?

"Do you see a stream over there, Lily? I don't remember that," Eddie said, taking my gaze in another direction as he swings the glasses around for a better look.

The silvery lengths might easily be mistaken for small streams glinting with the newly opening sky, but there are no streams in this entire area.

"Believe it or not, I think it just might be galvanized roofing and look, further to the right and down the hill, it's everywhere in pieces and even long strips. That had to have been those high-pitched screeching sounds we heard. They must have been airborne from all directions."

What a difference the view now. A week before the hurricane's arrival, trying to get a better feel for the house, we had eaten dinner out on that once welcoming terrace taking in the scent of frangipani, still hoping against hope that a miracle would happen and we wouldn't have to close it all up and block out the loveliness. We had only given casual notice to the other houses scattered nonchalantly over the hillside within distant sight of each other but knew that like so many homes here, they were all put together with care given to their plantings and panorama.

"I still can't find any of the other houses, Eddie; it's like they've vanished."

"I hope those folks are okay. My guess is it was much worse down there and we really were the lucky ones. And there's no way of telling until we can get through."

Slower scanning reveals evidence that the metallic proof on the earth meant that large gaps in the structures would now be exposing our neighbors' worst nightmares. The evidence of destruction in this less hurried look extends for miles but circling back here, another glint of metal reveals the bulk of a car partially hidden under the fallen tree unnoticed through the door, so shocked we forgot we even had a car. When the tree fell onto the shed, that structure took much of the brunt but our little vehicle was partially flattened, shattered glass left as evidence and a flat tire caused by the weight. It was thoroughly covered by the bulk of the trunk and the few bare limbs left and will take great effort to remove. Not that we would be able to use it without a road since that is now also obscured.

Finally, Eddie, seeing the top of the mast he's been praying for, grabs my hand and pulls me forward ignoring my objection.

"We have to get down there and see how bad it really is!"

"How on earth are we going to do that with all the trees blocking the roads as far as you can see!"

"I know it won't be easy, but we can do it. Besides I'll really need your help; I doubt if anyone else can get through yet, and I know Russ won't stand a chance of getting through town this morning. I promise, I won't let anything happen to you."

I'm thinking more about the unknowns than doubting his concern for me. He's always had certain strength of purpose, but never at my expense. No point in struggling over this question…it is our home now. Looking out over all this wreckage, I know that the town apartment, with its exposure to the sea and wind elements, didn't stand a chance against this onslaught. It was too vulnerable.

Even though the bay is a little more than three miles away, I'm surprised how quickly Eddie maneuvers us down the mountain. We crisscross the road dodging the fallen limbs and many partial trunks as well as downed electrical poles, being vigilant where danger lay in the path, much of this made possible by high levels of anxiety and adrenaline pumping through our systems. The worst of the wind is over, but it's still tough going.

My initial relief at finding the entrance road to Long Point Cay is quickly tossed aside; we still must climb over and around debris, smashed dinghies, metal fencing and even a broken window still encased in its frame lying on a heap of what is left of a young tree. There are a few battered doors and some marine equipment scattered about too as everything was obviously tossed aloft in the overnight hours, left to rest helter-skelter in front of us. And someone's abandoned car was forced from the entrance lot to the edge of an embankment and turned on its side by the wind. I remember clearly what everything looked like a couple of days ago, but much is now missing and much has been harshly rearranged.

It looks like the swath of the storm cut its teeth on everything yet somehow missed objects in small patches of obscurity—noticeably a small storage building set along the perimeter, leaving a bush to stand as sentinel while all else was gone. Standing out also was the prominent hulk of a large powerboat, now stripped of its exterior equipment and quite a bit of its dignity. Both had somehow shown their might against all odds, and the rest all but demolished, leaving only the masts of two smaller boats sticking out of the water like tin soldiers. There appears to be no pattern or sense to the placement of things. It had all gone up with the wind and landed as the wind tired of carrying it.

"There she is!" Eddie exclaimed in sheer joy.

The *Wanderer* sat amidst it all as though she'd had a protective shield surrounding her. The dinghy that had been lashed down was missing and despite the evident hull damage from flying debris that created jagged streaks in her once pristine blue paint, two broken cabin windows that meant water would be inside, and the vanished navigational gear, she was all apiece and afloat and to us looked very much a thing of beauty.

This is our reward for all the agonizing hours.

"Now what?" I asked, looking at the sky, feeling the first warning drops slap my skin.

The elation doesn't last very long. While we've been absorbing the impact of this one area, toting up all the work to be done and where we would begin first, the sky still a sickly gray, opens up with a new barrage of rain that is quite literally breathtaking.

"What do we do now? There's no place to take cover and even if we find someplace, all of this on top of what rain we've had could wash out the road if we try to wait it out, leaving us up that other well-known creek!"

"Our only choice is to make a run for it back to the house," Eddie says again, grabbing my hand too fast for my rebuttal. I didn't want to stay and I was too scared to leave.

Racing faster to find our way back, we have to dodge more tangled wires and poles while trying to reconstruct our downward path that is quickly becoming invisible through the pelting water. More 'stuff' is floating and small ruts and little gullies are beginning to form because the earth is already so saturated, promising to become a mudslide that'll mimic quicksand before long.

Eddie grips my hand tighter and begins to pull me upward as he jumps ahead, and I keep losing my footing. The rain is working against us with angry bursts that sting our pores making it impossible to see where we're going. I have an instantaneous flashback from my second or third year on the island rushing to get home before the roads flooded due to a milder hurricane that caused monumental rain. I distinctly remember looking to my right at the most bizarre scene where a small compound of wooden houses were stacked haphazardly against the sloping hillside and were beginning to collapse under the heavy torrent. It had loosened the soil beneath and the rushing water had made its way inside flushing out the belongings. I'll never forget the sight of a refrigerator and other household paraphernalia tumbling down without restraint, over and through anything in their path and that kind of fear acts like an invisible hand pushing me upward to meet Eddie's grasp.

Now our clothes are plastered to our skin much like the leaves to the side of the house. Shoes nearly come off in the mud making the climb all the more treacherous. Because of the heavier water, we have to climb over rather than around fallen trees to make better time. I'm suddenly uncertain that the events of the night before were the worst of it. We could actually die out here with no one being the wiser. We could be buried alive by something as large as a fallen tree or someone's refrigerator. Screaming out of desperation as well as pain as Eddie instinctively yanks my arm with more force, we reach the top and see for the first time even through the torrent, what looks like a construction site. The house set apart like an oasis in a desert of mud, is still whole and dry inside.

Once behind doors and protected from the scathing rain and with nearly exhausted limbs shaking from muscle strain, I strip off my wet clothes while going in search of some towels as well as the rum. Eddie rummages our hastily packed suitcase for dry clothes and for once I don't care if anything matches.

"Here, let me dry your hair."

I note the pensive expression and sense he is brooding over his prudence in tackling that hill so soon because this is very uncharacteristic behavior. And for once I don't respond. The rum helps after such a frightening climb, and brings some color back to our pallid faces. We're safe for the moment.

Flopping almost guiltily onto the bed, total exhaustion setting in rapidly, I am absolutely positive that many will now be without a bed to rest upon, or possibly any dry space or clothing to change into, but the exertion causes Eddie to sink quickly into a deep sleep. We respond differently at these moments, and I'm unable to settle with the full realization of what has happened, drifting instead into a semi-conscious state, bolting upright at each strange new sound. The rain is continuing to pound harshly, finding its own rhythm.

Eddie murmurs something incoherent and rolls over making me jump; I must have finally dozed off. He's obviously struggling with his own terrors. Moving away from his flinging arm, I'm again aware of the onslaught of the wind, and I know this personal nightmare won't be over for a long time to come. But as long as he sleeps and the rain prevents the work that will follow in the hard days ahead, I have no choice but to reclaim this time for myself.

Just as I had been doing during the last couple of days, I again feel a need to slice through the past, therapeutically and clinically, dispensing my own medicine, perhaps with a few lines in my salvaged journal. It is a way of enabling myself to find something of joy that might still be left, something to strengthen and bolster for the coming days, which are quite obviously going to be rough. Though I'm comforted by this remarkable gift we've been given—an escape from total destruction—I'm also acutely aware that our gentle, guileless way of life has been drastically altered forever.

The volume of his bad dream changes again as he remembers things I can't decipher. But it triggers my own forgotten thoughts, ones stored for posterity under the category of happiness, like when he and I first met, more than likely because of our lengthy conversation earlier. And now I can't tuck it away without rewinding it completely.

Chapter Five

Time had passed quickly and with pleasure after the surprise interruption by a man called Eddie Tremain on a small strip of rocky turf I'd claimed as my own. So much so on that morning, finding myself reluctant to say goodbye to the charming island stories and the man who told them so well, I walked him to his battered jeep with tools sticking up at odd angles, lingering a bit as he drove away, keeping his broad shoulders in sight until I saw his waving hand retreat through the window. As I stood there it hit me just how close I'd come to giving up my dream altogether, and that this accidental meeting could change all that. A new surge of excitement bubbled up inside me. Job possibilities as well as the tantalizing thought of having made a new and highly interesting friend—all because of a wonderful chance happening.

While I watched, transfixed, the air quickly changed and the anticipated raindrops began slipping out of the clouds that had cast their own mood all morning, dampening my light windbreaker but not my spirit.

With so little time left, I took everything Eddie had said to heart, knowing it might be my last opportunity to connect with those who could help make my dream come true. In doing so, just two days later looking my best in the perfect sundress purchased during one of the brief shopping stints in San Juan with Rosa, I found myself en route to Starfish Bay Resort. I had also added a bright yellow hibiscus (after brushing off the ants) to offset the pretty green cotton, tucking it into my hair for luck before setting out to keep an appointment with the manager, Tim Brownell.

The resort had been at the top of Eddie's job hunting list and I wanted to believe that the motive behind his choice was no more than a helping hand to a new visitor, but that was becoming difficult the more I thought about him.

Left side driving was only a bit easier to manage in the small rental, but I had finally mastered the difficult stick shift, which gave me a better chance to observe more fully all the abundant beauty the island so effortlessly displayed. Enjoying the sound of the engine created by shifting, as well as the sense of freedom it gave me, I tried not to miss anything. And as I passed more than a few small houses set within all manner of trees—mango, banana and papaya with the occasional citrus mixed in—my eyes took in many with a bit of makeshift fencing obviously only intended to keep small animals penned.

Smiling to myself with the air of hopefulness and new possibilities, I confidently maneuvered the winding road leading to the resort, catching sight of a man off to my left where he stood amongst his small forest of mangos hanging voluptuously from their branches. Sunlight glanced off the tip of the machete as he moved about looking a bit like the pied piper with his small goats and chickens roaming freely behind in his footsteps. Hearing the gears shift into second, he turned and lowered the large knife from the branch he was trimming and doffed his worn straw hat, uncovering a bold striped bandana, and generously offered a wide semi-toothless grin. I waved back enthusiastically like an old friend and immediately felt the warmth of this sun-drenched land envelope me, and remembering Carlos' intervention, sent up a silent 'thank you' in gratitude.

And as I neared the hotel the profuse greenery at once exploded with bright hues of pinks, orange and magenta formed by the heavy bougainvillea bushes crowding walls as they reached for the nourishing sun. Then suddenly, it was all green again, convincing me to leave the car in the higher elevation parking area so that I could take full advantage of the labyrinth of ferns directing guests toward the entrance. Its walkway was bathed with luscious giant leaves fanning out in every direction, then opened onto the spacious hotel lobby that seemed whisper quiet except for the activity at the fax machine behind the counter. The entire space was awash with flowering anthuriums, philodendrons and species as yet unfamiliar, all thriving in bold-colored pots.

I introduced myself to the petite clerk who, though outfitted in a simple dark skirt and white blouse that I took to be the standard front desk uniform, happened to have a red hibiscus tucked in her hair and felt it a good omen. I questioned the lack of noise and hushed atmosphere and she informed me that the guests were mostly at the pool or out on the beach at this time of day, having indulged on the generous breakfast menu made famous by their local chef from foods grown on nearby farms.

There had been a brochure I'd glanced over someplace in town, featuring the many amenities and proudly showing a few of their specialty breakfasts through colorful photographs. Items such as banana crepes, cheese soufflés, and a lime bread loaf with a drizzled glaze, surrounded by papayas, mangos and varied fruit toppings. They were glossy portrayals of mouth-watering creations to be tucked away for future reference.

"He's expecting you, Miss Harmon, just go down that corridor and it's the first door to your left."

Tim Brownell was sitting behind a cluttered desk with a very organic shape. I recognized the style; it had been made exclusively of native mahogany by a local woodworker utilizing natural forms for his furniture pieces. It was perfect and placed advantageously in front of a huge window overlooking the sea. Before I could stop myself, I made an immediate comparison between his phenomenal backdrop and my own New York cubicle that overlooked more cubicles in one direction and more windows in another. Could this extraordinarily beautiful view compete with the glitz and glamour of New York, I asked myself, because that is the question some will ask if I stay. Would it be enough?

Tim was what might have been referred to as 'rangy'. He was slim and quite tall with straight blonde hair giving me the impression he was of Scandinavian heritage. His striking blue eyes peered out through serious horn-rimmed glasses that were in direct contrast to his gleaming roguish smile, changing his entire appearance. When he stood to shake my hand warmth emanated genuinely in his greeting and it put me at ease immediately. But that movement also pointed out a slight limp as he brushed against the many documents nearly falling from his cluttered desk, indicating that he didn't actually have time for the interview. He seemed in desperate need of help, and I presumed the paleness of his skin also spoke of this shortage of time to indulge in the readily available outdoor activities.

He caught me eyeing everything. "Old skiing accident," he offered regarding the limp.

"You've found me at odds with the situation here; too much to handle alone, and no time to figure out where to start."

"I'm pretty good at multi-tasking," was about all I was willing to say before hearing all about the job.

That interview was unusual to say the least, both in his gentle manner as if we were old friends (a quality I'd begun to admire already in my short time in the tropics) and his ability to so quickly get to the heart of things. His management skills allowed him to glean my life story as he balanced the conversation with island living, obvious differences between wardrobe needs as well as the abandonment of heating or air conditioning bills, and housing cost versus pay scale that concerned me most over the course of the next two and a half hours— possibly the longest interview I'd ever had.

I could tell with certainty it would be an interesting job not only as his assistant but also with the inclusion of the many perks associated with this small resort. Then he switched gears and took on a rather fatherly demeanor that I shall never forget. He had thoroughly gone over my detailed resume that I'd shakily thrown into my duffle before leaving the City—not knowing if this was by premonition, but I was certainly glad it was now in his hands.

"While I think you could easily handle the responsibilities, Lily, and would require less training—which right now really appeals to my schedule— I frankly don't want to take a chance on hiring you if you feel that you're the type to bolt as soon as this new 'island fever' wears off. That's happened too many times before to many of the businesses here; not at all uncommon given the romantic ideals this place represents, mixed with difficulties of isolation from the mainland. Promise me you'll think long and hard and be completely honest with yourself about this move. And, please, call me first thing in the morning."

Tim's remark had struck a nerve and I knew a real commitment on my part was now necessary. No more vacation thoughts; the test of my mettle was on the line. Leaving the interview with a promise to call leaving my lips, I was at once hesitant to leave the grounds, instead choosing to wander about as though a registered guest and drink it all in.

It was still impossible to imagine actually working here in this beautifully contained setting that presumably would be like this year round. Maybe this is what Eddie was thinking when he made this place number one on his list, that I would be too smitten by the sheer beauty, if not immediately by his charm, to leave.

Walking out onto the terrace, I saw bananaquits, the locally known sugarbirds, pecking away at scattered sweet fragments left on the tables or right into the packets; their yellow-breasted bodies outfitted with a perfectly slim curved beak designed to handle the retrieval of whatever sugar was left behind by the diners.

Then came tiny flashes of yellow green ribbons flitting around me flowing off the silky heads of the fast-moving hummingbirds as they passed by looping and diving, stopping for what seemed like just seconds to grab the sweet nectar. This was their floral heaven nestled into another of the verdant displays I'd found by now so commonplace, utterly charming, and never ever tiring.

Prominent in the scene and breathtakingly beautiful, however, was the view beyond the enclosure, a portion of which had been seen through Tim's window, nearly tempting me to hurry the interview. But now, exposed to the air again, the same salt-scented sea breeze that quietly rustled the heavy fronds also swathed me tenderly within their movement, changing ever so slightly as I walked out through the clearing between the many plantings. This beautifully configured opening led down a path of strategically placed stepping-stones directly to the beach and beyond.

The breeze also carried a welcoming fragrance of frangipani and citrus all but dominated by the smell of coconut oil as bathers splashing in the warm surf sent up a glittery spray creating miniature rainbows around them. Others , transported from the ordinary by the cocoon of heat, lay burnishing under the bright cerulean sky oblivious to the activity.

Lured by its magnificence, I slipped my sandals off. I needed to feel the searing heat from the nearly ankle deep sand, relish in the baking granules even though my soles would bear the brunt, still novices to this barefoot existence. Then because I wasn't sure, I removed my sunglasses for only a moment and the surface gaily sprouted a jewel box of color, dizzying my eyes, forcing me to look away. Put together it all created a stunning montage, even flaunting large hammocks strung between tall palms for a nap or a novel enjoyed in the shade. Letting out a sigh of wonder, I slid into one for just a few moments pretending, willing it to come true.

It was almost too much, making my head spin. I knew there was nothing remotely as pleasing to return to. Not because New York didn't offer everything imaginable twenty-four hours of every day, and then some, but because it obviously lacked the fluid beauty I was now nearly addicted to as it pulled me in closer and closer to its epicenter. Yet I couldn't take Tim's comment lightly. I understood his major concern and knew that I was in for a night of struggle between head and heart both already full to brimming with every emotional response possible.

I drove back into town much more thoughtfully this time, taking in everything as a framework for residency and trying to imagine more realistically my day-to-day exchanges, allowing audible sentences to stave off warnings when they crept between the bouts of euphoria. Admittedly things appeared much different after that conversation, especially when I reached the now familiar hub of the open market square in the center of town—always colorful and noisy, but today perhaps a bit more so as I found myself creating new scenes within, even though it was late for customers.

The local women were closing up some of the stalls, sweeping out the day's rubbish, loudly scolding some idle men nearby. Someone was cutting open a coconut and a few little children were running around with genips, throwing the little balls of fruit at each other. I could tell something had been cooked recently, and though I couldn't distinguish what, the scent made my stomach rumble; I hadn't eaten.

Because of that earlier conversation, and with all these newly presented opportunities, the world around me had suddenly changed, looking brighter, as though dressed out like a carnival. The painted buildings that I had almost begun to take for granted all became more prominent—whether just small non-descript wooden structures with tin roofs housing the simple wares for the daily shoppers, or the larger ones proudly looking like venerable old ladies in high contrast, exhibiting their extra frills of heavy painted shutters or white gingerbread trim and more solidly built. The entire array, a veritable rainbow of pink, yellow, ochre, blue and red, and surrounded by nature's backdrop of lush greens that I'd already learned grew without fuss or intention everywhere, had me taking secondary glimpses as if seeing them for the first time.

This pivotal exploration with thoughts of permanence rather than simply passing through led me to the turn in the road to Essie's house along the outskirts of town among a row of whitewashed buildings, a ritual begun quite by accident immediately after my arrival. I had quickly become lost probably because of always being on the 'wrong' side and seeing a young West Indian woman walking along the road holding a basket on her head, the other hand swinging a small bag along with her hips to some imaginary tune, I had stopped to ask directions.

"Me son, you come by just right; my feet them hurt in these new shoes. What you doin' out this way?"

"I think I'm lost. I've just come through town looking for the newsstand and took the turn off Market Square. My name's Lily Harmon by the way."

"I'm Essie Caldwell, and I'm mighty glad you be lost ta-day!"

After becoming totally captivated by the unusual patois of her singsong lilt, and her cherubic manner, I ended up driving her home. These visits had become a high point in a very short time and even more so when the neighbor ladies were outside. I'd sometimes catch them in curlers and bare feet, bantering with each other while doing their chores, small children always underfoot. More amusing still, to find them gossiping in the shared island jargon, hanging out of their brightly shuttered windows, always keen on including me. These little homes, plain except for the colored shutters and choice of curtains that blew in the daily breeze were lovingly cared for by women with big hearts, and bigger smiles, always eager to laugh.

Dear Essie, making me feel especially welcome each and every time with an offer of her well-known guava tarts and johnnycakes she sold at the market, always reminding me of the day she'd been heading home with her empty basket and we'd had that providential meeting.

I often found her outside trying to perform some task with her baby Georgia sitting in the crook of her arm as though physically attached. Essie would turn her lovely caramel-toned face at the sound of my car and immediately rush inside for the tin of tarts. Then juggling Georgia who gave up a soft round fist in welcome before ducking her head shyly back into her mother's shoulder, she would pass the tin, her contagious smile exposing a small gold tooth.

Sometimes I would stay on longer than anticipated to help her fold the sheets not only as an assist, but in truth I think it was because the fabric smelled like heaven after hours hanging in the warm sun as if the sum of all the island scents were deposited on each piece. Essie would often tell me in the years to come that she saw my destiny when she watched me holding the sheets up to my face relishing the unfamiliar freshness, and the joy of being here was written all over it.

She had become a special friend and the first person I wanted to share in my good news about Starfish Bay, and she turned out to be not only a good listener, but also a keeper of stored minutiae about the island for me to draw upon. And as we talked excitedly about the new possibilities, enjoying our exchange with her multitude of suggestions, all the while nibbling the tarts that emptied their contents of sweet jelly onto my chin, it somehow created a comforting sense of belonging, emboldening my already blossoming spirit of adventure.

Her great lead on a little studio apartment that would be perfect, mixed in with the prospect of a new job and at least two new friends, bolstered my courage even more. So nearly swallowing whole the rest of my treasure, I tenderly bussed Georgia on her dewy forehead, and set out to claim my own personal odyssey.

Chapter Six

The walls were at first blurred and unfamiliar as I pushed through fluttering images of white sheets, feeling Eddie's touch trying to wake me, and then unfortunately all the horror came flooding back.

"I guess I finally fell into a really deep sleep," I said, untangling my hair.

"You must have because you were really rambling, something about trees and Essie and even flowers, none of it making any sense at all. I hated waking you, but the rain finally stopped and knowing how much work there is down at the boat, I'm afraid we'd better figure out how we're going to tackle everything, at least in these next few days."

Then he rolled over and wrapped me tightly in his arms with an unusual urgency to it, a survivor's hold and I clung harder because of it.

Dawn, against all odds given the day before, had broken through the relentless gray with welcome sunshine. But even with that small gift of bestowed brightness shining as though nothing bad had happened, streaming in through the still fastened window crying to allow in fresh air, the injustice from a storm bearing that much fury would now be completely exposed. It would surely carry that same overpowering impact to every waking person and my chest heaved in despair.

Without appetite and no concept of where to actually start, Eddie brewed some coffee over the little Coleman stove while I made peanut butter sandwiches on bread that was already feeling stale. It seems this practical task opened a hole like an exit wound for every word previously held in check. All of the things meandering through the mind that hadn't already been said, now rapidly spilled forth. All the pent up feelings caused by our isolation poured out onto the table making us sound like kids let out for recess, nearly talking over each other's words.

"Just from what we saw yesterday, the rest is bound to be even worse and our future here might be at stake for the first time; we won't be able to work, so I don't know what's going to happen. I knew I should have insisted you leave on that last flight when you could still get off the island. You, at least, wouldn't be in this predicament if I'd done that."

"Eddie, slow down, we already talked about all of that and there is no way I would have left then not knowing how I would be able to reach you to know if you were safe. This is my home, too. Whatever happens, we'll figure it out together just like everything else we've done."

"The thought of losing you during all that havoc made me realize even more how much I care and how much you've had to handle over the years, especially out at sea. I don't suppose this might be a good time to ask you to reconsider that marriage proposal that you've rejected so many times before. I realize this isn't exactly a romantic moment to be doing that but maybe the storm has weakened your resolve a bit?"

"I may be feeling vulnerable but I've told you, I don't need a piece of paper to make me stay and after my divorce, I've never wanted to go that route. Please try and understand, again."

"I always have, but you can't blame a guy for trying. And who knows, you might still change your mind one day.

"And on top of everything else that's been running amuck in my mind, there's been all the worry about the *Wanderer* and that led to thoughts about all our cruises. And then that made me think of that horrible mess that happened after our last boat delivery and all the things that went wrong. I realize it could have been worse, but like everything these last few days, it's made me appreciate having you by my side. Hence, another failed attempt at a proposal."

"Now I know the pressure must have scrambled your brain because it's not like you to dredge up the past quite this way. What have you done with the real Eddie Tremain and where are these thoughts coming from? You can't blame yourself for my stubbornness and my need to stay here during the storm. I needed to be here with you!

"And, this business about the *Melinda B* that we all agree has eaten away at you far too long, could not have been predicted. The outcome lay at the feet of the owners and their hiring of such an inexperienced crew to replace us. And we had no choice but to leave when we did, you knew that. We had other commitments, so there shouldn't be any guilt on your part, and I really hate seeing the way it still affects you."

This was not the time for rehashing all of that with everything else on our plate, and anyway I hated focusing on that trip that had begun with excitement and promise and all the expectations one would have for a voyage to explore the Great Lakes, but ended up as one of the few truly unhappy events that had ever occurred in all our time together. It had been only one of the many assignments as crew on a variety of interesting boats whose owners had needed Eddie's expertise, which had turned out badly. So badly, it resulted in the loss of a magnificent yacht and heartbreak for her owners. The only time since he acquired his desired captain's license that shook his confidence.

I am well aware of resurfacing of old doubts, dreams and fears, especially because of everything we've just experienced; who wouldn't be? But knowing how bringing up that particular episode again will only raise his hackles as always, I'm not prepared to go there, not just yet. It didn't make sense then and with the exertion of the past days, it won't make sense to him now. I know much of what he's feeling has been brought on by physical strain, and how this event is going to affect our entire existence, as well as the shock of the visuals. We both know there is little spare time, at least for the moment, for sorting through anything but the pathetic scene spread out garishly directly in front of us. And my gut feeling is that what lay ahead, without the ability to work in our usual way, will be an overabundance of unwelcome free time in which to cover that disturbing subject once again.

And though not anxious to see it all again, going outside might get us off this present tack; obviously, we have to start sometime. Taking

our coffee along like a Linus blanket, a normal leftover from those
carefree days when that was such a common thing to do in the morning
hours, causes a weak-kneed unwillingness to stand before it all again.

To begin, we must first remove boards from the windows that once
back inside will reveal the horror but at least eliminate some of the
claustrophobia. Then we'll have to tackle a great deal of loose debris
flung onto the deck, none of which is immediately identifiable, giving
me horrible thoughts of where they had belonged. For the most part,
this early assessment will give us a roadmap we can use for future
repair and cleanup but that is still difficult to imagine. There is so much
I can't figure out where to even begin. And the work on the house will
also have to be juxtaposed with that of the boat and that need now has
to come first. The inside of the house is fine but it is imperative we deal
with the water inside the *Wanderer.*

While we worked, what little conversation we shared still seemed
lifeless. I tried repeating his attitude from our nighttime talks to keep
our spirits up, to impress upon him how my world changed because of
him, so it might help snap him out of his mood. We were obviously
struggling with shock after all. And as I rambled on, I saw a twinkle
coming back to his eyes and could tell, at least for the moment, he was
switching gears.

But suddenly my rambling went the wrong way and I remembered
my beautiful office at Starfish Bay and my face crumpled into tears
leaving me standing pitifully, nail can in hand and Eddie totally
speechless and very confused. He reached for me and tried to wipe
away a few stragglers but not before I caught his bewildered
expression. I changed the subject before I made it worse.

"After what we saw yesterday, how are we going to find everyone;
the roads are so bad? Or how will they ever get to us?"

As soon as the words were out of my mouth, I realized that I'd
touched another nerve. Eddie knew how difficult things would be all
over the island with his grasp of the topography and because of what
we'd witnessed at Long Point after our hasty and dangerous expedition
to the marina. But we both knew what depth of sadness and impact that

same scene would create for our dear friends. Heaped upon everything else they were going to be facing would be the ruin of this last vestige of better times.

Hidden within that tiny inlet that had not only provided necessary shelter, were also housed the echoes of many boisterous hours of shared fun-filled gatherings. We had agreed many days earlier that this would be the best meeting spot, a head count of sorts, and we would all do our best to get there, no matter what. I felt myself choking up as I watched his own concerns move across his face and I understood that the thought of it all, ruin and loss, would soon become a predominant theme. We would all be forced to digest much in the coming days and I recognized with unadulterated certainty it would bring forth many questions, more reminders, and many more tears.

"What about Moses?" I exclaimed, remembering his dear aging friend and part-time confessor.

There was no holding back now. Thoughts were discharged as rapidly as they entered the mind and all those early months and years on the island together flashed like a kaleidoscope of images and began spilling over.

"From everything he's ever told me, I always thought him to be as strong as those mighty mahogany trees and just as resilient. But it doesn't stop me from worrying especially since I don't know which of his relatives he was staying with and it will be a little more difficult to find him. I hardly think even he's experienced one like this, but as soon as it's possible I'll go look for him or at least find someone who knows his whereabouts and that he's all right."

"The first time I saw him was such an unexpected surprise that it's stayed with me all these years. Before my hours at the resort prevented it, I passed that same spot practically every day on my way to Essie's, and never resisted the urge to stop for a branch of genips from the little schoolgirls waiting for their rides. They had me picked from the beginning as an easy target and I nearly always made a mess, almost as bad as the way I eat mangos.

"Those darling girls were so unique in their sameness, with pressed uniforms and matching ribbons in carefully plaited hair, with their captivating smiles, behaving like little girls everywhere, giggly and shy. They had a fascination for both my jewelry and my hair color, so I'd always have to bend down and let them examine up close, and each time I'd imagine Essie's little Georgia doing the same thing when she grew.

"I know I told you about the one day I really regretted leaving my camera behind. I'd glanced across the street as I was kneeling for the smallest girl to reach my new earrings and there he was. I know my expression surprised them because in their young minds, Moses had been around them in some way forever.

"I'll never forget; the impact was this striking composition. He was wearing what I like to think of as our tropical uniform, the usual white cotton, and was surrounded by all these baskets in different shapes and sizes, working on something new. Even from a distance the immaculate shirt stood out as the sun captured and highlighted some of the material. And even with the most unimportant looking rope tied loosely at the waist of the worn trousers, he still looked almost regal and I just knew he epitomized the gentleness of the West Indies.

"Of course, the fabric just exaggerated his gleaming skin so weathered and dark it looked like molten chocolate. And those hands, how can anyone forget. Watching him work, his long fingers moving with determined expertise, as if they'd be comfortable gliding a seine over water or holding a chalice in a religious painting."

"I know, Lily, he has that effect on everyone who sees him for the first time. When I first saw him sitting alone on a bench at the waterfront, he seemed like this great sage who could dispense all the wisdom I might need for life. That encounter took place when I was really struggling and worried about the lack of work; I told you about the diving. He told me with such great truth in his eyes to have patience and faith, among many other things, and I believed him. I knew somehow that he would be someone I could look to if ever I had a problem. He's never let me down and he knows more about me than most people have forgotten and I've always been grateful for his friendship.

"But he was never much for small talk as I found out very early on—really likes to tangle with a problem and find solutions, but once I brought you over and introduced you properly, he took a real shine to you. Even began asking for you whenever we crossed paths."

"Yes, and since I never neglect to wear a hat out in the sun, he's stopped scolding me and just winks and offers a huge smile and says, 'Listen to Moses, ya heah?' He'll even allow the occasional conversation, as long as I don't prattle on. That he will not abide!"

The floodgates are now mutually open and unlike the first day outside, we are more anxious to just talk. There is a different kind of urgency in this need to cherish the people like Moses as well as the many familiar images because what has happened will have huge impact on memory—the quaint outdoor patio restaurants and second floor havens filled with rattan and ferns and conviviality. The food enjoyed, centered around the many fresh catches from the sea that made gastronomic history and brought in visiting food mavens on holiday.

To be remembered are all of those wonderful meals shared over time with each other and our many friends, the best the sea had to offer; fresh dolphin fish that some called mahi mahi, wahoo, mackerel, and tuna all served creatively in various forms with the local chefs trying to outdo each other. Eddie even competed for attention in our own circle, with his creation of fresh caught tuna topped with thinly sliced onions, a fresh squeeze of lime juice and a healthy splash of rum, all wrapped in a bundle of foil and baked until the delicate steam floated out and pulled you in with an aroma of combined flavors.

I know we are stalling, but it's okay. These emotions are not easy; we're still baffled by the entire ugly truth, the enormity of destruction and daunting tasks that seem too overwhelming to put into any kind of order. And, I know in this moment, that we are also utilizing this tactic as a method of keeping that all at bay, even if only for a little while. There is little else to cling to in this instance, especially since it is now a foregone conclusion that there will be next to nothing left anywhere on the island resembling its old self.

"I think we both know it might not ever be the same after this; there's never been anything to compare. I still can't believe it's happened and I'm afraid to let go of the many treasured moments, tough times and all, no matter what happens next."

"I know, and even though none of us have ever been tested like this, it all goes back to what we talked about that first time we met. This place is different. Bonds are formed so tightly that through everything we seem to get stronger, at least I hope that's what will get us through this time. No matter what, we're all in it together."

As he said that I thought I heard much of Moses' influence; he sounded wiser than his years.

"Speaking of experiences, I know my stored journals must be gone, lost to the weather along with the shells. I thought of them a lot last night, hating the idea of losing everything that was documented. It is amazing how much of our lives are in those pages. Thankfully, I managed to grab this when we packed. I had it tucked into the emergency bag next to the first aid kit and already made use of it while you slept. After all, I do consider them almost medicinal," I said, waving my treasure.

"I'm so sorry. I know how much those journals meant. I only wish we could have protected them better, but I'm afraid in our hasty preparations they got moved to the bottom of our 'to do' list."

I knew I should only feel gratitude. We hadn't lost the *Wanderer* after all, but I also felt extreme sadness for everyone who attempted to protect the things cherished, like my journals. Very quickly the futility of all their efforts would be laid bare as eyes begin to take in the total wrath of an angry wind.

For me, the importance of documenting much of the lifestyle imbued by Carlos and his friends had been foremost and done with dogged determination, hoping to glean much from these islands and what lay beneath our crystal waters. I had done all of this from the very beginning, and now, those journals are gone and so is he and this new ugliness stirs it all up like the muddy waters of the hurricane hole. Much of this is bringing about yet another obstacle halting the many chores, and it is called lethargy, giving way to old feelings.

Just as the loss of that yacht has been tormenting Eddie, the loss of those volumes unearths many things that have lain dormant for a long time, forcibly plunged into the deepest recess of my mind. Now that the wind tore apart more than the houses, it is no surprise that the sadness surrounding Carlos' tragedy have once again emerged, taunting me as before.

It was horrible and had occurred well into my new way of life on St. Margeaux, and became a reminder to us all of how quickly events could unfold and turn sour. It is no wonder now that we've managed to survive all the nighttime horrors of a demonic hurricane, that I also find myself confronting this again.

"Since we can't stop bringing up the past, do you remember the events surrounding Carlos' disappearance? I need you to know that I will always be grateful for the unquestioning help you gave to me and particularly Rosa. I think I fell in love with you all over again; you really stepped up when I needed you most."

"I do remember, but I only did what I would have wanted done for me if I were in trouble. It was not something any of us were familiar with and I knew how much your friends over there meant to you."

It had been a long time ago, and Eddie and I had just returned from a fabulous weekend at Prospect Island and a dive into the caves only to find a number of messages from my dear friend Rosa. Eddie knew little about the time spent on Puerto Rico and what he needed to know was easily told. It wasn't terribly unusual to get an occasional call from her asking of my well being or thanking me for a birthday remembrance, but the number of messages alerted me to something far worse. Those instincts had been correct as I sadly recall her words.

"Lily, I am sorry to have to call so much but I'm *frenetica*. It's Carlos. It's been three days since he missed his scheduled flight with my guests and he's never done that and I can't reach him. I called Jonas and he hasn't heard from him either, but like a man, he thinks Carlos is just off playing somewhere and forgot his schedule. That's not my Carlos!"

"Now Rosa, don't think the worst. Maybe he is off chasing after a lovely lady somewhere and time got away from him."

"No, Lily, something is very wrong. I'm afraid to contact the police because I don't have enough information to tell them and they will think me *estupida,* a foolish old woman."

"What can I do, Rosa? I haven't talked with him in a very long time," I said, picturing her struggling with the unruly strays of her hair that somehow always broke loose from the beautiful tortoise shell comb.

"I don't know, Lily, but I needed to tell someone before this makes me crazy. Can you think of anyone or anything that would help?"

My first reaction had been, why me? I knew through our occasional contact that she always harbored the misguided idea that Carlos and I were meant to stay together, that I would never leave San Juan. That was her way and I loved her for it. Possibly she thought I kept secret information about his whereabouts or that I would always know just from habit. I was baffled how to respond.

"Give me just a little time, Rosa. I've just come back to my office, and I can't think of any reason why this may have happened. Of course I'll do what I can, but I'm doubtful I'll be of any help."

She knew I kept a journal, but what possible information written there would help?

"I wish I had more to offer, but I promise I'll go through some papers when I get home tonight. Maybe something will trigger a memory or provide a clue about somewhere he liked to go." I said more to appease her. "I can't really see how anything I wrote down would help, but please try not to worry too much; you know him, he's probably off courting the new love of his life."

All I had wanted was to bask in the weekend idyll; the newly seductive underwater habitat that I'd discovered snorkeling in the caves. I had done my homework, spending time between the stacks at the local library feeding my curiosity that had continued to grow exponentially and quickly. Much of it spurred on by the West Indian 'seer' I'd visited. When she learned of my English lineage dating back to the 16th century, she was convinced there must be a sea captain or two causing me to become so entangled with Caribbean history and made me promise to find out.

Instead of relishing in the many fish coloring the water—the playful yellow tails, sergeant majors, blue doctors and parrotfish, or thoughts of the green turtles off St. Margeaux that had captured my heart the very first time one poked its knob of a head out, daring me to swim along, I found myself being drawn into some melodrama not of my own making. Carlos and I had shared some wonderful times that even if not recorded, would never be forgotten, but I believed his disappearance was more than likely about a new woman in his life. After all, he had taken quite a bit of time off when we became involved which quite naturally hadn't bothered Rosa at all then, since it was pretty much right under her nose.

But that night back in my tiny apartment fueled by her concerns, I put aside the usual joy of coming home to my miniscule view of the turquoise bay off in the distance and dug out my box of stored treasures. I'd carefully wrapped the first journals recording my new love for San Juan, the awakening of my deadened spirit, and first impressions of St. Margeaux realizing their importance to my new life and found myself quickly enmeshed in the pages as though yesterday. I could see clearly the emotional self-talks regarding all the changes I was experiencing back then. There were blushingly sensual scenes infiltrated with flowery descriptions about the island and a few unattractive phrases regarding Rob and his dastardly deed of infidelity.

I was enjoying a glass of wine, relishing the end of the day colors from the terrace, tracing back with a bit of daydreaming over my discoveries, nearly forgetting my true purpose on Rosa's behalf, when the book fell off my lap, bending the spine. It was then some colorful green ink caught my attention. I'd forgotten that being new to the process of recording everything, I would occasionally make notations in the margins, usually in alternating colors just because it was easier to

go back to a section in question. This green ink scribbling must have
been an afterthought for a name that I'd referenced as an antique dealer
and art collector. I apparently had felt the need to underscore it since
my work in New York had me connecting with people at the
Metropolitan as well as the more obscure antique shops such as
Samson's Treasures on the West Side or my favorite, Chamberlains on
Third.

As I read along, there was one passage nearly at the end of my stay
in San Juan where I'd quoted Carlos grumbling about something that
'just didn't fit'. What did that mean anyway? Too much time had
lapsed by then but perhaps it was in reference to the man as a
prospective client intimating that something made Carlos curious or
even cautious. It wouldn't have been enough even back then for me to
question it, not really understanding the inner workings of his
businesses or who he did business with. That was not the premise of our
relationship.

Besides, after reading it all again, there wasn't much to offer except
for things I really didn't want to share, even with Rosa. Possibly Carlos
was hired to fly somewhere differing from his usual routes or that he'd
been required to transport small cargo to one of the islands with buyers
waiting. Nothing seemed unusual in that, but not notifying her that he
would be unavailable to her guests, was. I had called her the next day
with my tidbits including that name and she let out a small gasp.

"What's the matter, Rosa, do you recognize a name?"

"Si, Si, Lily, only because he was so unpleasant when he called the
posada. He somehow knew of the *viajes* and he asked a lot of odd
questions. I'm thinking Carlos is avoiding him so he called me, but then
he was so *grosero* when I refused to answer them."

"Can you remember what he was asking about, Rosa? It may help."

"*Jo no se*, I tell him when he asked so many questions. He wanted
to know if Carlos still flies to Copper Island. I know nothing of this
island and tell him that he doesn't fly to a special one, just all around
showing my guests the *vistas*."

I knew Rosa broke into more Spanish when she was nervous and I could imagine her carrying on if pressed, but now I was getting an odd feeling about this, that kind where the hair rises on the back of your neck. In order to calm her, I promised to make some calls since I already had someone familiar with the antique world in mind. It was a wild card because none of it made sense. But it was a starting point.

That evening, hoping to eliminate my worries, I placed the call to Gussie Carter, long ago shortened from Augusta, a name she detested. She and her longtime companion, Detroit Chamberlain, ran a wonderful old antique shop on Third Avenue. We had built up a good friendship with our mutual interests in the various museums, galleries and affiliated dealerships, and I valued her knowledge. She had once saved me from absolute embarrassment when a colleague's illness forced me into her slot as benefit organizer featuring early bronze statuary. My knowledge of the Buddha pieces from the 15th century would have me looking a fool, but thankfully, Gussie knew her stuff. She also knew of my situation with Rob and had been keeping tabs on his relationship with my sister, none of which interested me. But Gussie's heart was soft and we were like adopted strays in her mind. It bothers her still that we've been estranged for so long.

She answered the phone with the remembered cigarette rasp and I could picture her slender, still youthful frame holding the receiver with fingers tipped a deep red, her perpetual favorite.

"Lily, what a lovely surprise. I can't remember the last time you called. We are long overdue for a visit," she said with a smile evident in her voice.

"I know, Gussie, I miss you too, but not life in the City. How's old Dee these days?"

"Same as always, battling his weight and ogling the young women who stroll past the shop; but he's still a dear. It's all harmless fun, and just his way of continually baiting me. Keeps our lives interesting, right?"

The first time I met Dee, the name used only by his friends, was when I was one of those women strolling past for him to ogle. But once inside their treasure trove of goods and getting to know them, it became one of my favorite New York haunts. That's how I learned a little about their story. Dee's mother had apparently fallen in love with the city of Detroit during the speakeasy days; hence the name for her son. He had fallen in love with archeology and Gussie while in college and together they traveled the world to satisfy their need to see artifacts preserved and fill their shop with saleable treasures appealing to the doyennes of Manhattan.

After some time catching up on gossip, special events and my new island life, she casually mentioned that Rob stopped by periodically, mostly on the excuse of the odd piece of mail to be forwarded to me. He only knew that I'd left New York and that she would be my contact in the event of emergency. I also knew that she still harbored a small hope that once hearing how miserable he was, that I might soften in my resolve to have any contact with him. All I could do was laugh at the absurdity but I knew she meant well.

I briefed her about the miniscule amount of information I had from Rosa regarding the man in question and his supposed connection to the art world.

"Gosh, Lily, I don't recall that name right off, but Dee might; he's always better at dredging up names and dates. Unfortunately, he's at a board meeting tonight, but I'll be sure to ask him when he gets in. I know at the very least, we can make some inquiries for you; who knows what might turn up?"

"Thanks, Gussie, I really appreciate it, and don't forget you've promised to visit me here on St. Margeaux."

"I know, but it is damned difficult to get Dee to leave this city. He might, however, if you promise not only to visit us here but maybe you can coax him with a sail on that boyfriend's boat you're always going on about."

"Okay, okay, it's a promise, to both of those."

Less than a week later, Dee's search turned up sketchy information at best, but I still couldn't turn my back on Rosa. The name I had found was not of a man well known and no blatant criminal activity was noted, but also brought forth no proud credentials within their circles. But because of that lack I received a forewarning from Dee that this might be out of my league and to be careful.

Small alarms were still going off in my head and I knew I had to make some kind of attempt for Rosa's sake to find out what might have actually happened to Carlos. But I didn't have the means and knowledge of the area to do anything productive. Thankfully Eddie did, enlisting his friend Boomer whose dive contacts throughout the Caribbean could put out feelers on our behalf. Without any knowledge of a flight plan or a reported mayday, there wasn't much for us to go on. Whatever Carlos had gotten mixed up in, he left little trace behind.

Fortunately, because he had connections at all the marinas, it wasn't long before Boomer was able to obtain bits and pieces of information through a friend working at the one on Beef Island and the story began to unfold very strangely from there. He learned that a Boston Whaler had been found abandoned, and then a body discovered on Copper Island but wasn't sure at first if they were related events. But once hearing the name of the island, my heart beat a little faster remembering Rosa's conversation.

He also found out that the local island authorities were investigating both as well as any connection to an anonymous tip from a pilot spotting that very same boat, occupied by a lone man seen hauling a mysterious bulk half in and half out of the stern. It all coordinated with the time frame from Rosa. Without knowing, I was convinced that Carlos was okay, certain that call had come from him, at least that's what I wanted to believe.

Then a new twist when the identification of the body found was discovered through a marina rental form for the Whaler. That led the police to learn from the property manager where the slain man had been staying, that he was a writer supposedly researching material regarding mineral rights as well as salvage rights to use for his current manuscript/mystery novel but, strangely was also in the employ of the man connected to Carlos.

When the body was discovered, his backpack had been filled with samples of malachite, quartz and some other unidentified specimens that could have come from Copper Island, as well as a brochure for Palm Coast Charters. In a pocket they found a small gold object encrusted from time in seawater. What did that all mean? Was Carlos helping him with his research in any way? Were they all working together to transport some sort of treasure? Or had Carlos stumbled upon something revealing much more sinister aspects in their business dealings? This might indicate the reason, if that was Carlos placing the anonymous call, and any possible danger to him because of it. What if he found out that this client was responsible for the stranger's death? That would place him in grave danger.

By now the phone lines were humming as we all tried to coordinate information obtained. During that time Rosa had been visited by a couple of Puerto Rican detectives who were investigating the case in conjunction with British island authorities since the charter business was registered in San Juan, but they found no new leads, although they still believed Carlos was somehow tied up in something illegal.

Not once believing that theory, Rosa then hired a private investigator because her main concern was still finding Carlos and she felt the locals on Copper Island might open up more freely to him rather than being interrogated by a uniformed officer. His private conversations with the owner of the rental unit that had been occupied by the victim uncovered a larger plot about the discoveries in the caves and profiteering by modern pirates but even that could have been due to his writing. Still too many unanswered questions with no sign of Carlos.

Through all of this Rosa kept her vigil, exhausting herself with the hope that Carlos would walk through the door of the Inn with a happy grin and a bride on his arm after eloping mysteriously or at least something as fanciful, but this was not to be.

His plane was finally discovered when someone sailing along the northern shore of Jost Van Dyke spotted a piece of orange metal protruding from the water glittering in the sun like an S.O.S. By the time the divers located the spot, they found his remains still strapped into the small compartment. I was told that an exact identification had been difficult and I had no doubt when hearing of the area and its heavy wave action as well as the presumed amount of time it was submerged. As far as anyone knew, Carlos had been returning to San Juan when his plane crashed probably due to mechanical difficulties. An underlying notation passed on to Rosa by the investigator stated that he had been in the employ of a New York antique dealer to ferry him between islands on business.

There were still gaps in the story large enough to drive a car through, and a few people wanted as material witnesses. Without finding more clues and direct ties to all the loose ends, it had become a 'cold case', leaving all of us even more disturbed. In my heart I knew Carlos wouldn't be mixed up with anything criminal and was more than likely a pawn, but it didn't ameliorate the loss.

I had flown to San Juan at Rosa's request, for the scattering of his ashes and found her visibly shaken, looking older than her years. I had only seen Jonas during my time with Carlos, but he seemed a bit thinner than I remembered and kept his dark glasses on his still boyish face to conceal the tears he couldn't hold back. Carmen and I had stayed in touch periodically by phone until she left for Chile and the Museo in Santiago for an art-related sabbatical, losing contact after that. Our meeting was not the reuniting we had hoped for. We clung to each other on the deck of Rosa's brother's boat off San Juan Bay, stepping aside a bit as she and Jonas like mother and brother, somberly placed the ashes in the direction of the prevailing winds freeing them forever.

It was one of the most difficult tasks I'd ever taken part in, especially when I thought about all the times my girlfriends had asked me why I never went back to him. I never had a proper answer except to say it had to do with timing, and now he was lost forever. But this day, because of the attendance of the many he touched, celebrated a life lived fully.

In a totally characteristic move, Carlos had left a will naming Jonas as executor and it outlined certain monies from his father's business was to be given to Rosa's favorite charity, a local orphanage. For those of us who knew him well, he left behind a legacy of good will and high spirits sprinkled lovingly across his favorite sea.

ళళళ

Eddie had been listening attentively, waiting for me to compose myself after exposing these long buried, painful memories. "I understand your emotions my 'water Lily', and I know how much remembering still causes pain, but I think we have to put some of this on hold for a while.

"I know it's been necessary and surprisingly good that we've taken a little extra time to pull ourselves together; I'm really glad we slowed down after what happened yesterday. And I know you're not going to like this, but now I have to ask you to go with me back through the mess outside again. We have to get back to the boat."

I loved Eddie's endearing name coined after teaching me to sail and snorkel, but I don't want to follow him outside even though I know I must. The thoughts of death have made me very sad, and I think possibly what has happened outside is like another death and my sadness is going to stick around.

Taking my sandwich with me for comfort more than hunger, I follow him along a bit like a child sent off to summer camp that dislikes the counselor.

"Come on, Lil, don't be upset. Take my hand."

I did of course and even planted a kiss to make up for my moodiness and because we took the hill more slowly this time it wasn't as grueling, and when we reached the marina, we had a surprise waiting. Those that could, had made their own long and tiring walks in the sun and stood there, appearing just as we must have, slightly shell-shocked and wickedly tired and unkempt. They had all remembered we hoped to use the single sideband radio to reach the mainland and had set out with no idea that anything would be left of that hope.

Nessa and Russ, safe though stunned, were there among the group, my happiness at seeing them forcing me to throw aside the earlier thoughts of death. Most of their house including the bedroom wing and kitchen with its high countertop that was a pass-through to the terrace, was in ruin leaving them a very small space in which to live. Oddly, the vaulted opening was perfectly intact but quite naturally had allowed in an awful lot of water, which in turn flowed across hard tile surfaces and out into well built drains. A miracle of design; I still wasn't quite sure.

Mick and Tasha lived in the other direction and so far hadn't arrived. They were a bit isolated on that hillside beyond us and I worried that things might be even worse for them, more so because there was no way to reach them. It was going to be an anxious couple of days for many of us.

Essie sent word with one of her friends from the marketplace that she and Georgia were safe and staying at the Mission until she could get back to her house and assess the damage. I made a mental note to get over there as soon as it was feasible. At least they were all right.

It wasn't long before the group grew as word was passed on that we had indeed opened the boat. With each call stateside, we had to relive the horrors experienced as it was related to the many friends and families over the static of the marine radio, waiting for the sobs to subside between the formalities required for the transmissions. The untold losses were monumental and grew by the hour, leaving even the radio operators long distances away in tears. This necessary eavesdropping told us everything we'd begun to suspect, that many would await the first transport out until their situations on St. Margeaux could be sorted and homes rebuilt where possible. And as Eddie and I listened to each and every heart-wrenching story, we knew our plight paled in comparison.

For those that a journey is impossible, time may quickly become the enemy. There may be many who will never recover and damage that can never be undone, and overall, a pall that will hang over us even when the renewing sun comes out to play, and it will prevail for a long, long time. But the one constant among us all, growing louder with the crowd expanding, was the mantra of gratitude at simply being alive after such an ordeal, a near euphoria brought on by survival.

Chapter Seven

The days are now dry, so dry we are begging for rain. It has been nearly five weeks since the mother of all hurricanes and while heartened by the humor used to fill in old cracks, I would really love some rain.

But we are adjusting. Getting to and from a desired destination in ninety-degree heat to find supplies that are now being flown in through emergency channels is a continuing challenge since many roads remain nearly impassable. Dust and dirt now dwell everywhere and there is no escape from it. We've been tested often, stung by wasps and bees that could try the kindest souls. Without trees and foliage there is nowhere for these tiny beings to inhabit and they are angry and confused, just like the rest of us.

Had it not been for the trail of destruction left behind, the eerie calm on the day after the hurricane would have us deny the entire event. And when everyone was finally able to come out of their shelters for the first time, they found what we had, desolation and wreckage everywhere and at every turn. And each time we witnessed something unimaginable, a situation more wretched than another, a worse one would turn up.

Boats were high aground in the most unexpected places, more on land than in the water; their hulls dry and angry looking at the assault to their size and predicament. Some of them ended up on front stoops or dooryards or in some cases were swept away leaving behind a smaller broken reminder of their existence.

All types—sail or power, big or small—could be found in the middle of a street or upside down on top of a car or wind-driven onto a side coming to rest on a beach heavily damaged by salt water with sand filling in the empty spaces. Damaged utility poles were evident everywhere too—either askew, broken in two or displaced from their original location, and displaying a tangle of cables hanging and twisted as if waiting to ensnare a larger target. Others simply vanished forever.

We now understood from the extent of the damage that it would take many months and a massive influx of heavy equipment with crews transported in to refit the entire island for new power and wondered again and aloud whether we could wait it out to live as though in a third world country. The blazing sun was laughing at us.

For those who had sought protection in the calm muddy waters of the 'hurricane hole', hell's fury must have been awakened and unleashed by the outrageous noise of the wind and been angered to the point of creating mass destruction for anything in its way, making me abundantly grateful for Eddie's last minute decision not to join them.

Vivid descriptions circulated around the island from sailors injured but lucky to be alive, telling of the agonizing and frightful night when many of the boats were upended so that they seemed to be flying, landing them on shore, into each other or simply coming to a halt upside down in the water and mud during all the chaos, disorienting anyone who braved the night on board. We knew that photos of the complete and utter destruction rained down on us would eventually surface, but we also knew that the indelible print of the enormity of it all would be burned into our collective memories forever.

And almost as a footnote to the storm, for many weeks afterward a simple tropical wind could cause near panic to those already traumatized, fearing a repeat performance. The heat and moisture in the air, unable to be eased by trees swaying in a cooling breeze since there were none, caused one to believe the Sahara might have shifted from the force of its winds. It was all becoming too overwhelming to comprehend.

Reports began circulating through island authorities of the actual wind velocity as well as the enormity of the damage. Quite a few small private planes had been overturned and wings sheared off to fly alone across the island, and in at least one case, ending up in a front yard competing for space with household remains that had been uprooted by the steady 150 mph-180 mph winds that actually gusted as high as 200 mph. Debris was everywhere and the equipment used to record speed was also damaged beyond repair when those same winds went beyond believable limits. The entire island had taken on a slightly shiny appearance from all the scattered galvanized metal lying about and questionable items strung like dirty laundry hung limply anywhere they could.

One of those damaged planes I found out belonged to one of the legends of St. Margeaux, a woman who'd made her reputation long before I arrived and was in her late seventies when the hurricane hit. She was an acknowledged storyteller and hotelier leaving behind a trail of rumors of spying, love affairs and daredevil flights, all before disappearing into the tropical sky on a new plane. She must have lived an incredibly exciting life in these islands, just the type of person that would thrive and create awe wherever she went. We have all benefited from her ilk, those who have found their place in the sun just as she did.

By now I've come to understand much, and the outcome of this most unfathomable event has definitely reaffirmed that, for us, we people from away, we transplants, fun seekers, and romantics alike, arrived here without ever truly knowing what we would find and in the bargain we received so much more. But though we may have reached a limitation stronger than we can ultimately triumph over, I'm convinced I couldn't have asked for more—wacky friends, low maintenance wardrobes, retired snow shovels, abundance of seafood and the ocean as our playground.

We've been told that tornadoes were spawned that night, somehow sparing a few of us as we held tight, yet creating even more indignities for others to be suffered on top of the already mounting list. When roofs came off, furniture and belongings were sucked up and out of the openings. Whole balconies at apartment units were sheared off leaving great chunks of concrete and metal exposed and looking as though bombed by enemy fire. Mattresses were found lying about as the days passed, lying as though in wait for their occupants. Much of what was left scattered but not totally annihilated was confiscated by whoever could carry it away. Looting became a natural occurrence with stores laid bare and open to the masses and the elements, inviting to many in dire need and a blot on the conscience of others.

Eddie and I now find after having the chance to talk with many more old friends and acquaintances in these past weeks, that we've been among the very few fortunate enough to survive relatively unscathed not only throughout the storm, but having the *Wanderer*, however damaged, to still call home. She took on new and precious meaning when we returned to begin the cleanup process.

For others without places to work and homes to care for with broom or dust cloth or recipes to be tried from cookbooks lying in wait on the shelf for a party planned or guests coming for a visit, creativity will reign and give additional meaning to their survival.

The one place we quickly discovered that hadn't fared at all well, much as we'd suspected, was Eddie's small 'crow's nest' apartment. We'd not only been using it for storage but also for the odd overflow from the *Wanderer* by visiting friends or ones who didn't fancy staying on board a boat for more than a couple of hours. It was located over one of the oldest and now most damaged hotels, leaving an empty void where it should have been. I had always loved the look of mystery within its cool dark space created out of the beautiful and timeless appearance of brick walls and scarred plank flooring that creaked wherever a foot was placed.

Before all the damage, the so-called nest sat smartly atop Yolanda's Hair Salon that occupied the lower floor of that wing of the hotel, which she also split as living quarters. If he chose, Eddie could watch the ladies preening as they left their goddess of hair to attend to their daily business. The only decent view of the water was seen through slim white double doors, adorned with an ornate, though rusting, white iron railing much like those visible on the larger French island hotels. The already decaying façade of the building only added to its timeless charm. This opening gave him a vantage point from which to watch the

Wanderer as she bobbed peacefully in the small town harbor under a postcard sky, serenely awaiting his presence.

Eddie, always the consummate storyteller, had quite early on in our relationship filled me in on Yolanda's pet Macaw, Figuero. When on occasion we shared that living space, I received my personal introduction to this large bird's unusual habits the hard way. At the first peek of sunrise the parrot, his beautifully feathered blue and gold body poised with importance on his large perch made of a citrus branch, would belt out arias from "Carmen" at the top of his little lungs. This would continue until Yolanda took him out of his cage.

"That's bad enough, Lily, but I'm up early for work anyway and at least it's not foul. It's around dusk when the light is changing when old Figuero turns into Captain Bly and spews out the kind of phrases that would make even a pirate blush. Even worse, he directs them at the women who pass by. There've been some pretty close calls in fact because his salty language usually followed by whistles, are perfectly timed to my exit making me look like the culprit. I complained but Yolanda doesn't believe in stunting his questionable talent by stifling it under a cover. Can you believe that crap?" Eddie says, offering some of his well-known comic relief to the dreary scene.

"I so loved that small romantic space, even with that unruly parrot. Even now looking at all this, I can't stand the idea that we might have to leave it all behind; it represents so much to both of us."

"I'm not ready to face that yet; seems like it was only yesterday that I found that apartment. I took that place not only because of the proximity to the water, but also to the Sea Crest Restaurant where all my friends hung out. Remember the night I found you sitting on the terrace over there? It had to have been just a couple of days after meeting you; I'd come over to meet Russ. You didn't see me come in and I admit after your initial reaction at the cove, I was afraid to disturb you, especially since you looked deep in thought. I wasn't quite sure if I'd be welcome. It sure seems a very long time ago."

"It really does, and looking around at everything here, it's hard to believe any of that ever happened." Spreading my arms wide, "This is like a bad dream; I can't wrap my head around all that beauty reduced to this.

"But I do remember I had been making one of my often used lists of pros and cons on a large yellow pad, having just been interviewed in depth and at great length by Tim. I was confused, and anxious, and slightly attracted to the idea of getting to know you better as well."

"You never mentioned that part."

"Well, I didn't tell you everything back then! I also remember that I was in awe like never before, gazing out from that lovely back terrace watching all the harbor activity. From up there it was like looking at a moving stage with little vignettes of island stories. Such an ordinary room in many ways, and so wide open to the breeze that swept across that eclectic mix of wicker and wood, all of which was nearly devoured by the huge potted ferns. Wasn't there even a small tree growing up through the deck in one corner?"

"There used to be, yes, and someone had named it the 'wishing tree'. One of the locals who waited tables there talked of a terrible illness in her family and each day she said she would go to the tree, touch a new leaf and make a wish. The person she talked about, I think it was a brother, survived and ever since, people have been making wishes on it."

"I wish I had known; it would have come in handy during those long hours I sat there trying desperately to imagine what my life would be like on a daily basis, permanently a part of all that the island seemed to offer. After all, till then, I'd basically been on vacation. But something kept gnawing at me to stay, a sort of hunger for things I couldn't explain even to myself. It was all tied into the spontaneous feeling of belonging here. Nessa and I have talked about that a lot and she said she had the same experience when she arrived. Maybe that's why I've always felt so close to her.

"And then the longer I watched the activity grew with boats coming in to unload passengers or their day's catch. I wanted so much at that moment to know more about everything I was witnessing. I could just barely make out the bantering as the occasional shout or laughter reached me, but couldn't help noticing the beautiful skin tones that had so much range, adding warmth to my vision of a life here, as they stood alongside tourists having been careless about sunscreen suffering the effects with bright red burns. It was all being toted up on the pro side of the list. And then you showed up and plied me with drinks and a fantastic seafood dinner and I was hooked, line and sinker!"

"I was rather charming, wasn't I?"

"And extremely modest!"

"Well, it's a good thing we have the way things used to look indelibly seared into memory; hell, that may be all we have left to sustain us for a long time to come. The island and everything on it may be changed drastically no matter what our decision about staying. Not only are homes gone or nearly so but also the entire center of town is a complete mess. Many of our favorite spots are now just rubble, and as a footnote to that, I heard that even Lew's barber chair ended up hanging off the second story of the Top Deck bar, like it was just ripped out of the window, but not even a shard of glass from his signature red and white striped pole is anywhere to be found. The worst part for him is that he really hated that bar, wouldn't set foot in it. There was some stupid feud between his family and the owner's family that's been going on for years. Of all the places that chair had to end up!

"That great terrace you loved is also bare and filthy from everything that flew through. The wishing tree is no more and we could all use a bit of that right now. But even though a few areas like that one can be cleaned up eventually, it's still going to be a terribly long and hard road ahead for everyone."

There was much to be pessimistic about regarding the future, and yet so much to laud of the past. It is a crushing blow to view destruction as a total package in the way we've all had to do. But that particular terrace holds a special place for me and always will, not only because of Eddie and all that grabbed my heart that day, but the many hours over the years spent lunching with my dearest friends, mindful of the fact that we were lucky in its openness in case 'walls could talk'. At least our many conversations could drift out into the universe. Those hours as regularly scheduled as possible where troubles could be put out onto the table and shaken out as easily as the napkins when the meal was done and the burden lightened were the backbone of our friendships.

We relied on each other during the trivial household squabbles, job challenges, boyfriend troubles and wardrobe mishaps usually relating to bathing suits and platform heels, and for the saddest and most horrible of losses. We reinforced and bolstered each other through everything that came our way. And when a severe illness took one of the dearest among us, we celebrated her as close friends do, keeping her spirit there with us through shared stories honoring her with the laughter she had so enjoyed when refusing to give up.

Had anyone been eavesdropping, we could be heard sharing innocent local gossip, political woes that were always newsworthy and colorful and a constant punching bag for jokes, as well as old and new recipes. I had experienced a few kitchen disasters when trying some of the Puerto Rican dishes I'd been introduced to by my dear friend Rosa, settling on one that was pretty foolproof and eventually used for many a potluck dinner. They made me copy it for each of them, committing it to memory due to the repetition.

Arroz con Pollo
   1 package (2-3 lb) chicken pieces
   1 tbs. olive oil
   2 small onions, chopped
   3 cloves crushed garlic
   1 green bell pepper
   1 small can tomato sauce
   a pinch of saffron
   2 cubes chicken bouillon or stock
   1 cup beer
   1 10 oz .box frozen peas, thawed
   1-1/2 cups uncooked rice

Using a heavy skillet, sauté chicken in oil till brown and remove. Add onion, garlic and green pepper to pan, cook till soft. Then stir in saffron, bouillon and sauce, returning chicken pieces to skillet. Cook for another 10 minutes and add rice, reducing heat to low. Add beer, simmer until rice is tender and add peas and thoroughly heat through. Salt to taste.

While I had adapted it for use on the boat by substituting instant rice and canned peas in order to save time and space, each one of them tried it adding or subtracting something of their own, earning their individual praises.

Sometimes, sounding more like tour guides and travel agents, we shared our experiences of other islands visited over the years. Each of us had very quickly discovered within each new island, a marvelous history of an indigenous population that lent it authenticity and charm. We all felt that the smaller and less tourist oriented were better suited to our personalities, making it easier to learn about its residents. And we all found ourselves drawn to the marketplace on each new island where everyone gathered, sampling the wares those islanders had to offer, because that gave the clearest picture about a way of life in much the way I'd learned about St. Margeaux.

And these moments were never far from my journals. And while I had documented much of what I'd learned about the island's fascinating tribes, it wasn't as popular as some of our other conversations. They were polite and listened to my newly acquired information regarding the fact finding I'd done on both tribes, the Arawaks and the Caribs. I thought it only natural with my own background to be drawn to those pastoral peaceful Arawaks, vastly interested in the arts, known for their cave paintings. It was not easy, however, for my new passion for the rock shelters and theories on treasure hunting to gain much ground over lunch. I tried using the excuse that I was certain much of my quest was because of my gene pool and certainly there must be a sea captain speaking to my very soul, and they retorted that for what she charged, the reader of palms and cards had gotten the best of the deal from my repeated visits.

Even I realized how boring it must have sounded, but I felt vindicated that at least I didn't talk about the other tribe, the Caribs, who were a nomadic warlike group with a major reputation for cannibalism. My diatribes may have been interesting to me, but obviously that was not a topic to offer up at table in place of the more important ones...those about men.

Nothing was sacred and as we tossed it all up like a sumptuous salad, we all added stories of excursions with the odd mishap thrown in and, of course, every place reached by water and there were many. I also loved extolling Carlos' virtues and the many delights of San Juan and ensuing days exploring in that little orange Piper and how that had actually planted the first seed of bravado for my new life. That recounting always encouraged them to match me in stories of their own love affairs of the past, leaving us flushed and giggly as schoolgirls each and every time. And they were the ones I turned to in order to suss out the facts and my feelings when Carlos died.

These wonderful women were the only ones I could talk to when things got a little crazy between Eddie and me, and I found myself questioning the need for such a serious relationship. We all knew, some from first hand experience, that flirtations were easily explored just for the asking because of the abundance of single men, and dished often, and always with the intent that not one of us should suffer an unintentional hurt through any of their misguided theories. There was an abundance of feminist ardor always at the ready.

Always opting to focus on the more fun aspects of life in the sailing world of our ken, we had a particular favorite that stood out; a handsome blond Australian that revisited each year to participate in a large sailboat race featuring the best men and women sailors. Because of the rarity of those races that included women, this was often the topic of conversation because it was such an arduous race and some of us had already given up the quest.

The men looked forward to this once-a-year bash with high anticipation and many stories of triumphs of the past, and the women who still raced looked forward to outrunning their male counterparts, which they'd as yet been unable to do. They also looked forward to seeing the Australian.

As usual each season, he crewed for the skipper of a fast Ericson 36 that often maintained the lead especially when they hoisted its spinnaker with its odd combination of Easter basket colors. But he had something else up his sleeve he'd stolen from a sailor down under to be used only if in dire need in extreme circumstances such as falling behind to the feminine contingent. If that should happen, the crewmen would all stand up in unison, turn their backs to the ladies and drop their trunks, a tactic intent on grabbing their attention away from the pressing win.

It had never failed or so the story goes, and obviously it hadn't failed on our island either when in unison the women's voices could be heard from a great distance, across the large watery gap while they were being mooned, "Oooooh look, there's Ollie!" This had the desired effect but caused great curiosity among the other men as to why only one naked bottom got all the attention, not understanding that for him the preamble to many a race was spent thoroughly scouting the female competition. It was said the clamor of women's voices could be heard for miles.

I am constantly reminded in these hard days of the many simple stories like this, their content overflowing with good-natured humor and grounded in friendships that flourished here. It may have begun with the pull of the trades, but it all compounds the agony over the possibility of being forced to leave.

And as we discussed everything about our lives on St. Margeaux, and no matter which one I could have chosen after my preview in Puerto Rico that would have done justice to my daydreams, I was positive each would have made me happy in the end because I would have fulfilled my destiny to live life to the fullest on an outpost in the tropics. But I know fate brought me to St. Margeaux and now, sadly, that same fate has just dealt us a new and unruly hand.

It is heartbreaking but because of it, I more fully comprehend the havoc, injustice, confusion and general disorder to a way of life that could just as easily have occurred on any of these insular entities. And because we all sit in the pathway year after year of ominous threats that are gauged by charts indicating longitude and latitude, current and wind direction, it is a price for the most part we willingly pay. But this time, the price is possibly too high. Only time will tell.

Chapter Eight

For those of us left bearing witness to the many weeks that have now entered into months and the full realization of the length of time it will take before and even if known lifestyles might return, we fully recognize how much the initial euphoria over having survived such a staggering event is being put to rest from wear and tear. Life on St. Margeaux has become increasingly difficult not only by the very lack of services and basic creature comforts, but so little has advanced.

Whatever foods can be obtained is still cause for a gathering and the creation of a meal no matter what or where it becomes available. Sometimes that might be the blessing of freshly caught fish when the catch is large enough to share. No one can tell us how some of the animals survived, and I know many did not, but if the occasional chicken could be bartered for, a communal meal turned into a mouth-watering feast talked about for days.

And as I talk with anyone who will listen since the litany doesn't alter much, I find each new day brings hope that some plantings may have lasted the scathing wind and rain in order to pop its shoots up to the new and constant sun and provide a fresh taste so craved.

Essie and little Georgia and all the neighbors from Old Town Road outside the marketplace survived their own horrors, and lost most everything they owned when the roofs on all their homes were assaulted and split apart in various ways forcing them to stay at the Mission until enough of the repairs are complete and they can put their lives back together.

But never to be outdone in her creativeness, she managed to locate a shopkeeper who had salvaged a sack of flour, protecting it from looters like a prized diamond, and agreed to trade just enough of it for some of her salvaged jelly. That in turn allowed Essie to make a few batches of the longed-for pastry gems using the oven at the Mission with the help of a generator, providing in turn moments of happiness for the friends and neighbors of the *Wanderer* always grateful for the kindness of this brown-skinned sprite.

The dripping guava freshly scooped from canning jars always at the ready when I visited, carried importantly by my small friend into the Mission ahead of the hurricane in place of her sparse belongings, brings back reminders of excitement in a time of hope in the life of a young woman so desiring of becoming an islander. It is difficult to remember myself now as I was then. I feel worn and tattered like the frayed sails flapping around us without purpose.

My emotions are being pulled in so many directions that when no one is watching I try to find solace out on the deck under the stars counting my blessings, fearing that I may be forgetting some of them in this time of turmoil. I know well that all across the island there are many with far less than we've been able to obtain and I marvel at the strength of many of these people that have endured all of this and more before me. That is when I know I must choose as part of my personal survival not to look at the negatives that could pull me away from my passion for them and their place in this vast sea of humanity. Rather, on nights like this I need to commune with the stars that have always provided insight, being both a source of pleasure and comfort. And as when lying at anchor in a quiet harbor, they enforce how really small we are here on our tiny island, graced by their presence.

They quite naturally offer up many romantic thoughts to anyone seeking and seem particularly close in this part of the universe. If you study them long enough, they appear to be hanging from the wall of blackness as if waiting to be hand-plucked out of the broad sky, their bright glow bringing enjoyment as well as guidance through the bleakest of times. Difficult now to conjure up all the names with my mind in as much clutter as the surrounding area—Orion's Belt, Seven Sisters, Big Dipper and all of the astrological signs that studded the night and the Milky Way galaxy as far as the eye could see, crossed only by fast moving comets or orbiting satellites and all twinkling as though making contact.

I sense as always a relationship to this miracle of the night and comforting source for sailors everywhere. The water that now moves without fuss under our hull as if it too has had enough of the storm's assault, this fluid sound that lives in the tiny discoveries of my own.

Through it all, I can still hear my first Caribbean friends expounding about the fortitude and will of those traveling through my now favorite sailing waters of Drake's Passage where Sir Francis himself kept watch over warring ships. I had fallen in love with the sea and could easily believe that this is the type of night, witnessed by those others using their sextants, focused on their course, or just casually standing out on a deck in contemplation.

This by now comfortable awareness also constantly had me searching for more of the same through the written word, and with everything I learned I also discovered rather quickly that the Leeward Islands were rife with shipwrecks. Though a terrifying story, the history of the famous Rhone was the one that stood out and captured my full attention. Perhaps because I couldn't imagine how a 310' iron hull could be torn in two by striking a rock, but she was after all trying to outrun a late-season hurricane possibly as ferocious as the one we experienced. She was only two years old when that happened in 1867 and now I cry inwardly for the vulnerability of her crew placed in the way of such fury and could only imagine from our encounter on land, what hell they must have endured. And again the past and the present collide in my imagination.

I feel a slight breeze and hear the plashing water underneath the dock as the ripples hit a different obstacle and as I listen, I try to envision the dives yet to be taken at that once wished-for location. I know there are strange and beautiful things that came out of that horrible wreck because over time she has become a highly sought after natural reef with divers from everywhere enjoying the creation. And after so many years, she is occupied by a multitude of fish that dart throughout her bulk while her frame offers a home to the colorful sponges and coral that share her with the many other life forms in our warm waters. And while I'm certain things here will eventually improve, I continue to whisper prayers for those beautiful things I'd sought.

For Eddie and me and many of our closest friends having been presented with the many harsh facts foisted on us by this natural disaster, much of being able to cope and get through each day has come from sharing with each other, not only supplies but time. And much of that time is quite naturally spent in the litany of re-telling the stories that often revert back to the beginning when each of us first started to call this Peter Pan wonderland home. We uniformly agree and have much to say about our first impressions of the water, the interminably beautiful weather and importantly, our complete and lasting friendships, and somehow it all adds strength to our resolve to get through this toughest of challenges while not knowing if that is even possible.

But life is definitely in slow motion and we cannot help but notice even the absence of the annoying tiny creatures that crawled or flew and normally inhabit these islands and no one could tell us if their species would be rekindled over time. The ferret-like mongoose, the palmetto bugs called flying roaches, the centipedes and the precious tiny green lizards I'd taken a shine to ever since witnessing its larger cousin, the more intimidating iguana; all were missing.

The fruit bats too that customarily flew through the palms as dusk fell, marking a ritual passing of twilight on those late afternoons when work was done, while we all sat watching the sun set into the horizon in that magical way of appearing to drown inch by inch into the sea, hoping for the storied 'green flash' to appear at the end. If anything did survive, they were in hiding, waiting as we all were for things to change.

All in hiding except for the tiniest of insects desperate for new housing. On the boat we were more fortunate than those whose homes were missing windows with screens; that is if they even had windows left. There were mosquitoes and no-see-ums adding to the misery on top of the already abundant presence of noisy bees burrowing wherever they could find shelter. Dipping into the water was one of the few ways to avoid anything that flew but it also presented more of a hazard in town where sewer lines were broken creating another set of serious problems.

However we came together now, it is but a modest form of our old selves, yet it is enough to create a sense of harmony that will bolster us, and keep us from spinning out into the universe and out of control. And all that we had to anchor us with any validity and strength in these gatherings of congregated friendship was a union with the past.

And while life here wasn't always easy, that part too would somehow be turned into comedy when it suited. Our island life was charged with many firsts. Some of the more memorable ones for me seemed to involve power outages. In the early days these outages were frequent, changing up the day's routine or interfering with set plans. More than once I'd been caught covered in soap from head to toe when the water abruptly stopped. Awkward, yes, part of a pattern to be fed into what would soon become the overflowing coffers of our storied life...definitely yes!

And when it came to water other than that of the sea, there was importantly the education of its conservation because of the periodic arid conditions and the need to collect rain from the roof into cisterns beneath the house. This conservation often times caused an inability to flush regularly. That in turn, seemed to burgeon into humorous jingles—'*on our island in the sun we don't flush for number one...*' Those then turned into a trilogy of rhymes to be printed out and displayed in the anointed place. These signs also inviting graffiti experts wishing to hone their craft on the walls of public spaces and they did it with the zest and flare of a bard. A bit of laughter could often be heard behind the closed door of a stall inside many a public restroom.

At times an unwelcome visitor could be found in a household cistern. More than a few comments could be heard at the checkout counters of the hardware store regarding these small coqui (tree frogs) that somehow managed to infiltrate that sacred space. Worse yet, to be awakened in the middle of the night with a 'splat' as an escapee of the cistern dropped from the ceiling onto a cool tile floor. It was impossible to understand their patterns or whether these odd moments occurred during a particular mating ritual, but the hardware store was well stocked with long-handled nets.

And what we'd have given finding ourselves now after this holocaust of nature, idling our days in isolation without the formalities of an infrastructure, just to be in the endless waiting lines for car registration or local government services required to become a resident. Those nearly always three lines necessary for anything to do with a final tag or document, never given easily and always an annoyance as well as a marvel at the mechanics of getting things accomplished at all.

In the past in better times, necessary cocktail party fodder could always be found in the long and comical accounting of someone waiting nearly a day to finally reach the head of the line only to find they'd been in the wrong one, adding one or more days to the entire process. Then if papers were not in order, there would be no cajoling an employee with the smiling innocence of being from away, a phrase conveniently used for those not *bohn here*. Days could go by just longing for the extremely important and final stamp only to find as you reached the last hurdle, the little barrier counter-top window being lowered with authority by the smiling clerk pointing to the clock on the wall.

Even those inconveniences that perturbed so many venturing to make this their home for the long haul would have been welcomed with open arms now that we've been reduced to so little.

And while many of us still shared the communal bath water of the sea, soaping down with dish liquid well proven by a boating community for its use in conquering the salt, we had to be mindful always of the sharp objects hidden beneath in sandy tombs created from the boiling activity of the water the night it pushed ashore and everything went flying.

Being in the salty water all I could think about were the many times we all swam, snorkeled and windsurfed, sailed or fished as if each day was a holiday because these simple pleasures could be had before work, after work or any given weekend. Time never mattered and rain rarely hindered anything you set out to do on any given day.

Nessa and I would every so often find that our timing coincided when performing these daily ministrations in seawater that we'd now been reduced to, and would end up rehashing many of those former activities. We were never at a loss for words about anything that made up our life on St. Margeaux, but there was one event that stood out for the two of us specifically from all the others. Occasionally we had been cajoled by Russ and Eddie into sewing up ballyhoo fish to be used for bait primarily because the art of stitching and darning would obviously benefit from our more nimble fingers. These bait were much needed by the anglers in our lives anxious to at last lure the 'big one' during the major tournaments held in the more challenging waters offshore, fighting for the elusive trophy. We would usually meet up at Mick's, dressed in the oldest of clothes, hair hidden under old sailing caps, for a project that could turn messy, all except Natasha who absolutely refused the assignment, somehow each time due to a fresh manicure. By the time our fingers became sore from using those large needles necessary to pierce the flesh and we were ready to quit, we'd notice we'd done them all. I think we may have had a bit of misguided pride in the act, however, since we never found anyone else to compare notes with.

The fish were then placed carefully into well-iced coolers, awaiting their ultimate destination the following day where they would tantalizingly gleam in the early morning light, taunting their prey. Then we'd gather around a grill heaped with burgers and roasting potatoes listening to tales about the ones that already got away but not without the good fight.

She and I milked that situation for all it was worth, claiming of course, that we would gladly accept the many perks and rewards known to be available even though it wasn't as difficult as we made out. We were acutely aware that we were indeed much faster at it than they would have been. It just took a little getting used to at first, but the fish were fresh, so the smell was tolerable. Those fishing boats have also all been destroyed and all that's now left is the ability to savor that once glorious chance to watch a marlin or sailfish take the bait and rise out of the churning water as it met its match.

The overall demeanor of the business landscape has also changed for the time being and most everyone is idle. Eddie's found himself without crew or equipment and does what he can with less to help our neighbors. His storage unit he'd tried so hard to shore up also took a heavy toll leaving little in the way of tools with which to work. Everyone still pitches in wherever needed with whatever they have, to clear land and rubble and replace a roof but not much more. It will be a long time before there will be building of new homes on slabs left by discouraged owners.

And from the air the blue of thousands of tarps being used as a temporary patch over exposed openings continue to dot the many hillsides and valleys, replacing the lush bounty nature had previously endowed and which had been taken for granted. That same bounty I'd rushed headlong into with Eddie taking the lead.

Before all of this, our island had been grandly gifted with blazing color; much of it seen in the tremendous array of the yellow flowered ginger-Thomas, the orange flamboyant and the red-blossomed African tulip. And all of them enhanced mightily by nature's gift of blues and violets contrastingly placed by her gardener with a very good eye. This vibrancy punctuating the verdant greens was seen as a bonfire of hues that brought everything into focus, and now in the aftermath of the storm, no one could predict what will be reborn. But as long as there is sunshine and rain, there will be new color.

One of the earliest casualties to hit our immediate group came when Reno and Max had to give up the hope that they'd be able to re-build everything in time and were forced to leave, creating an empty void even before their departure date. The remaining cars on their lot at the time of the storm were the targets for everything that flew and many were simply damaged by their overturned placement or heavy object that landed on top of them. Their tall sign, Vincent's Rental Cars had been the largest object on the property and when it fell, it covered quite a few cars before smashing through the storefront window. They had simply lost too much and could not endure the long wait without new resources.

I've been told through our grapevine, as predictable as any ancient drumbeat, that Max has already set up space in their stateside condo for guests needing an occasional reprieve from island drama. I know she will be revered in her new home as much as she was here and wherever she is, there will always be a party.

But even with the many that have had to forego their plans, dropping out because of necessity, there are still some among us whose determination has been ignited, for whom life under these new circumstances takes on a new rhythm. It appears to be created out of that necessity, showing strength of their endurance during a crisis as well as their need to remain in a unique society, one in which their own uniqueness would thrive unlike any other place. These individuals gave up the idea of returning to the mainland, possibly having no place to go, or simply feeling it more important to carve new ways out of the rubble, much like early settlers anywhere had done. Wholeheartedly they began taking on a positive attitude about change being good even when forced upon us in such an ugly manner.

Eddie and I understood that sentiment also but were still feeling in limbo about our own future. We hoped through the closeness with those left that a bit of that much-craved outlook would rub off on us and looked forward to spending however much time possible in their presence without worry or those saddest of thoughts again interfering. And when that time was available sparked by that same heartwarming attitude, I would find myself quietly holding back rather than participating in the usual give and take in order to better observe. And what I saw was a heroic effort, grabbing for that foothold of animation that had always kept us going. I understood it well and admired the bravado and scanned their faces to imprint them forever, these dear people that made up our wonderful world. My greatest fear, unvoiced, was that too much had been taken from us already, hoping against hope that I was wrong and we could stay.

During all this time we still continued to pool our food with our close boating neighbors and others who could make their way from town, a ritual easily developed since we had very few facilities left for such purpose. Because of that we found ourselves sharing not only the food but trading stories much the way we might have over campfires of our youth.

Surprisingly, the simplicity of island life, other than waiting lines, always weighed in against that which was left behind on the mainland. And life had become simpler yet in this post-hurricane time making most of us realize that which we truly valued. This in turn forced us to use every resource at our disposal to fill in the blank spaces and recreate whatever possible.

A resource like a salvaged guitar turning up, more than likely held tight under a pillow by a frightened owner hiding in a tub, would allow us the momentary pleasure and healing powers of music. Minds could drift peacefully for a few hours with fears and worries temporarily muted by the echoing strains of the occasional hymn thrown aloft into the darkness and carried out over the water to touch another soul.

Every so often, the high drama of a lightning storm could be seen out on the horizon, so far away as to be silent, but its far-reaching flashes and bursts of light against the soundless inky backdrop could conjure up an 1812 Overture in tribute. Each new flash seemed to appear in sync with the imaginary cymbals and triumphant canons of the musical composition. The lights blasted into the sky meaningfully, matching the fervent wish for a triumphant outcome to our torn apart way of life, a visual drama put there to enrich us.

If the mood were just right and it had been a good day overall, the inevitable sea shanty would spring forth and with very little encouragement. Or a 'Parrothead' formerly disguised as a blues man would pipe in with…*"nibblin on sponge cake"*…, and in honor of Jimmy Buffet we'd join in, picking up the lyrics, continuing until we ran out of songs. He after all knew much about islands and storytelling and was revered by many as being simpatico to an adventuresome spirit, real or imaginary. We all knew how curative songs and fresh laughter to be for our ailing hearts, and clung to that notion at every turn provided.

And at other times our friend Matteo Cruz, a non-boater but a wonderful entertainer, would provide a change of pace with his romantic Latin music and popular tunes that he could no longer perform at the now destroyed Top Deck bar. There never was much to the space, just a lengthy slab of mahogany with Matteo's favorite stool sidled up to the end abutting a corner wall, a dart board well used, and light fare offered daily at the small crowded tables. But a watering hole nonetheless to quench the thirst of its happy patrons after a long day of slogging through whatever their particular stumbling block happened to be. But importantly holding within its plain walls shared feelings and ideas, creating that element of solidarity that had always been our claim.

That had been one of Eddie's favorite hangouts with his old diving pals, grabbing a beer after work to reminisce about those early years. They were all a little wiser than when they first met, holding down important jobs or businesses of their own, but still young at heart and still taking Eddie under their wing when necessary, and still romanticizing their early misfortunes.

And the bar's weekend music man, Matteo, part Spanish, part Italian, looking every bit of both was handsome, charming and what older folks might call a 'bit of a lady's man'. That was especially true if one took note of his seductive smile that curved toward his haunting black eyes while he sang. I often wondered if Nessa would be swept away by his charm since he seemed to favor her company when we all met there, focusing his ballads in her direction and causing a blush to form across her high cheekbones. It would have been easy left on her own during Russ's obstinate moments, but as she confided, she continued to hold out hope that he would one day 'see the light'.

I, on the other hand had been overjoyed when introduced to his brother who had been visiting. He had Matteo's looks, but as the elder by three years, Marco was a reminder of Carlos and what had intrigued me about all Latin men. He was introduced to me at a time when Eddie and I had fallen apart over my not wanting to get married. When word got around that a new man was in town escorting his newly released girlfriend, Eddie did something quite astonishing. Showing up at my door, flowers in hand with two tickets protruding from their stems, he willed me to accept his invitation to fly to St. Martin, using a look I had never resisted, knowing I'd never been there, taking me completely by surprise and giving our relationship a second chance.

By the time he left the apartment the next morning, thoughts of Marco had faded; Eddie had made his case very convincingly. So I added that memory to the many competing for penned space, of those nights on another magical island, one with the divided flags of the Dutch and the French cultures. It was made to order...sunfish sailing offered in the azure blue that flowed onto white sands of the Dutch beach outside our door, very romantic gourmet dinners enjoyed on intimate terraces on the French side savoring the views there, no longer cognizant of the division of countries, and everything else in between. We were back on track with Marco a thing of the past.

Now however, Matteo is here on the *Wanderer* to provide succor as necessary as the foods we needed to survive. Knowing people had only each other to count on in their small neighborhoods he would make the rounds to any of these intimate gatherings throughout the island, trying as always to offer his musical talent to those in need of a bit of uplifting in these wearing days. This kindness was in-bred and respected. And as I watched his face aboard the *Wanderer*, dipped slightly as his practiced fingers ran the strings, I knew we were all filling up on a sumptuous meal at last.

Thankfully, for those rare times that marked a birthday or a longed-for food specialty finally obtained from the hands of a stateside benefactor, even more boisterous laughter could be heard as each of us with the help of a glass of rum somehow always turning up, brought forth another story. How could so many events have been tucked away? Had we really lived so much life in these past years while we weren't looking? I made myself listen with a new attentiveness, a custodian of their content.

And as always, I was aware that emotional convalescence was becoming our biggest challenge, the order of the day each day, especially because so much of the progress and outcome was still out of our hands. We had been experts in the art of living and pulled together fiercely, digging deeply into our collective consciousness seeking the reasons we had all chosen to stay on an island given to many hardships and our willingness to sacrifice many things over the years because we still couldn't face the thought of leaving.

My treasured journals, some no more imposing than black and white covered composition books, had been heaped with these experiences and I had turned them all into stories about the good times as well as the difficult, adding new twists and turns to the episodes of life. With all of those now gone, I can only try and recreate some of those meaningful events through all the storytelling out here in the open air. And these small notes are now placed meticulously into what is only a rough imitation of my very first one. I await with great anticipation the new ones to soon be brought back with the items far more important to our daily living than journals. For me, however, as everyone had long ago discovered, they've become nearly as important as the foods for which we hunger.

There are already favorite passages holding claim to the few blank pages remaining, so necessary now that we had developed this new pattern, much like the night we were sitting around with a molding board game rescued from dampened belongings.

As was becoming habit, we were joined by Russ, Nessa and Mick who'd already dropped Natasha at the airport, as well as a few townspeople somehow just turning up looking for a bit of distraction. Tasha, the only one among us who can still look good without trying was the unanimous choice for the trip and was on her way with a long grocery list of items to send back. The flights were coming and going with better intervals now that most of the cleanup had been completed at the airport and she was my angel of mercy regarding journals.

That night was really no different from the many previous ones, but somehow judging by the tenor of their conversation, something had sparked a story that would have Russ and Mick holding court bringing out the big guns in their own inimitable manner. They often used our impromptu stage for their renditions of events that they fit together haphazardly from the many yachting excursions taken, with their telling always becoming more raucous as the night wore on.

Eddie had long ago gotten his captain's license, what the Coast Guard called a six pack, the type required for delivery of the boats whose stateside owners were unable to make the long crossings necessary to reach the islands. Even though our work schedules only allowed for the occasional longer trip and it presented me with my own daunting anxieties during the early days of our relationship, the license was still at the ready. I knew he hoped it would provide for an interesting future when we could afford to permanently leave our jobs for the open water. In the meantime whenever we were able, we shared many of those nautical miles with the capable and delightfully funny band of mariners we gratefully called friends.

Busying myself with getting extra glasses from the galley for the few stragglers lured from a nearby boat by all our voices that seemed to grow louder by the hour, the noise beckons thoughts from a time before life as we knew it changed so drastically, times of high-spirited joy.

It has become very obvious as we sit night after night in the cluttered space of the deck, that the *Wanderer's* exterior is not as pretty as she once was and below even worse and definitely in need a lot of attention. But those now distant times are deeply imbedded within her frame. They've become the melodies and lyrics that have accompanied us on our short junkets and long peregrinations like pilgrims seeking mystical destinations, our connection to each other joined in mutual celebration of our way of life that we consider anything but ordinary.

Whether local cruises or yacht deliveries requiring a more rigid schedule, the responsibilities differed little, but once at anchor, there was never a lack of fun and enjoyment to partake in. Mostly our shorter cruises were to the number of islands reached within a few hours or less. And of course, within those there were a few that would require wonderful hours in those marvelous caves because Eddie had learned to indulge my obsession and everyone loved being in there.

There was no mistaking that after my initial flyover of these very same islands, I had felt mesmerized by what seemed like some sort of utopia, and then with Eddie's help, at last had the opportunity to see for myself the rare beauty hidden beneath the ever-changing surface of our cruising waters.

It was never difficult to be lulled by the lore if you allowed your imagination free reign. Call it paradise or just pure bliss; the warm waters always beckoned. And when opportunity arose, Eddie and I sailed alone and heeded that call and eventually spent some very romantic hours inside the grotto at the Baths. And when we came together as lovers within those walls, I clearly felt the sigh of thousands of women reaching satisfaction as if waiting for love to set them free.

Even though my search of all things regarding St. Ursula only turned up a scant connection between those giant boulders and the eleven thousand virgins and I finally claimed defeat, it still allowed the simple unspoken presence of all myth and mystery to envelop just as I had been advised in that little plane by a very wise young woman named Carmen. I had occasionally written to her about this, knowing she would be pleased at my persistence but lost touch before filling her in on the rest. That I'd been seeking the help from an island woman eager to engage my whims, acknowledging the claim I was still searching for in this most beautiful water-born sanctuary.

Mariah had made it clear that she believed in many things having to do with the oceans. She spoke of goddesses and mermaids with the confidence of someone connected spiritually. More often than not, she'd bend my ear with one legend or another and had me checking my own favorite conch shell for evidence of a goddess's first gift to humans. Mine of course lacked the proper response.

And Mariah had encouraged it all, wanting me to investigate the past within the maritime world saying that one day, I might find a real connection, or at least satisfy my stubborn curiosity. While I wanted to believe much of what she offered simply because it would have been an easy way out to my own intrigue, my own desire to tie up the loose ends to the gnawing inside, I knew that discovery wouldn't come easily and possibly not ever.

But she did warn me to expect the unexpected. My instincts could just be a longing, a crying out from somewhere deep within the past of my ancestors. She had seen a lot of cards and spoke from her experience as well as her heart. These things happened; people died at sea leaving untold mourners and the heart's longing could be very powerful indeed.

I had to admit that made more sense to me than mermaids, but I also had nothing to go on. And unfortunately, all of that would have to wait until we get through the present disaster. I didn't even have access to the books I would need and might not for a very long time.

Our friends were well aware how much I wanted to believe and find answers to this persistent yearning I have talked of along with pirate bounty, for as long as they've known me; always searching, never fully understanding but never giving up. And I knew full well those stories would find their way into the agenda along with so many others as soon as these new guests settled in with their drink and there would be good-humored laughter, sometimes at my expense, since there would be differing views about everything.

Their male bonding is hardly unfamiliar territory for me, but I had no trouble remembering the time that started it all and brought us so far. Who could forget my initial indoctrination party attended by this melting pot of characters and personalities? Fortunately, there had been many more parties just like that shared with those having that same zany robust zest for life, and all making a lasting impression on me as I came to know each in their turn.

For many it was their simple zeal over anything island related that attracted me to them, or even sports-related events if one considered the type of games played on any given Sunday afternoon at Long Point Cay assisted by copious amounts of rum, to be sport. It might be a dinghy race to see whose outboard was fastest, or a rowing race with a damsel always in the prow holding the custom burgee of the rower, and even another race to see who was the fastest to hit the floor. Someone would yell "Red" and the deck would be awash with bodies flat on their backs holding their legs in the air, imitating the dog bearing that name. Anyone failing to do so would be responsible for the next round. Only the tourists laughed—the rest were dead serious. The tab could be outrageous!

A great deal of our time together that didn't actually involve making fools of ourselves included traveling on our boats in tandem to many easily reachable destinations, as often as was possible. Occasionally, that might even mean a brush with danger, especially if the weather changed unexpectedly or unforeseen problems occurred hindering the operation of the boat itself. Whatever the situation or occasion, it melded into the years that grew an infinite bond between us; we could always count on each other.

The closeness forged also gave way to hilarity that flourished easily into an overabundance of fun. I realized with pride as soon as I became a part of them, that we may have appeared outwardly different, but here in the islands appearances and antics never disguised the hearts and souls that were indeed open to anyone in need, the real story of a society the likes of which will hopefully linger on even if only passing the lips of those to come after us.

Chapter Nine

As I write, many more weeks have slipped idly by while the voices drone on in this continuing theme on deck. It's so easy to space as I listen, and yet sadly, this is another of the many evenings we've come to depend on as if to prove our existence on an island that has lost its compass and has us feeling adrift in a sea of rubble. It has been too long, this waiting. Right now I hear my name being called, which can only mean another new arrival and at least that keeps me moving. It seems even though this is a small marina, it has begun to represent a haven to many more as the monotony sets in all around. Word has gotten out and they are always welcome.

I dislike that we've been reduced to very mundane snacks, always having enjoyed the creativity of planning for a party, making something unexpected for a galley cook. But tonight we're going to have to settle for the unimaginative can of assorted nuts I found in the bottom of the storage bin, one of the last.

Taking this small token up top I'm relieved and happy to find that the guests are a couple newly arrived after their harrowing night at Sweet Bottom and fortunate completion of at least a few of the necessary repairs, enough to bring her home to their old slip. So far there have been only a few other sailors that made their way back into the bay, either by tow or limping in on their own auxiliary power, and even though we're still missing many within our community, this is encouraging.

By the time I came out of the companionway, Eddie has already begun telling them about our first sail together though I can only imagine what triggered that discussion, and I know full well his version

will be scaled with drastic differences from mine. He had thoroughly
charmed me with promises of sailing as soon as we'd begun dating and
said he would teach me all I needed to know. I thought him confident
and almost cocky as he talked about the knots and sails and currents,
initiating me into the jargon of a sailor about to embark on a much
longer voyage. Then of course I simply fell in love and never did figure
out whether on that day it was the sea or him that made the best
impression.

My version of that day is remembered more correctly not only
because I had taken the time to write it all down when that had become
a daily habit, but also because I had learned quite quickly how he
embellished his stories for new audiences. It actually went this way:

By the time I arrived at the town dock, heralded by a blazing sun
that was already casting glancing blows onto the white deck, the lightly
swaying palms nearby could do little to shield from the heat. Even then
the deck's glare was enough to shock without sunglasses, so I was
anxious to be on board under the small bimini top.

Tossing my canvas bag into the cockpit, Eddie let out a hearty wolf
whistle in acknowledgement of my new periwinkle bikini that I knew
accentuated my coppery hair streaked by the sun. His eyes told me he
was noticing quite a bit more as he reached out a strong hand to help
me jump aboard his prized possession. She was a beautiful 44' Gulfstar
sloop with a gleaming dark blue hull and a captain that had already
inspired confidence.

Even though I began the day with first-time jitters, he turned out to
be a patient teacher. And before long, with the wheel becoming a more
natural fit in my inexperienced hands, even I could actually feel what
he called the slot in the waves, holding the sails at the perfect angle to
catch the ever-present trades and smoothly propel us through the water.

It was such a clear day we could see the hint of the island chain far
off in the distance resting in a violet atmospheric haze, each topped
with a perfect whipped cream cloud. The compass heading pointed us
toward his favorite spot, Robin's Bay, and with little conversation

needed there was only the repetition of the hull slicing purposefully through the deeper indigo water with that swooshing sound as it softened each wave, smoothly pushing the bubbly froth from bow to stern.

The sea was perfect according to the skipper—under two feet and wind velocity increasing just enough to get us to our destination quickly, but not too much to cause us to heel over uncomfortably. And, he had timed our arrival into the picturesque anchorage well before our stomachs would begin rumbling with thoughts of lunch. We had the entire day ahead of us.

From a distance I thought the island appeared a bit unremarkable, but as we drew closer it was stunning to the eye in a way that could only be seen to be believed, especially as the darker blue once again turned to the shoreline color that had already seduced. Then turning aqua with the addition of a hint of green, it fronted the dense growth that encompassed the length and breadth, more intimate than most and void of a sandy strip, replaced by smooth, oddly flat stones heating in the sun.

We were alone in the bay, free from other boaters and life on shore. But for just a moment as I squinted against the bright sunlight, I thought I captured the sound of a bosun's whistle, spurring on my imagination with the illusion of a massive wooden schooner, dark hulled and mysterious. This would of course contain pirated treasure hidden deeply in her bowels, just as its heavy rigging was being readied to set sail on a perfect sea.

The spell broke as something caught my eye and I let out a screech sounding like nails on a chalkboard. I had spotted a very large barracuda not far below the surface where Eddie intended to drop anchor, completely erasing the mythical schooner and its intended journey from my mind.

"It's only George." Eddie tried to reassure me as though he were a personal friend.

"He's been here ever since I found this spot a few years ago. The clarity of the water is deceiving; it's really deep and George simply likes taking the shade in the shadow of the hull."

To prove his point, the anchor went zinging overboard into the depths until I saw the white cloud rise up through the clear water after finding its mark on the pale sand at the bottom.

"He's far more frightened of you and I'm sure he'll move away quickly the moment you put your lovely flipper into the water."

"Well, if you say so. I do not want to give up the beautiful swim and snorkel lessons I've looked forward to because of a spoiled barracuda!"

Looking back upon that entire weekend as replete with total joy as possible, I know that was when I officially recognized what the future could hold. All I needed was to keep my mind open about the chances I'd taken hoping for this exact opportunity. I had been acting on my dream to have such an exceptional lifestyle, and I found surprisingly, it had come without struggle.

We swam and talked and took our shade from the intense sun underneath a larger awning spread from mast to stern, allowing time to stand still and a chance to elaborate even more about our worlds outside of St. Margeaux, all the while savoring the lunch I'd taken great care to prepare. This already had the earmarks of being much more than the simplicity of time spent together to date because of our heavier work schedules.

And until then I had been listening to all the anonymous voices in my head telling me to be careful, we were getting too close, but now I could feel my resistance breaking down as I studied Eddie's face. It was becoming obvious we were headed into new territory. The brief encounters with other men while trying to understand what I was looking for after my divorce didn't match up to the life I imagined when I was with him. I had been fleeing any permanent emotional ties and had found such pure joy in that release of pain after being with Carlos, but I sensed Eddie was not going to settle for brief encounters of that nature. I still was not sure, but his amorous attention was becoming very heady stuff in the meantime.

As we sat there sipping the refreshing cold wine, it was so obvious he was set on making me feel at ease in these new circumstances as a novice on the water. And with good humor he generously took a great deal of time sifting through all of my in-depth material about what early dwellers referred to as 'rock shelters', and seemed taken with many of the same stories about the various sailing ships that had roamed the waters of Drake's Passage. I had come to realize he found my curiosity extremely appealing. My ongoing interest with the many myths and legends of the Leewards had already taken a strong foothold, and I saw that Eddie was taking great pleasure in being the one to bring some of it to life for me.

He took advantage of the day's rhythm, unhurried and relaxed, making light of his own versions about the explorers that built watchtowers along deserted beaches and hidden coves in order to attack passing vessels, mentioning that some of his friends were quite taken with my persistence in wanting to know more about the surrounding geography. They as yet had no idea how much this new land had quickly come to mean to me. I knew my inclination for research and my newfound love for journaling played a role in that persistence and I hoped over time they would fully understand. Little did we know then, how many stories would end up in one of those little bound books.

It was quiet except for our voices and a faint lap of water. Even the birds seemed to be napping and the shaded awning enveloped us, our conversation soft so as not to disturb. Certain topics garnered more attention, not only because of his knowledge of the Caribbean and the pirates that sailed the seas between the 18th and 19th centuries, but we found we had mutual favorites. The pirate Blackbeard was one of them.

It took very little time to realize that Eddie was a great reader of history and had already tapped into many of the books that had taken over hours of my time while sorting through the volumes available at the small library. There were differing details of events of Blackbeard's career that we each had discovered, as well as his physical description and even the spelling of his given name. Even with written accounts, many of them still seemed to me like storybook characters but then Eddie's way with storytelling managed to fill them out with their own personalities, and he seemed to enjoy playing along. His was a very compelling presence, perhaps more than I was prepared for.

"The only pirate I'm at all familiar with from childhood," I added, "is the one called 'Black Bart' Roberts, known as the Admiral of the Leewards, the one with that skull and crossbones flag."

"Even though I've been devouring island history ever since I came here, there was only one small story on him that I vaguely remember. And it was about a particularly notorious pirate who tried to break ties with Roberts, but never achieved the dreams of wealth and glory he sought. But I think that was what caused Roberts to flee the Caribbean for Africa."

Eddie was enjoying our history session and I was enjoying his company. And the more we talked, I realized how fully all of the reading was more than the stuff of legends for me because so much was purported to have happened in the depths of my constantly moving backyard. I also knew I would continue seeking answers that would create even more questions and sensed that the time needed would be something Eddie would be quite willing to share.

Finally, turning his attention back to the moment and the glorious surroundings, he said, "I promise we'll bring Mick and Natasha back with us the next time to do some real exploring over on Prospect Island. You've done your homework but you need to see this for yourself and I know they'd enjoy it.

"They're old hands at this, but I want you to be more comfortable with the gear, especially the mask, before we go into the caves."

"I really can't believe this. So much of my being here is still like a dream come true without my ever knowing that the dream even existed, or that I would have such a thirst for it. I'm almost ashamed to say how little I miss of my life back in the states. Don't you think that's odd?"

In reply, he simply reached over and kissed me with such amazing tenderness that it seemed to say 'welcome to my world' and 'I'd like to undress you' simultaneously. Both fit the circumstances and what followed provided the proverbial leap from a heart hiccup felt during that initial dinner at the Sea Crest to joyously span the wide range of emotions, bringing them to the fullness of an operatic crescendo.

"I know you have trust issues, Lily, but I need you to trust me. I'm not like Rob and even though these feelings are scaring me a little too, please don't run away from them," Eddie said gently, again pulling me in tightly.

Long legs entwined, murmurs of long awaited words, and a heart-song of unrealized wishes pierced the last of my protective armor. A couple of hours later, utilizing my full quotient of feminine intuition, I knew I'd finally met the man I could again love deeply and completely against all odds after that cold December morning I stepped aboard a crowded jet with despair clutching at my heels.

We napped briefly and made love more slowly and richly with this knowledge and later contentedly swam in the light blue dream and watched the ripples circle lazily around us as each small movement broke the surface gently and without sound. It was enough to simply *be*. It seemed that feeling was somehow conveyed to George, who was still dozing far off to one side where he appeared quite unthreatening. He too may have been dreaming of a mate rushing to him in this aquatic jewel-toned world.

Refreshed and renewed, Eddie provided another lesson with snorkel gear and fins, tantalizing me with thoughts of eventually graduating to scuba gear. By then I didn't need much more to reinforce my longing to stay on St. Margeaux, but of all the new delights being stacked one upon another, the offering of this unexpected and enchanted underwater world thriving with a life form previously unknown to me, was the pinnacle. The nooks and crannies of my heart expanded to capture all the gifts placed before me on this boldly bright Caribbean day.

Later when hunger called and the sun changed the world around us yet again, Eddie put the small hibachi, two thick steaks, and the rest of the gear into the dinghy while I put the finishing touches on the salad.

We had gathered edible wild greens onshore earlier—just one of the hundreds of new finds he had already pointed out.

As I watched him from the galley port, warmed by the afterglow of the previous hours, I understood that by letting me into his life and teaching me the things that made up his world, he had already eased his way into my heart. It was almost as if he had been waiting for his other half while I never knew I could have one. And I sensed that I would always be able to trust him, even with my life.

From now on I would no longer have the need to compare him to any man, especially Carlos. Yes, Carlos had been the one who first opened my eyes about the tropics and the many dormant longings. But this relationship with Eddie would not only be joyously romantic, it would also be multi-faceted with a mutual give and take of interests satisfying to us both; one that sustains everything. It was all there, just waiting for me to accept it.

I kept watching his purposeful movements as he prowled the shoreline. While the steaks were cooking he looked to be foraging for plants, tossing them into the canvas bag with care, a seemingly natural habit for him. Besides the genuine affection and sexual desire newly expressed, he'd already begun sharing his own broad perspective on those things work related that helped me to grasp some understanding of the flora and fauna of the islands. It was all so far away from the concrete jungle of my city background, and I was learning literally from the ground up.

As with these new-found greens he'd made sure to spend some time driving me around St. Margeaux, so that he could show me others that would amuse as well as educate me. Those with the names *soursop*, *seagrape* and *breadfruit* and many more even stranger sounding plants like *monkey puzzle* and *pipe organ cactus*. I had already noticed the puzzle being utilized around the Resort where their stinging configuration acted as protective barriers surrounding certain storage buildings.

And if it hadn't been for Eddie, I would have been poisoned by the innocuous appearing tiny green apple of the *manchineel* tree while roaming one of the small beaches along the eastern shore. I was one of the lucky ones because it was told that many early explorers had come to their untimely deaths from these very apples, not a pleasant thought.

No sooner had my daydreaming taken hold again, than I heard the oarlocks dropping into the dinghy as Eddie tied it off to the cleat, followed by the thump of heavily loaded canvas onto the stern. That was followed by a hard rolling sound that turned out to be a few smaller interestingly shaped rocks he thought I'd enjoy keeping. I now understood there would be many more days like this filled with pleasure and discovery and even a few possible mishaps. After all, I was new at trusting. I could at least avoid the near misses of things as dangerous as poisonous fruit but the door was now open to all the possibilities and that created an exciting menu to choose from. Boredom would never be on that list.

The finished product of his efforts proved wonderful; a satisfyingly simple meal lacking for nothing, and heightened by the rarified air of the late afternoon light and tropical breeze. As a final touch to an already perfect day, Eddie retrieved his favorite Spanish brandy kept cradled in the bulkhead storage, to be savored out on the deck. I'd already discovered that darkness comes early in the islands but in the quiet calm of a protected harbor time nearly stands still.

Nestled into the cushions of the roomy cockpit, there is only the velvety softness of water as it meets the hard surface of the hull, the sound creating a soothing balm to lull us into a dreamlike fugue. All tangible signs of time are missing and the telling is gauged by looking up as the darkness deepens and the horizon disappears. Stars abound with a new brilliance unfettered by lights from land, bringing to mind the magnitude and roundness of the planet.

Finally, Eddie took my hand, not wanting to turn on the lantern and break the spell and led me below where we curled into each other in the wide cozy berth made warmer still by the generous placement of gleaming dark wood and our sun-baked bodies cradled in the gentle rocking motion, a world away from everything except our own desire. Any leftover concerns I may have harbored at last disappeared, drifting away with the last vestiges of thought before they found their place in deep sleep, spinning through space as fast as the earth.

The morning after came with the now familiar bell tones of a laughing gull announcing another bright day had begun and a new reason to greet it. Glancing over at the sleeping form, I knew it wasn't a dream, and I wriggled quietly out of the berth and slipped naked into the sea for an early morning swim to celebrate my feelings.

No other boats had arrived and the day looked much the same as the one before, but now giving credence to newly identified feelings, I happily discarded the niggling fear that this sameness might somehow become monotonous over time. Then I caught a whiff of strong freshly brewed coffee and turned over to see Eddie on deck in his trunks ready to sail again, holding up a huge mug in salute. My breath caught with happiness at the sight of this adventuresome man who would soon fill in the blanks to the many pages of journal entries silently calling out.

వావావ

The edges of the unknowns had rounded out pretty quickly after that small voyage with our declarations made clear, my intense love for my new job and a wealth of new friends. It was easier than imagined to embrace this unusual environment that caused adventure to sprout up nearly as fast as a seedling.

And there were many more intimate dinners aboard the *Wanderer* while anchored in the town harbor, leaving the 'nest' on those nights the draw of the water pulled us more deeply, allowing me to become more familiar with her galley and comfortable interior. She was perfectly outfitted for the needs of cruising as well as ample storage required for provisions to feed all our sailing friends at anchor or underway. The dining table was so well designed around the interior base of the mast, that we could seat six in a pinch using the two long built-in settees if weather prevented us from being up top. Those seats also made for extra sleeping areas that would prove beneficial when we began more extensive long distance cruising. All of this was fostering the beginning desire for a future life aboard.

On those evenings that we stayed aboard, we would also take advantage of the harbor location for an evening stroll. We tied the dinghy to the town dock and enjoyed the historical aspects of the area while dreaming our plans out loud but also taking pleasure in our immediate surroundings. It was a beautifully quaint village, built with the characteristics of many generations of different nationalities, rainbow-like with its tropical tints and totally filled with charm.

And many of these walks quite naturally evolved into conversation filled with the lore of the West Indies. When time allowed, I was still continually visiting the past, retrieving interesting information and feeling that in some way it honored them. Eddie knew that my appetite for all things Caribbean had grown exponentially and quickly, and he never once seemed to find that unusual.

Because of our desire to make our dreams a reality, we talked candidly about our fears as well as the excitement over everything we'd ever read or heard from other long-distance cruisers, hoping to stockpile enough information for the adventure of a lifetime one day. And while there were plenty of modern day tomes to read, one of my favorite books was about Joshua Slocum's voyage, *Sailing Alone Around the World*. And another about his barque, *Washington,* wrecked after dragging anchor during a gale, as well as those about pirate ships sailing the Leewards and being overtaken by hurricane winds, causing the occupants to give up their new plunder in order to save themselves—crime didn't pay. The scariest for me were the frightening stories of well-known dangers occurring while out in some anonymous location of deep water as one sea crossed into another where it seemed ships and crews were mysteriously lost.

And as if all of that wasn't enough, we'd mull over Caribbean travel guides for the Windward and Leeward islands that always sat on the shelf opposite the galley next to a copy of Chapman Navigation, just for the fun of it picking out hoped-for destinations while enjoying our morning coffee. We immersed ourselves not only in the pretty and romantic aspects of sailing, but also the many frightening endings into an abyss of darkness.

Eddie, also an avid reader, enjoyed the give and take. He loved to read aloud of ships adrift or lost at sea during the stormy periods in the tropics and all the related high drama and dangers encountered, especially given the lack of life saving equipment of the modern day sailor. It made the research more compelling and more fun as I listened to his narratives voiced with theatrical emphasis. Even his account of a brigantine crew he'd read of who had to relieve her of all her guns and provisions since the masts had been dismantled by a huge storm, leaving them to fend for themselves on the stormy sea. That particular one was more than I wanted to know about, but that imagined fear still made its way into my dreams, especially on a stormy night.

After my decision to stay on St. Margeaux, I discovered to my delight that one of the most colorful buildings, one I'd already claimed as 'venerable', housed the library. So my spare time was often split between locating sailing adventures to dream upon and island vegetation to better cope with the needs of the present. I had become an eager pupil beginning with the first days at the Resort, and Eddie was an amazing storehouse of information, bringing me either samples or photos. If I didn't know better I would have thought his last name *Appleseed* instead of Tremain.

Added as footnotes to his contribution in my journals, were the unusually named woods located on the island. One was called *purple heart* and the other *lignum vitae*, that one being termite resistant and so strong it was used as propeller shaft bearings on earlier ships, giving pause to its connection to the studied pirate ships we'd now thoroughly covered.

And because of my dear friend Essie, I had become completely intrigued with the names and types of multi-purpose trees she was always going on about. She loved to share her family stories about the many different species that grew on the various islands that had been utilized for islanders' needs throughout history.

There was the *calabash* with its large gourds that when dried out could be used as containers for food and drink as well as musical instruments. And there was the fruit of the *tamarind* tree that could be drunk or placed in sauces. I also finally found the *bay* tree whose leaves are used for perfumes, food flavoring and the ever-popular 'Bay Rum'. I'd even occasionally catch myself creating little jingles about the shiny-barked turpentine tree known as *gumbo limbo,* easily envisioning a group of friends at Long Point Cay shimmying under a thin pole to spirited music on any given Sunday.

Then with the help of her tutorial, I located the *jacarandas* and various citrus trees scenting the air as well as the many forms of cacti that sometimes got lost in the mix. But all of it was specific to the markings on the globe that denoted this sub-tropical climate of the West Indies. And all of it a continuing labor of love and cause for enchantment of the place I now called home.

But best of all were the hours she would spend teaching me about the so-called *spirit* trees. These seemed not only appropriate to a place built upon years of strong legends and people to pass them on, generation to generation, as part of their important culture, but gave Essie an opportunity to fill my head with much of the folklore passed down to her. And she did it with gusto, but only and always after we'd finished baking. She worried I would get caught up in the stories and forget the ingredients, and it didn't bode well to let that happen. Her baking was sacred!

She loved the taste of the syrupy sweetened condensed milk and with our abundance of limes taught me to make key lime pie. We expanded that to lime bread and then turned her prowess to the available coconuts and coconut bread and, of course, the guava tarts she made with such simplicity. Using her own lovingly made jelly, she would drop a spoonful onto pastry dough, cut it into squares and fold it into triangles like an empanada. These would pop out golden and sweet, fill the room with the scent, and make their way to the hearts and stomachs of her friends. These were all generously given up but also quite emphatically noted to encourage me to learn to prepare them all in order to "keep he full up on goodness" knowing how much Eddie loved her baking.

Once satisfied with our work, she'd sit me down at her kitchen table to relax and enjoy a glass of lemonade. Then, rocking Georgia on her lap she'd add the spice of a new folktale, watching my face change expression, enjoying her role as each one came to her. Essie's mother had sat her on her knee and her mother before her and the myths exploded into timeless stories just as they probably did in many a West Indian household.

During these hours that I was beginning to thrive on, she explained the various forms and sizes of what she considered to be those special *spirit* trees; some even considered a bit more sacred than others, like the very old *tamarind* on this island. But, and this is where she would really get carried away with her own childhood memories, there were also the ones to frighten small children into coming in at night should they forget the time because those trees housed the *jumbies* and they were called *baobob* trees. Then her voice would change as she stated in a more somber tone, that this tree was the one made of up water and when it dies, the water evaporates turning everything to dust—always making me unsure whether to believe her now serious composure, yet afraid to laugh just in case. As a scare tactic, I could only imagine how a story like that would sound to a truant child.

There is also a tree known as the *strangler fig* that devours its host tree, and although possibly not considered sacred, certainly sounded frightening to me. Essie elaborated about a few other *ficus* species that held a place among the *spirit* trees but the one I came to love the most is the *banyan* with its unusually huge tangled root system and enormous canopy of leaves that could, it seemed, shelter an entire village. The bigger the tree, or so it was as Essie told it, the better it could hold an entire congregation of *jumbies!*

How could I not become absorbed and enraptured by these stories? And there were also times when I sensed I was really beginning to believe them, especially late at night walking in their midst when a slight breeze could cause a tremor of leaves sounding very much like whispering voices. Essie and Eddie had created a united front when it came to scaring me witless.

When time permitted, and I wasn't engaged in baking or research, I also managed to do a little snorkeling near the boat, making myself more confident for the next opportunity at Prospect Island so that I would be able to keep up with everyone. I considered this to be like a small hunting party, exploring the depths of the unknown, finding treasure. I couldn't help myself; I'd been reading too much and been touched by a sorcerer's wand. Besides, Eddie had already agreed we could make that into a wonderful sailing weekend with Mick and Natasha.

Between work and my voracious reading, I imagined lovingly cooking up a feast in the galley for all our friends, hoping to prove to myself that it didn't require a lot of square footage to throw a great party. I felt it was just calling out for my feminine touches to Eddie's ordinary cruising fare and slowly moved aside the old cans of Vienna sausages and Spam. And of course I had Essie's recipes. Fearing I would not be up to the task she'd encouraged regarding Eddie's stomach, she'd taken the time to throw in a few easy to prepare stews. The rest would be up to me.

So in those earliest days of discovery, I would take off Essie's flour covered apron, leaving Old Town Road behind and head for the library to do a little fact checking before going home. I spent so much time in the process that at first it caused the lovely librarian to wonder aloud at the number of books. Finding me cross-legged on the floor one day, that same woman approached me wearing a badge indicating her status: M. JARVIS, Head Librarian—although there was only one.

She had kind dark eyes that were in contrast with her imposing stature and was outfitted that first time in a navy and white batik print with matching headscarf wrapping thickly braided hair. Long gold earrings jangled slightly in tune with a few gold bangles on her slim wrist that I could hear clearly as she closed in, reminding me of a teacher softly ringing the morning bell. She would quickly become a very relevant teacher extraordinaire that I might respect island culture. And under her guidance I had a chance to slow down a little and actually smell the roses. Like so many things about this island, I had to learn to give way to the pace and once done, it made all the rest worthwhile and it made Essie stop scolding me.

علی علی علی

I didn't realize how deep my thoughts had gone when Russ's voice suddenly broke through the maze of it all: Robin's Bay, romance, and sunken treasure and more. And now on top of that, I've been reminded that along with all the destruction will come the need to replace so many cherished books and that will take almost as much time as rebuilding our island, if not more.

I had nearly forgotten about the library and those books in my worry over everything else these past months, but at least I had learned that M-J, her chosen nickname, was safe and had left the island on one of the first departures available soon after the storm. There will be much to do when she returns, and I know she will. The books were her treasures and always lovingly placed, opened with care and gently date-stamped, before being turned over to a new reader. She would often be found examining the returns with the care of a paleontologist looking for life forms. Oh yes, she will be back.

By now from the sound of Russ's monologue, however, the rum has taken hold and as is his habit, he probably won't stop the teasing until I put in my two cents or we run out of rum. It is understandable since these nights have now reached far beyond wishful thinking for it all to be behind us, and our island made whole again.

Of course, each time anything pops up during these gatherings even hinting at the many hours spent in all that was available to us within the little harbors, bays and beaches, our thoughts once again pick up any thread from the past that strikes a fancy. The threads of our memories are intricately woven and spill out only to disappear over the water to join the lace that is always hiding in the waves. We'd always taken for granted the easy availability of so many of those places and have been blessed by much here in this Caribbean playground and fortunately for us all, there has been much to hail.

Before all of this, visitors would arrive and it would be another excuse to ready the boat for a small excursion somewhere. With such good weather available and as custom dictates not only national but also many island holidays to celebrate, coupled with well-planned vacation schedules, we all became practiced at creating our happiness on 'island time'.

We still get letters of gratitude from Eddie's old college friend, whose visit occasioned our first ever sail to Nevis with its aging and pictorially charming port. It had been alive with tiny children practically lying in wait for the boats to arrive and their antics to begin. And after twenty-seven long hours sailed, many during a nighttime downpour, we were greeted by whoops and hollers from an adorable band of small people home from school on a Saturday full of mischief. They wanted nothing more than to keep us company as we stretched our sea legs, so we filmed them as they hammed it up as though it was an everyday occurrence—and perhaps it was since they seemed very comfortable doing it. They waited for the coins that would come for showing us around and their angelic faces made it difficult to wave goodbye.

And on other specific springtime holidays we'd form a contingent of boats for our annual trips to Antigua and would join forces with people from all over the world arriving there not only for the superb racing but for the well advertised and highly anticipated race week festivities known throughout the Caribbean as one of the best parties held anywhere. This is to say the least, a testament to the best of the best—boats of all sizes, class, color and age; wooden ones with layer upon layer of bright varnish showing off high spirits, or fiberglass boats with sexy lines and bold crews.

There was an abundance of heavily manpowered sailing machines with high tech masts reaching for the sky churning up the water at the rate their specially crafted sails could propel them. And each year their owners met newer challenges, bringing with them updated materials, equipment and ideas. Those strong, beautifully designed forms witnessed by all as they pounded away at their competition, came with many descriptions but none suited them more in my estimation, than purely romantic. And at the heart of it all was the perfection of nature's combination of the warm blue sea, tropical sky and fantastic sailing wind, and that made for days of not only the best racing conditions but in equal parts gave way for zany parties to turn up often and in high gear.

Perhaps it is an unusual thing, but I shall always remember the sound of a boat hull parting the water at top speed, causing a powerfully sculpted form of white froth to envelope it, rising up to meet the strange invader and then with a practiced precision, drop innocently downward, falling behind to silently ready for the next one. If I could name the sound it might be closer to an operatic movement but with the volume notched up by the freedom that came with the thrill. And yet I might say it is also whisper perfect like a fine wine savored, hinting of things to come, inviting and complex. How could it be called anything other than romantic? The sea, from my very first initiation, became this strange enigma; veiled with uncertainty and awe inspiring, to be played in and at times feared, but never taken for granted.

And always as the sailors rounded their marks and headed for the downwind leg of the race, I embraced along with everyone watching, the individuality that took center stage through the use of colorful spinnakers; these sails that somehow seemed perfectly matched to the more colorful personalities of their owners and crew. They might turn out in bright stripes, bold solids, or bearing the many insignias or colors touting wacky slogans appropriate only to their particular clubs or organizations, but always worth the wait.

And as the ever-grateful observer, I felt what I realized others might not; that is side by side in my imagination with the bravest of the islands early settlers. The ones who might take pride in seeing these shores evolved into all that it is today. And not to be forgotten were those that would come after them, the many prominent historical figures seeking their future and their fortunes, filling the many pages of important documents.

But even with all my gratitude and imagination, I had no doubt the placement of sleek modern race machines coupled with all the activities staged at Nelson's Dockyard year after year could not have ever been envisioned by even the far reaching Christopher Columbus.

But it is much easier to imagine, however doubtful as it may seem, that the young, ambitious Admiral Nelson holding his new command of the *Boreas* stationed here at English Harbor, might have envisioned a bit of this frivolity. Perhaps he would have even ordered a small race to commemorate the completion of the buildings done sometime in 1788 that still have a place here.

But the crew of the *Wanderer* was more fortunate than those early types, having front row seats on her deck, and happily watched as sails and rigging were adjusted, maneuvering the many masterpieces of technology toward the finish line. And like so many in attendance, we never gave up a chance to partake in all the non-racing activities.

Through the years, I had learned first hand and much to my dismay, that my love for sailing and regard for these highly developed craft, would not be matched by my own abilities. Even with Eddie's caring guidance and years of practical experience, I lack the natural instincts or that elusive skill and daring that I see in Eddie or many of the sailors on these coveted machines during this hugely popular event.

Instead I'm left to relish my pure love for them and the satisfaction that comes from their unexpected beauty simply because of my good fortune to share space with them. This acceptance releases me from any angst and gladly allows them to become a standard by which all that power and weight influence me, all adding to the bountiful gifts I gratefully took for granted with my newly acquired life on the water.

There would also be the inconsequential things that I hold dear and whenever I watch a race, it brings one of those back to me. It was on a day when Natasha and I spent a few hours so out of the ordinary and one that did not tax either of our skills at sailing. The event was short lived but of such pure joy. We had been guests on a boat larger than *Wanderer* and the skipper who loved to surprise called this little game, 'laying in the sails'. What we called it was freefalling. As we stood near the bow, the boat heeled over throwing our backs against the jib—over far enough that it was like lying in a giant hammock suspended outwardly, hovering over the soft waves. It was such a small thing, but did much to charm me into my love affair with all boats.

I was too much of a novice about rigging at that point to understand the dynamics of sheets and sails accessing angle with precision, but it didn't take an engineer to be stunned by the overall effect of movement, light and color. The taut material held not only our bodies forced flat against it from the momentum, but also the smell of the sun and salt now strongly imbedded into the dampening cloth, our weight nothing against the large triangle pulling us forward picking up spray as we moved. The stays were singing through the air along with a few indecipherable phrases in Natasha's native tongue.

It is in these small happenings mentally noted and mused over that informed my spirit and made it easy to adapt to a Caribbean lifestyle. And Eddie in turn reinforced and encouraged it all. And as always, there were more islands to visit.

When Eddie and I sailed to Guadeloupe, we found ourselves anchored in a tiny harbor with nondescript cafes that served wonderful French food and good French wines that we quickly discovered were available in even the smallest eateries. And it is a colorful island with a colorful people, speaking in a mix of French and Creole. Small, unexpected treats came in the form of long jitney rides enabling astounding views and the discovery of freshwater pools nestled and fed by small waterfalls. With salt-imbedded clothing, it didn't take long to act much like the children we'd enjoyed watching on Nevis, diving and floating at leisure. Not surprisingly, a few well-crafted stories came out of that episode as well and again, Eddie's memory somehow managed to grow the events into a wonderful tale.

I know Eddie will forever remember St. Barts, as if anyone would let him forget—sophisticated as islands go, being so French with its topless beaches and food no one could pronounce, cooked by chefs wearing high hats and white jackets with names embroidered importantly. When there were only the two of us, this island offered a chance at the ultimate romantic interlude. It was an intriguing island and Nessa said that it was the only place she and Russ seemed to relax into their role as a couple and she cherished their time there; perhaps it is a French thing.

The only drawback to flying in is the extreme proximity of the airstrip to the hilltops. As the STAL aircraft dropped down, one could see the widened eyes of the shocked drivers winding along the road beneath the fuselage, causing the urgent palpitation of heartbeat for everyone involved before the plane startlingly came to a halt on the runway below just yards away from the ocean.

On our first morning there, having flown instead of sailed, celebrating an anniversary of sorts and the chance to be quite alone, we were anxious to be on that delicious white sand that awaited us—we had already picked our spot from the air. We were deep in conversation as we wandered down a narrow shady path from our room after consuming the most magnificent warm croissants ever tasted. They alone would have enticed us back—the pleasure of rich dark chocolate filling oozing as it melted within the buttery envelope, gratefully received fresh to the room from a nearby bakery.

While walking and extolling the virtues of the chocolate, telling him that I would definitely share this with Essie as soon as we returned to St. Margeaux and we would create a recipe of our own, we suddenly found ourselves confronted by two lovelies returning from that same beach. This should have been an ordinary encounter, but one of the women lowered the folded beach chair she was carrying with a slow natural ease, revealing beautifully rounded bare breasts while simultaneously extending a typical "bon jour" in greeting. As they split aside to make room for us, I quickly averted my eyes while responding in kind, but poor Eddie couldn't manage a fast recovery. As they passed, all he could muster was a stammering "bh, bh, bh" to their retreating giggles, leaving behind an echo of that attempt that I'll likely never forget.

We were so smitten with the island, however, that we returned there many times, hoping to make this a yearly habit following race week events in Antigua; then always accompanied by our entire entourage. And each and every time we returned, Eddie took his 'mates' along that same hotel path, a pilgrimage of sorts, hoping on the off chance for a repeat performance. Their lips, however, remained sealed on that topic.

One such visit I recorded in bold red ink for its bold outcome was of the time while anchored in Gustavia Harbor. Apparently not enough excitement and challenge had taken place on Antigua in the days before. Having exhausted all manner of folderol on that island, our homegrown adventuresome 'wannabe' swashbucklers found themselves in need of something more to expand on all that fun in their own inimitable way. And they wanted it to be something that would include all the boats returning to St. Margeaux.

They came up with the idea to hold a special race against the other yachts within our group, unsanctioned by the bothersome and more official rules of the Antigua event. THEY hadn't had enough fun yet, so in their quest to beat the pack back home the crew of the *Wanderer,* putting their heads together which some might say was always a bad idea, ended their search at the town dump finding the solution for the most original and untried race ever concocted.

Nessa and I still marvel at the ingenuity on that occasion which is one of the few she participated in and maybe one that will make her think twice about yachting as a whole. Not only were we racing against the five other yachts heading back to St. Margeaux, but a personal challenge to our sister ship, *Glory,* another 44' sloop, was offered with extra incentives. The start led by locals already apprised of the shenanigans would be at the sound of an air horn.

What the captain of the *Glory* did not know was that the foray into the local dump had produced the best possible object to keep his boat from leaving the harbor on time: a slightly cracked, but still in good shape, yellow porcelain commode that had probably been left over from a remodeling project. Well, it would be disposed of quietly and in short order by a couple of divers fortified by their usual beverages and imagined sounds of cheering accolades awaiting them at homeport.

Extra shackles and lines were found in storage and a few dives later, this unique anchor was set in place just before the captain of the *Glory* returned from dinner. Everything was finally ready and all on board the *Wanderer* were certain to sleep well off their watch shifts with the knowledge they would surely be the ultimate winners. The hour arrived as the sun cast its last glow over us all before sinking behind the bordering hills with all at the ready, waiting for the 'committee' on shore to sound the horn.

It split the air overhead loudly and with meaning and everyone on all the boats standing at the ready simultaneously hauled anchor and hoisted sail, heading their boats quickly out of Gustavia in front of the last of the good light with one exception, the *Glory*.

By the time the captain replaced the embarrassed, heavily straining man standing at the bow perplexed and dismayed by the weight far greater than should have been, and after a great deal of effort and not a little swearing, he brought the newly designed anchor up himself. By the time he saw the source of his trouble, we had been given a tremendous head start.

It was a beautiful night to cruise homeward with a good moon to watch and dream over but for the expletives that kept blasting out of the radio from a very disgruntled sailor. Let's say we paid dearly for that excursion; even though this anchor, a wonder of imagination nearly made it into production by an overzealous bunch thinking they'd found the one thing that hadn't yet been tried for fun, the crews that subsequently sailed with us stopped foraging and kept their competitions to simpler things, like hermit crab races.

ৠৠৠ

So with all that in my back pocket of memories, some possibly a little more exciting than others, there is yet a particular escape into another time when my mind was filled with pirates and hidden secrets. That must be the one Mick is referring to since they somehow manage to take turns and often at my expense, and I hear him gearing up for another yarn to tell. It is up to me to hold my own against the verbal barrage once again. Honor is at stake after all, and I don't like backing down on a good story, especially about anything related to those watery caves.

"I realize that while trying to impress you all with the tons of research I'd printed out for our initial cruise over there, it may have been overkill, but in my own defense, I was really excited at what I thought was easily just waiting for me to discover. It all sounded good on paper. But even before setting sail, there was that near catastrophe at the dock. Do you remember Mick, all the commotion?" I said, jumping headlong into their conversation.

"You must mean that guy hanging onto the piling for dear life."

"That's the time; and just to fill you in on it, Russ, if you can still concentrate, it was my first time taking the boat out of the slip. If you remember, Eddie was a stickler about my learning to handle it by myself in case of emergency and even had me taking classes. On that morning he and Mick had been readying the sails, Natasha was at the bow handling lines and I, struggling for confidence already having the boat in reverse and nearly clear, when we heard an ear-piercing scream. That noise was coming from this really petite woman all alone in the cockpit of a 33' sailboat, that detail remembered only because of the For Sale sign taped to the stanchion rail. My impulse was to stop, but Eddie said no. She had this look of horror on her face and she was yelling. "Guntherrrr! Helllp!"

Her boat was drifting backward, but she did nothing, couldn't make a move. In the meantime, he was hanging on that piling for dear life, screaming right back and obviously in a lot of pain because it was covered in barnacles. I can still see his sweat-stained face getting redder by the minute. Hard to know what was worse, the searing pain or his anger at his wife.

"But you didn't panic, Lily, that's all that mattered. And there was someone close enough to help her; you just didn't see him," Mick said kindly.

"Well, I was more upset when I found out that she had never handled the boat at all, let alone at the dock and he in his arrogance, hadn't taken time to show her what to do. All he had done was toss out directions that she couldn't understand, making her get even more flustered so she backed away while he was loosening the lines."

Eddie piped in, "He'd probably stepped on the bow rail and lost his footing. The whole thing was stupid; he knew she was inexperienced."

"I thought he damned well did deserve what he got after hearing the way he was reacting. She was terrified. Why do otherwise rational men always yell like that on boats?"

"Always the feminist, my darling," Eddie said.

"But then you knew that when you met her if I remember correctly", Russ piped in.

"So you do still remember that first meeting when I thought you would have to be pried from your chair?" I said to Russ. I was slightly chagrined over my change of heart from thinking him an odd sort when he appeared as rumpled as an unmade bed, to the bond of friendship that now existed and the homely truth of relying on first impressions.

"Tsk, tsk, don't be disparaging my old habits, Lily. There was a great comfort in that old chair and the sameness of my routine that gave me lots of time to contemplate. Wouldn't I love to have that chair right now? It probably flew to the other side of the island during the storm where it ended up as firewood for someone's dinner."

"Speaking of dinner," Mick interjected, we treated you gals to a pretty terrific dining experience on top of everything else, if I recall correctly."

He was referring to the grand finale to that same weekend spent in childlike delight in those emerald waters. We had so little to do these days but reflect or listen to others doing the same, clinging to straws of memory in an uninvited idleness. And I did the same, as though it had just occurred....

જાજાજ

I had turned the wheel over to Eddie after witnessing the fiasco at the dock, still feeling a bit shaken. Mick went about trimming the sails while Natasha and I made things ready below. Then trying to find a comfortable spot for the ride, I noticed the change in the water immediately as we neared the narrow cut in the reef. When conditions are calm as Eddie pointed out during that first sail, the opening is very visible, welcoming the sluicing hull with ease. But when conditions are questionable the opening becomes an angry swirl, making the run as difficult as threading a needle, necessitating complete and careful attention and a perfect angle to enter it.

There were white caps beyond and Eddie began flinging instructions to Mick, quickly cranking the winch as they pointed us into the wind. But there was a flurry of butterfly activity in my stomach and Natasha was already turning a light shade of moss. A usually shy woman, she became stonily quiet as soon as we retreated to the high side to keep from being seasick or getting wet, but listening to the noise from below it was apparent that we hadn't secured everything as well as we should have and neither of us could go back below deck. Without taking our eyes from the horizon, hoping that would control the nausea, our bodies moved with the boat, up on a growing swell and then slapped down before the next one with a forceful lurch, sending poor Natasha to the rail more than once.

It dawned on me as this pattern of rise and fall continued that while boats were in many ways visions of romance, the actual act of sailing in tough seas might not always be that—at least that was what my insides were saying. And as if the gods were listening, a second hearty wave slapped us with a huge dose of seawater. It would be a very wet sail for the next three hours but as I sat in agitated discomfort, I watched Eddie's easy joy and contentment that probably any sea condition would create for him, and realized that no matter what, I was in it for the long term.

I also learned how quickly those 'green' feelings could dissipate nearing land as the water levels out, always erasing the previous discomfort. It only took a few more tacks and we were gliding through smoother water surrounding Prospect Island, putting all the discomfort easily behind with our attention focused on the awaiting fun.

Mick dropped the anchor into an incredible shade of light jade while all around us the sparkling sun hit the soft ripples exposing an interesting mix of bright orange clownfish, yellow angelfish, and some lapis blue tangs, all twinkling an invitation like submerged Christmas lights. There wasn't a beach on the entrance side to the cave, but the water was clear enough to see white sand evident in the shallows near the openings and each little fish casting its own darting shadow beneath.

While the sails were being furled, Natasha and I went below to try and straighten out the fallen gear and retrieve fins and masks that we had neglected to put in the lazarette.

"Thankfully we stowed the wine properly; we're not totally hopeless," Natasha offered as color began to return to her face.

"As soon as we're finished down here, we can get in a swim before lunch," I replied, anxious to test my new mask.

However, after lunch and a short rest with Mick enjoying his latest paperback and cold Corolla, it was at last time to go exploring and that's when I nearly lost my nerve. I'd built myself up with so much expectation as to the possible discoveries and easy diving and all the things I'd read about and now I was having a panic attack. Everyone else was in the water as I stood on deck trying to expel the feeling. Eddie was shouting for me to jump in; Mick and Natasha were already closing in on the cave, swimming easily with their snorkels bobbing and fins waving back at us. Eddie eased closer to the hull near the ladder and removed his mask, already sensing something wrong.

"I hate to admit it, but I'm really scared to go in there and embarrassed now that we've come this far."

"You'll be fine, Lily. Just remember to breathe the way I showed you and use your flippers and simply relax into it. You know how, and it will all come back when you get in the water. There's a big drop at the entrance and I don't want you to be scared because it levels out fast to around four feet and you'll be able to see the bottom and be up close and personal to all the fish."

I caught a glimpse of Tasha waving me forward and knew I had to try.

Putting his mask back on, with words sounding as though through cotton stuffing, "Now take my hand my love, and I'll take you to your treasure as promised."

Placing my mask on my already sunburned face and grabbing hold for dear life, I tried to concentrate on the empty pages awaiting new entries and feeding off the excitement that I'd allowed to build up in anticipation. I held onto those thoughts until we neared the outer rim, trying to release some of the fear. Then if it was possible, I held on even tighter because the water suddenly darkened and for the first time I couldn't name the color. Then both Eddie and Mick turned on their flashlights and suddenly the cave came to life. At the same time three red kayaks paddling out in single file, poked from behind the wall on their way out. The man in the first one with the flag attached was waving at us and motioning to the two behind alerting them of our presence.

"How is it in there?" Eddie called over.

"Fantastic, but really eerie until you round the first corner. The rest of our group has already headed back to our boat, but I had trouble prying these two away."

"Don't worry, Lily, I've got you." Eddie croaked through his snorkel feeling me responding with a squeeze, water lapping his face gently as he pulled me toward him.

Rounding the corner, they swung their lights higher and the cave grew larger and I could see markings and pocket-like holes placed almost strategically throughout as though someone had used them to climb the walls. I sorely wanted to believe it was all like those photos in the books I'd spent so much time with. A closer look, however, momentarily disappointing, revealed more naturally occurring striations and openings and water walls alive with coral and sponge.

The floor of the cave was not to be outdone by the walls when all our movement caused the fish to scatter in every direction making some of the sea fans dance in their hurry. I spotted one of George's cousins who seemed a lot more threatening in this confined space and as soon as I pointed him out to Eddie, he took off in another direction. The other two were way ahead of us now and in their element and I could see their playful movements somewhat magnified through the mask and wished for that day I too would be so comfortable doing this.

My only goal, however farfetched, was in trying to find affirmation for all my reading and I was naively determined to find some evidence of the documented history. I was pushed along in that determination not only because of facts regarding the wrecks and pirate booty, but mainly because I'd stumbled across an alluring article some time back. It was about a chest filled with doubloons that had actually been recovered in the early 1900's by a couple of men from a neighboring island. I just wanted to find any small thing to support that claim even knowing how unlikely that might be.

Eddie popped his head up, removed his mask and signaled to Mick, and though it hadn't seemed like we'd been inside for very long, the time had flown by in my complete concentration.

"We really need better lighting, Lily, but at least this gives you a taste of what's actually in here, however short the preview. I promise we'll come back again, but these batteries are getting low and I'm getting hungry again. How about Mick and I treat you lovelies to a wonderful dinner over at the Cliffside Hotel? We can make it easily in the dinghy."

Back on the boat, I felt more than simple delight at my accomplishment. I'd managed to offset some of that earlier fear and got to see what all the hype was about and it hadn't let me down. I knew the large cave went back into the mountain around seventy feet and that would have to wait for another time, but I was far from disappointed. There were visions of purples and rusts of the water walls with deep veins reminding me of rings on tree trunks indicating age; so many wonders in their history strewn accidentally or intentionally and supported in the many written accounts. Even without enough experience, I was left with a keen sense of satisfaction that all my research was well worth it. I knew I would return.

Looking at each other, cleaned up nicely after a bit of primping and lots of lotion for our reddened skin, the earlier excitement could be put to rest, temporarily replaced by thoughts of the special evening ahead. I was happy to now show off my cotton batik halter dress purchased in Tasha's favorite shop, agreeing with Eddie's initial impression that we would become good friends.

"Wow, look at you two!" Eddie exclaimed as a whistle went out from Mick's lips.

I saw that Mick and Eddie had put on their 'formal' shorts topped with nearly matching Indonesian print shirts from that same shop without telling us. They were definitely out to surprise and impress but stifling a laugh, Tasha moved in quickly to pull the price tag from Mick's collar before he caught flak from Eddie.

"Leave it to Mick," She said affectionately pecking his cheek while hiding the tag in her palm.

Arriving for dinner by dinghy was a wholly new experience and even coming in via the small dinghy dock welcoming all who lay at anchor, we made much of our rather grand entrance in our new clothing.

Walking smartly, hamming it up as always, "Ladies." Mick bowed, presenting the entryway.

"Look at this!" I exclaimed, taking in the room.

We were entering a forest of lantern style lighting high above and all around that scented the air with candle wax. It was a huge space but somehow they had created a sense of intimacy without the use of many walls and I could already picture Christmas décor and music, feeling a need to witness such a beautiful holiday here when the time came.

Just then the aroma of clove-studded orange peel floating in the liquid splendor of spice tea steeping in a huge silver bowl wrapped us in a welcoming hug. We had talked of nothing else but the well-known langouste on our ride over and could already smell the broiled to perfection creatures topped with melted butter wafting from nearby tables.

While we waited for that anticipated main course, a waiter came closer, pushing a cart ahead of him. On the cart was a simple cloth that evolved into something more important looking as it caught the intimate lighting. Spread out neatly were all of the ingredients necessary for our first course.

The scene was now set for a large Caesar salad to be prepared tableside in a beautifully honed and very large wooden bowl. Little did we know the highly dramatized performance about to take place was to be handled with a new tempo and with such flair by this muscular man. His arms richly tinted the color of golden rum were strikingly beautiful next to his sunflower yellow shirt, forcing them to stand out even more.

Seeing our expressions, he first took the cloves of garlic and rubbed them slowly almost erotically into the wood, releasing their oils. Then taking an egg from one of the small containers lined up according to need, he separated the yolk and slid it tenderly into the wooden bowl. Next, the anchovies were softened delicately, forming a paste on the side of the now fragrant wood and a fork inserted into the lemons, twisting the necessary amount of juice from them before he began to pour the olive oil slowly with one hand above the bowl theatrically, whisking it all together with the other.

I looked over at Natasha and she too was having difficulty keeping her eyes off him as he applied his capable hands to this obviously often-repeated skill. Suddenly it registered with our beaux, catching us blushing heavily. The waiter, who apparently had become quite used to female adoration, continued on by gently tearing the lettuce and tossing it all with a knowing curve of his sensual lips.

Amidst all the teasing and bantering that hummed around our table while the aromatic breeze held us in its grip, thoughts of treasure were tucked far away, and I was at once at peace and at one with Eddie who was sending loving glances my way. Looking from face to face, lost in my own special thoughts, the flickering glow from the candlelight made us all appear like the characters in a 19th century novel, but I knew happily this was real and just possibly the beginning of my own three-act play.

Not wanting to miss one moment of a perfect evening, we indulged in a decadent dessert and Irish coffees, enough to 'level those who supped too much', finally heading back to the dinghy and the Wanderer, the only thoughts left centered around a morning swim to work it all off.

The night's enjoyment was too great even for that bracing swim, and though feeling a little physically fragile, and somewhat sad at having to leave it all behind, I vowed to become more adept at diving and less hell-bent on fact finding. This time readying the boat we worked more in unison, having gotten used to maneuvers and each other and quickly made the boat ready for the sail back to St. Margeaux. The wind and following sea on that new morning gave us reason to set the sails wing on wing creating an opportunity for another first. The Wanderer now looked more like a giant bird about to take flight while being silently pushed along on a frothy wake.

Chapter Ten

The effects of the many months of this prolonged hiatus for our island's recovery were playing out everywhere. For us, this lengthy waiting game pushed the memory gates open wider still, with lamenting conversation night after night until eyes drooped and sleep became essential. It was then that I began to notice the odd thing here and there. Had Russ's sideburns become grayer at each passing, and were there more wrinkles on all our brows?

Finally able to tuck into our berth late into one of those endless nights, wrapped in the familiar comfort of each other's arms, I caught myself observing Eddie more closely as though I might have missed something I hadn't been looking for. After all, money was running short with lack of work and slim prospects for more. Stress had to be playing a part in even the smallest changes.

I caught a glimmer of starlight through the small cabin window. With power still out all over the island, the stars were even more magnified, like all those treasured memories we heeded daily and used to light up our hearts during this extremely bleak period. But I was becoming convinced it was not enough; we had been changed, perhaps just in appearance, perhaps forever. We all suffered the many lacks, even taken to cutting each other's hair, and my own was showing signs of saltwater abuse much like Boomer's, becoming even more odd where my natural highlights had been.

But more importantly for our little band, some imperceptible aging seems to be taking place. And it's not even in the deep creases and squint lines normal in the weathered faces always submitting to the sea and sun. Seeking the adaptability of my favorite chameleons in order to survive so many months has hastened my admission that I am indeed tired. I sense Eddie is beginning to admit to this as well since I'd overheard him talking with Russ and Mick recently about our future here especially if things didn't turn around soon.

Certainly there is some evidence of renewal happening, but at the moment only in the rebuilding of businesses necessary to infrastructure needs and the inevitability of a few new watering holes grown up out of empty stretches of beachfront land. Water is still a valued commodity and liquor is still cheap, so this does not surprise me. But there is not enough immediate growth to sustain many of us for the long term and I can practically see the ideas churning inside Eddie's brain.

The roads now opened for traffic carry products to and from destinations to aid workers from away desperate to complete the jobs assigned in unrelenting heat since it will take even longer for those famous trees to benefit. And more consumer products are arriving on a weekly basis. But predictions told for a full recovery now border on a year, and here we are near spring with temperaments running amuck. Our biggest problem is once again logistics. We are insular. Nothing is accomplished with ease. The excitement and awe of being on an island cannot incorporate all of these newer feelings of helplessness that have been pressed upon us from such a force of nature. We are well aware, and always had been, of the strategic distances, so we knew we were off the grid, possibly out of sight and out of mind.

More friends and acquaintances have already left out of desperation to seek housing and employment elsewhere. Nessa has been hinting at that idea, but I selfishly keep asking her to rethink it since I don't want to lose the closeness of her friendship at a time like this. I know this is partly because of her uncertainties about a future with Russ. He, Mick, and Natasha are determined to stick together no matter what, which leaves Eddie and me to decide our fate. I noticed he has been working on the *Wanderer* with a renewed energy so his latest news does not surprise me.

"I have an idea, Lily, and I want you to hear me out before you say anything, because it may sound a little crazy at first. What would you think of moving to Anegada? The guys have been brainstorming and you know many of the other islands have always intrigued us. We've been thinking about going into a joint venture so we can be working again at something that gives us some pleasure and fulfills us like the old days, almost like when I first arrived."

"I'll bite; what is it that you have in mind to 'fill you up'? And what is this joint venture?"

"Well, Boomer has a friend who is trying to sell his business over there so he can retire. It's a combination of small restaurant and cottage with enough room for them, and a separate space set up as a tackle shop for the deep-sea fishermen that flock to those waters. But best of all, there is a powerboat thrown in that, added to the *Wanderer*, would be a nice tender for a little charter business.

"Mick thinks the restaurant idea is perfect for them for at least a few more years. Said they have always talked about something like that someday, something really laid-back, quieter even than here, especially now with all the heavy equipment tearing up the island. And now that their apartment is trashed, they're even more excited. Tasha isn't getting anywhere with teaching here until the schools are finished and she apparently is crazy about being a chef. Who knew? Apparently that runs in her family."

"So what's Russ's choice in all of this?"

"He would be perfect to run the tackle business, don't you think?"

"So, let me guess, you would be the charter boat captain?"

"You got it; and of course, you would have to be my first mate. What do you say—you game?"

"Other than the fact I think maybe you've all had too much sun exposure and you may need a few extra folding chairs for Russ, I'm about at the end of my rope here too and I hate to hear myself say that. I'm probably crazy to go along with this, especially since there wouldn't be any escape from future hurricanes unless we wait them out in Venezuela, but I recognize the signs…boredom, listlessness, and all this inactivity. And quite frankly, I'm smart enough to realize you've already made up your minds.

"But what about Nessa; doesn't she get a vote in this?" I ask, knowing the answer ahead of time. Russ is going to have to pitch this idea directly to her and convince her once and for all that he needs her by his side.

Crazy at it all seemed; what did we have to lose at this stage? St. Margeaux will come back and so could we when the need arose. I had a feeling Nessa would not go along on such a bizarre scheme, at least not at first, but if Russ thought he really might lose her—maybe this is what is needed to finally bring them together. And I had to admit I've been really worried that if we don't take control of our situation in some way soon, we too would be no more than empty vessels waiting to be filled up by others.

Strangely, once this idea began to germinate, we found a way to use all that idle time to reflect and voice the ideas pertaining to the future and it began to feel good. This meant talking about what our needs would be, sharing ideas that would lead us in a new direction, that feeling of certainty that we could pull this off, rather than the continuing unpleasantness here that had been dominating our conversations. It was so refreshing to be thinking ahead that even I felt the excitement taking hold.

Then almost as quickly, the idea was all deflated, like a hot air balloon with no flame. We had come face-to-face with reality and with all that this idea would entail. Suddenly, our project didn't seem so attainable and our new dream was slipping out of our grasp. Even with Boomer's help, it would be difficult to pull it off from a distance, meaning they would need some kind of plan to position themselves physically on Anegada, and find ways to cut through the bureaucracy between flags. Not inclined to give up because this was not their style and true to form, Eddie, Mick and Russ put together their plan, convinced that this venture was indeed in need of more objectivity.

First they would fly to Beef Island, taking the only still operating seaplane before continuing on by ferry. They left us gals waving them off like airmen going to the front, blowing tender kisses till we met again. The storm had brought out the theatrical in all of us, a side we were determined never to lose.

Boomer had laid the groundwork prior to their meeting with the property owner, to coordinate with their arrival on Davis Bay. They would then have a more concrete method by which to assess the feasibility of the project. And though the project was enticing, I knew Boomer's well-intended motives were to have this settled. He missed the communal gatherings with his longtime friends.

There we stood, on the site of the tiny battered terminal, now missing the resounding phrase, "there goes the last goose!" It had taken me quite a while to realize the 'last' was simply the one always leaving and a comment certain to bring about the most sincere concern by waiting passengers fearing they might have missed their plane. In her earliest years on this island Nessa happened to be one of those passengers, but by then she had become used to being stranded in small airports throughout the Caribbean.

As she tells it, that offered as much fun as the planned destination—live music, single men apparently waiting to check out the arrivals, and a complete party atmosphere. Flying in those days meant hopping a small commuter plane, a seaplane or the only slightly larger Carib airliner. And it wasn't uncommon for the captain to adjust his departure time and delay the removal of the stairs to accommodate a late passenger seen running out on the tarmac. The uncommon part was that often a small rum punch would be handed over by the attendant the moment you crossed the threshold—a harried traveler's dream come true!

Fond memories sprang forward while I waved them off, thinking about my own initial response the first time I witnessed one of the pre-war Grummans now so much a part of our lives here. Once in a while a passenger got very lucky and was allowed to sit in the co-pilot seat during take-off and landing. This raised the line of sight slightly from those seated in the watertight belly of this odd looking bird. I know this from personal experience since my own first time in that seat definitely raised the bar on my already highlighted moments in the air.

The view from above was really no different; it was in the landings and takeoffs that one felt the thrill. There are those first powering up sounds that fill the cabin as the pilot accelerates and we wait to be thrust upward like an overweight object catapulted from the sea with force. Then, just for a few moments, the water hangs suspended like icicles on a Christmas tree until the Goose soars higher and levels out.

The landing is quite another story that I prize on its own. It is only a feeling, of course, but one that fills the mind with swirling images. The hefty bird upon touching down meanly plows up the sea, simultaneously forcing a blinding spray to erase all vision as it hits the windows. Then just as you think it can sink into the abyss, it slows and clumsily climbs onto a ramp as if on webbed feet, this feeling leaving me wanting to do it all over again as though it were a carnival ride.

It seems lately that I'm always on the threshold of other times, re-running old movies through my brain. I have tired myself in these empty days with the plethora of reasons leading me back always to the one constant that's now become in itself a platform for residency here—that depth created through this insular life where everyone and everything touches our feelings in some profound way almost daily, touches in a way that would have been impossible had I stayed within the anonymity of the larger New York scene.

And I'm convinced, just as the giant tentacles of the hurricane spread out and affected us all, the stuff of life here has also reached out and taken a vice-like grip on our lives. It has drawn us together in a continuing flow by allowing us, however briefly, to touch upon each other's lives whether through happiness or sorrow. No wonder it is so difficult to make the choices to leave and yet so necessary before the memories consume and the fresh start becomes less and less a possibility. I know we are not the only ones who've been feeling this way of late even though we truly believe there is still much hope for the island. Time is the real enemy, consuming that hope and being unkind to so many.

And it is because of this significance through our shared feelings, that no one has wanted to go too far from this base created by our lives here. It will be tough enough for us to do so even with this refreshing new plan, and especially since we know the decision wouldn't have come without dire necessity. But down deep, even with all of that in mind, another island no matter its size would be preferable to a return to the mainland. At least it would keep our little band together in the only way we know how for however long possible.

If I could turn the clock back on our lives, I could imagine finding Anegada the way I found St. Margeaux and at least, I reminded myself, this time around I will have love and friendships built in. But moving will not be easy for me. No more than it had been for any of those who have now gone before us. Nessa, I knew, shared my feelings on this matter. I saw it on her face each time she began to consider it, which may be the only thing holding her unless Russ steps up quickly. We are nearly at the end of that seemingly endless tether to a valued and cherished time here, and both still slightly afraid to let go for fear of falling.

I have been steadfast in the knowledge that Eddic had long ago become my anchor and the many written journals, an intimate lifeline to a path first chosen many years earlier on a larger island. But even with all that, for this woman from away, St. Margeaux would always be considered home, no matter how many miles traveled. I savor one journal entry memorized by now, that says doors open, and doors close, while life experiences fill the rooms in between. My rooms counted many and they have been richly filled.

As we now wait with a different kind of time on our hands with the men away doing diligence for our quest, Natasha and I left alone on the *Wanderer* hope to sort out the rest of the details here in our own way. There are still the logistics for the transition in the way of housekeeping, banking and supplies. And while I still had doubts about the move to an island so flat as to be mysterious, she has been so caught up in her excitement she began working up a small cookbook for island recipes using a post hurricane gem, a newly acquired three-ring binder large enough to hold a month's menus.

"Look, Lily, I think these recipes of Essie's will be perfect and give it more of an authentic flair. As soon as possible I'm going to try them out on you and Nessa. Hopefully, with practice they'll taste as good as hers," Natasha said, pointing to this newest addition of baked goods.

Johnnycakes:

1 cup flour
1 cup cornmeal
1 egg
1/3 cup brown sugar
2 tbs. veg. oil
1 cup milk
Mix all dry ingredients, add wet, mix and pour into square pan. Bake 30-35 min. at 350°F.

Key Lime Pie:

5 egg yolks, saving whites for topping
1 can sweetened condensed milk
5 oz. lime juice

Blend egg yolks and milk, add juice, mix well and pour into crust and refrigerate till it sets. Top with egg whites mixed with 1tbs. sugar for meringue and brown in oven.

Lime Bread:

1/3 cup butter
1 cup sugar
2 eggs
2 tbs. lime juice

1 tbs. lime zest
¾ tsp. vanilla ext.
1-1/2 cup flour
1-1/4 tsp. baking powder
½ tsp. salt
½ cup milk

Glaze:
   4 tbs. lime juice
   2 tbs. sugar
   1 tbs. lime zest

Cream butter and sugar. Add eggs and beat well. Add lime juice and zest, vanilla and combine all. Add milk and flour alternately and pour into greased loaf pan. Bake 1 hr. at 350°F. Then mix juice, zest and sugar to spoon over finished bread slowly and let cool.

Coconut Bread:

½ cup butter (melted)
3 cups flour
1 tsp. baking powder
1 tsp. salt
1 tsp. cinnamon
1 tsp. brown sugar
2 eggs (lightly beaten)
1 tsp. vanilla ext.
   zest of one lemon
   1-1/2 cups unsweetened coconut milk
   1-1/2 cups shredded coconut

Preheat oven to 375°F.

Mix flour with baking powder, salt and cinnamon. In another bowl, whisk melted butter, brown sugar, eggs, vanilla and lemon zest. Pour in coconut milk and whisk together.

Pour wet ingredients into dry and fold all together till smooth. Fold in shredded coconut and pour entire mix into prepared loaf pan. Bake for 1 hour to 1 hour and 15 min.

This bread is particularly good toasted.

I was so happy to see how this whole adventure suited her personality. Normally introverted, it seemed to bring her to life. She will do well running her kitchen; her Hungarian roots and love of food will serve her admirably. I'd nearly forgotten that Mick had mentioned a long time ago that one of her aunts owned a small restaurant in Budapest, so this would not be far from her comfort level.

"I'm impressed, this is wonderful. And I know Essie will be very proud that you want to use them and we already know they're delicious. As soon as it's possible, let's try these out on the whole gang," I said, looking at the neat script on the fresh pages of her notebook, already decorated with the cover logo.

As I watched her curled up with the booklet, making small tidy notations while inadvertently chewing on the pencil, I was certain these were just the first of many items that would be added over time as she found her stride. And at last I began feeling that in many ways we would find it easier now to be as enticed and maybe even wooed by it all, just as the men had been from the beginning. These things spoke of 'home' as cooking and food always did and would help unite against our longing for this island, when those inevitable feelings broke through.

Natasha had that hopeful exuberance needed and looked even younger without a hint of makeup, her tanned slim legs sticking out from a cutoff pair of shorts. And as she continued, I sensed she held some of that promise already, and it was catching.

I knew I wasn't wrong about their being wooed when three days later our very own buccaneers de-planed, confirming that with a new bounce in their step. There had been many high-jinx on the high seas, and even though this was new territory for us all, I was helpless to stop the trajectory already in motion. And down deep in my heart, I no longer wanted to. Life here had become too enervating.

But there was still so much to do to bring this whole situation to fruition since we would be doing business under another flag, on island time—same number of hours, different speed—and without any proven experience in all aspects of the businesses we were buying into. It was also essential to find an attorney able to cover the fine points of binding us in a way that no matter what happened, our friendships would remain intact.

The list grew; a solid business plan to be mapped out: licenses for the three phases yet to be obtained through British authorities and, of course, more trips to Anegada to meet with local fishermen and those supplying produce and all the other required items. And there were a number of small but necessary renovations to be made to the existing property. The previous owner had done much before putting it up for sale, so fortunately our work in that would be minimal and simply adapted slightly. As the new owners, we also felt it important to introduce ourselves to the locals in order to solidify those existing partnerships.

We had unanimously decided after one of our last well-orchestrated rum fests that when all was finalized the new corporation would be called "LaBelle Reef" and the restaurant would also bear the same name, unanimously overruling Natasha's Kitchen much as we loved her. Fortunately, she took no offense and it marked a beginning. The island reef, hazardous in the best of conditions, was approximately eighteen miles long and had claimed hundreds of shipwrecks, none of which seemed to bother our intrepid sailors, and that bothered me without knowing why so I quickly overlooked it.

Not totally unexpected, all of the preparations took far longer than we had wished, so we waited out the season of the infamous Christmas winds and extended the timetable for departure during the more placid springtime sailing conditions. And as always, we watched the calendar with anxiety since another hurricane season would appear soon after.

Delaying the Anegada project was making everything connected to the *Wanderer* more of a challenge. There always seemed to be something to put a snag in the flow of paperwork or items needed, but Eddie and Mick both determined as ever to move things along faster, managed to take the challenge in stride. They left Russ behind with us on many of their return flights since he was needed on St. Margeaux to keep things rolling at this end.

Then when we least expected things to go right, a beautiful yacht named *Artemesia* dropped anchor in the town harbor just before the sun set, casting a spell on us all. Her timing couldn't have been more perfect, especially finding out that her captain was an old friend of Russ's and we would be welcome aboard. Now the *Wanderer* could be spared to have the last of the important repairs completed, and would give us all a much-needed break.

Artemesia was a true luxury yacht, magnificent in every way, and beyond that by choosing St. Margeaux for a stopover before crossing the Atlantic, allowed us to take full advantage of that friendship by bunking aboard. Perfect timing, and after the months of deprivation seemed like Shangri la. We were treated royally, especially when the captain and crew learned what had taken place on the island. They had all spent their well-paid, highly trained careers and a lot of the owner's money avoiding all of the horrible events associated with bad weather and the type of hurricane we'd lived out.

Her arrival was also perfect for Russ since he had decided not to rebuild the worst of the damage at his house, instead choosing to sell the property as is, leaving the construction to new dreamers who will arrive when all this has passed over and the infrastructure is again sound. So everything seemed to finally be going as planned.

The following weeks in such posh surroundings made me feel almost selfish under the circumstances. A 90' motor vessel has more room and all the amenities as many a home and is a far cry from any of the ugliness that had infiltrated our lives for so long now. Yet we all yearned to be settled again, to feel alive and working toward our mutual goal. Idleness did not suit or complete us. And the continual rehabilitation of our once beautiful surroundings was getting out of hand, becoming perplexing and uncomfortable.

All of a sudden we were living in a contained bubble, everything clean, fresh and new, a foreign sensation. I was particularly happy to have Nessa join us, and I noticed a softening between her and Russ. I believe a small kernel of hope began on that trying night together when his home was destroyed and they had faced such danger. They may finally be recognizing how fragile their time together is. I selfishly hope for that too.

Mick and Eddie continued to fly back and forth to Anegada, sometimes taking Russ or switching depending on whatever needed to be done. But at least now, with a comfortable place to stay, life became a bit easier and the dream again seemed attainable.

You can imagine, however, that it didn't take long for any of us left behind to take up that mantle of storytelling in their stead, not only to an audience of new friends, but those still left, feeling fortunate to often be invited aboard after our many ragtag gatherings, and be moored out under the stars on a bright shiny deck glowing from within with grandeur. Our group had been dwindling as expected with the need to search out new occupations or locations in order to resume their lives in a more harmonious manner. In some cases, it was simply to take a welcome break from everything here. But somehow even with that, there were always enough voices to be heard and ears willing to listen.

I may have been happiest of all since I never found it difficult to be charmed by any yacht of this type no matter where they were moored and I would often find myself caught up in her many appointments and the ingenious use of space, taking me quickly out of whatever doldrums had set in. Yacht designers were high on my list of creative people and my admiration went deep.

Artemesia had immediately cast her spell when she first arrived in port. It was the one thing that could deter the constant emptiness and remove for just a little while, the surrounding shame feeding off the extended time of suffering for so many. It could set my mind to spinning and weaving true and imagined events—those yachts I'd been lucky enough to get close to and those I still desired to.

There had been a particularly grand one named *Ragtime* docked in a British harbor where Eddie and I had stopped during one of our island hopping excursions. No matter where we were, we would take time to walk the docks of various harbors to wistfully gaze at the fleet in for that night. It was better than any New York department store window that I had once enjoyed while walking along the many streets and avenues enraptured by the bright lights and pretty baubles.

Ragtime was what I would call a more classic model, a bit like a Victorian lady with lace curtains and crystal barware, but my reaction to her was very much the same as to any: spellbound. I absolutely knew she would have looked wonderful with men in straw hats, smoking pipes on the aft deck talking with women in sun bonnets and white dresses, sipping sherry. Or those men in pinstripe suits commuting from their homes to their offices when they weren't planning the Gatsby-like croquet matches on the estate lawns of their era.

She had been built in 1928, during the jazz era, and was a magnificent and welcome sight cruising the Sir Francis Drake Channel, steaming along in a manner that had me wishing I could go back in time. She was put together with cedar, oak and soles of teak with mahogany joinery and shone with gallons of spar varnish, but the on deck attire had long since changed to much skimpier bathing costumes.

The fine *Artemesia* on the other hand, I immediately classified in my own way as sleek, sophisticated and glowing with European style, a modern woman; a woman for our time. She had many of the same qualities as her older sisters, but glistened with far more stainless steel and chrome. Her furnishings too, were of a different look and feel.

Molded seating covered with fabrics rich enough to be tapestries in the main salon area, giving way to the colorful durable all-weather furnishings on the exposed decks. And enough wall space like many of these newer designs for priceless artwork.

The crew quarters even had the look of richness because of the intriguing use of different wood though clothed in practical fabrics, but it was in the master stateroom and adjoining bath, all extremely modern and highlighted with extravagant touches of Italian marble that the indulgence toward fine things stood out.

My reaction to her was no different in that something mysteriously unusual has always happened to me when I'm in the presence of any of these fine specimens, old or new. I become totally captivated by everything about them, but always especially drawn to the finely crafted rich woodwork. And I've been teased and mocked because I have always felt assured that wood truly comes to life under my touch, or so I've convinced myself, easing it gently through the harshness of sanding. Loving the moment when it is at last smooth as any silken fabric, and I can grace it with layer upon layer of golden varnish, deriving great pleasure each and every time I've done so. There is and always will be the extreme need to protect it all from the unforgiving rays and though it is hard work, for me the reward of the finished product makes it all worthwhile.

I never knew when I arrived on this island that I'd be given so many opportunities to not only appreciate the embodiment of beautiful boats, but would also be able to spend so much time aboard them. But whether just viewing them from afar, traveling great distances, or exercising plain old hard work to cherish their workmanship, I continually marvel at my idealized enchantment. Even more so when I try so unsuccessfully to remember that city girl with the manicured nails who had never even opened a can of paint.

And wherever we were, I never found it difficult to pick up on the joy and promise they held in the eyes of the experienced yachtsmen. These men from all backgrounds seen in every harbor across the waters, who treated them all like grand goddesses, tending to them as though a lover, and the loss of one felt just as painfully.

Now, surrounded by so much beauty I'm reminded again of another loss—the *Melinda B* was one of those, traumatizing and hard to ever forget. We all felt the pain experienced by her owners when she became a casualty of the sea with no one paying attention. Being on the *Artemesia* has surprisingly brought back Eddie's comments that so stunned me by his timing right after the hurricane when I could do nothing to console any further. He doesn't talk about that incident as a rule and since I know that Russ is one of the few who could understand, I'm comfortable doing so privately here while we are in this waiting mode.

Russ comprehends that misguided pain, a cerebral pill that Eddie has so much difficulty swallowing. We've been there, seen his level of responsibility and the care he extends. Seen him transform into this highly trained chaperon, bringing them into safe harbor without so much as a wrinkle in the paint and varnish facades. It is no small thing to lose any boat, even a dinghy you've cared for tenderly, but the loss of that one yacht in particular, hit us all like a death. She is mourned not only by Eddie, her temporary guardian, but by all of us who stepped aboard her with genuine pride. And now that it is again on my mind, I know it was as though a scab had been removed by force of the wind, revealing a festering sore that once and for all needs to be cauterized in order for Eddie to heal.

Even though Russ and I can relate the events, I'm convinced that healing will only begin when we begin all over again, filling up our lives with productivity and fun. I'm positive that will provide the opportune time for it to find its place in our history so that this unfortunate chapter will be put to rest, and I'm determined to help that along.

And though momentarily contented by the surrounding luxury, grabbing at all the mental straws willing everything to fall into place for the next phase of our lives, I can still bring her easily to mind even though I wish not to. Her beauty and size alone had generated an excitement and Eddie created an itinerary that would outshine many others. While Eddie is busying himself with his new duties, far and away from that story, I'm happy to take this leap on his behalf. And if absence makes the heart grow fonder, perhaps for him, it will also soften the need for any of that to rush to the surface with belated pain.

There will always be those reminders about the man who'd hired us, a stubborn sort always in a hurry, a man whose opinionated impatience led to ill-gotten gains by a poor choice of crew replacements in order to suit an impossibly rushed schedule. Even though scheduling was made perfectly clear well before, that sort of owner always would think he could get around such things and attempted to do so with us. When he realized there would be no compromise, he'd left his decision too late. That his new choices didn't present great credentials mattered less to him than their appeal to his wallet and his temperament and they honed in as if drawn by a magnet.

But then in the owner's defense, he really thought the last leg of the journey was the easy part, the one that would be mostly open-ocean except for the required fuel stops. Much of this was related to me after the fact when his very distraught wife was looking for a sympathetic female ear. I had found it difficult to lend one but the boat had mattered to me as well, to all of us.

I never knew exactly why it had happened to this very classic 65' Burger motor yacht except that it was among an elite few that had attracted the attention of the more modern day pirates during that period of time when drug smuggling was changing its forum. Instead of night drops using very fast 'cigarette' boats, they'd begun to get creative, stashing their loads within the unthinkable containers of cruising luxury yachts. The way the story was much later related to us, the *Melinda* must have become an easy target during one of the stops en route to the Dominican Republic, possibly along coastal Florida while provisioning her.

These men without known references but employed anyway, had apparently been careless with their conversations, more concerned about themselves than the yacht. They were likely followed without detection before being captured in Samana Bay. The lone survivor found on shore was able to piece together some of the story. From his interrogation, it became obvious they'd all been indulging on the highly prized *Presidente* beer, to the point of leaving no one on watch. That consumption had allowed them to be boarded at gunpoint by the men who would subsequently destroy her. And while the lore of pirates always fascinated me here in these islands and my many beloved books, those modern day ones had hit home and hit hard.

We were told that the yacht had been taken out of the empty bay under cover of darkness with no one the wiser, without realizing the man they'd left lying on the embankment had only passed out, more than likely from excess, rather than the bullet graze to his shoulder. With only that simple lead to go on, and after an extensive search by all necessary marine agencies, the damaged shell of her former self was discovered nearly six months later by an island marine patrol. An ugly paint job was responsible for the unknown name on her stern.

And she had been run hard with visible signs of their operation left behind, evident in her ripped out cabinetry and torn up compartments. Even her flooring had signs of damage, exposing a small residue of what had been there. Used up and nearly destroyed, she had been left to sink in too shallow a spot. The only good to come of that discovery was to allow the owners to at last put an end to their expensive and exhaustive search, though not their heartbreak.

Rehashing that knowledge with Russ, who'd been with us on that first leg, helped only a little as it again reminded me of the root of Eddie's distress. "Down deep, we all know there was nothing we could do, Lily."

"I know that and you and the others believe that, but Eddie takes this one very hard. I think in part because he really fell for that boat. You remember what beautiful lines she had and how she handled?"

"I do, especially the pilothouse layout where I spent most of my time, but her fate rested with the owners, not with him. They were stupid, plain and simple, for not thoroughly checking the credentials of those men who've paid a heavy price for their own stupidity."

Though misguided, we would always understand Eddie's irrational guilt primarily because the trip began with so much hope—another exceptional voyage to look forward to. We had flown into Michigan fresh and eager to take control of the newest grand lady in our charge and begin the route from the Great Lakes to Long Island Sound.

Now it's no more than looking through a maze of cobwebs as I sit on the open deck of this modern queen of the sea and piece together the specifics which brought us into the Straits of Mackinaw and on into Lake Huron. I can smell sauce from the galley; Natasha is making dinner tonight, triggering the memory of a craving for pizza at Port Huron. I think I must have smelled that heady aroma as we were docking there. Why else would I think such a strange thought now?

From the Huron River into Lake St. Clair, the Detroit River; all coming back to me, and then one of the most indelibly imprinted moments: taking our place for entry into the Welland Canal. Unfortunately, all the charts and paperwork for that part of the St. Lawrence Seaway's valuable shipping canal had been in one of the many boxes packed away. So much lost—memorabilia, shells, books, journals, a compendium of noteworthy experiences, gone as though a dream.

Back then, however, a trip like that still held great promise. Clearly, the reactions as we waited our turn into the monstrous lock system at Port Colborne on a grainy morning, made more so by tired eyes suffering the nighttime exhaustive crossing of Lake Erie, would be difficult to forget. But what grabbed our immediate attention was the framework of a white structure at first looking something like a six-story building slowly rising out of the bowels of the lock in that odd morning light. Then it got even bigger as it morphed into a huge oil tanker reaching our water level forcing us aside as she ground her way past, her darker hull mocking us with her size.

We had been instructed by the important voice on the VHF channel to "stand aside" until our turn to enter the reach with other pleasure craft. Quite a few boats had joined us by then, preparing for their turn into the first of those eight locks, most of which are over seven hundred

feet long and eighty feet wide, giving the tanker maximum berth. Not
that we cared to do otherwise. I was anxious and more than a little
nervous as I stood at the rail, one of two always on deck to handle lines
and whatever else might come up. This was too good to miss.

We no sooner had entered what was by now an obvious marvel of
construction and precision, with Eddie maneuvering into our necessary
position, than the threatening gray skies opened, making it even more
difficult to make out the shadowy figures some thirty feet above us. We
stood, rain pelting away at our impenetrable foul weather gear, to
accept huge cables tossed at us by those at the top. I grabbed on tight as
mine landed to my side and then for extra measure hooked my elbow
onto the slim iron ladder bolted into the lock wall already slick with
rain. The contained water, as we'd been told, did all the work after that.

Once closed in by a massive gate built to withstand the corralled
tonnage of water, the opposite one would open to release it. We would
then be moved forward toward the next lock opening to a new level,
repeating this sequential pattern that dropped us downward like a giant
slinky but with better precision, until eventually a clearing sky unveiled
monumental breathtaking vistas.

It took nearly eight hours but in the waning twilight, the last gate
opened, dumping us out unceremoniously at Port Weller on Lake
Ontario. A tiny nearby marina with floating docks was waiting for our
wobbly sea legs and so was more 'sauce'. It was an Italian restaurant!
No wonder this memory stays so strong.

In the morning sunshine, still rehashing the layering of the locks,
we set out again for the crossing of Ontario to the entrance of the
Oswego Canal that would connect us like the childhood game of dots to
the New York canal system and more remarkable notations in my
journal.

That particular cruise opened a new chapter for those of us with
misconceptions about lakes or canals being calm and tranquil waters.
We found out very quickly that in some cases, the surprising
combination of shallowness without width hit by spontaneous high
winds could kick up monster waves, even on a pretty lake.

But the canals, on the other hand, while appearing non-threatening and even mistily romantic were the ultimate challenge in navigation. Admittedly, some of it brought traces of the famous *African Queen* into the imagination or even novels exposing the reaches of southern bayous in terms that conjured up hot sticky nights and mint juleps.

Or better still, squinting your eyes in the milky morning light as it filtered through soft filled branches overhanging the edges of the river, you might envision a play being written by Tennessee Williams. I realize I might have been the only one thinking in those terms since most often our accompanying crew were more interested in the more tangible aspects of those challenges as well as the next meal.

We moved placidly and happily through the Barge Canal lock system, originally known as the Erie that encompasses four state systems, enjoying the ride. Wending our way through the small towns of upstate New York, there was always an opportunity to wave or have a quick conversation with bystanders enjoying their own views of the passing boats. And although not the length and breadth of the extraordinary Welland, still a wondrous accomplishment worthy of the experience and one that would eventually guide us into the Hudson River.

We navigated through strange and unfamiliar territory, always finding ourselves in either rapt attention or strong emotions, but never more so than when coming upon the 259' gray mass of the *M.V. Peckinpaugh* looming ahead through murky shade. We gladly gave way. The tranquil fluidity of this moving highway settled in with reflective hues nearest the edges of the embankments or spread itself out by great width built for just such an occurrence as confronting heavy cargo vessels...'tonnage has the right of way'... or could surprise even further and become narrow enough to invite a conversation from a biker along a parallel tow path and just as awe inspiring.

By the time we entered the Hudson River where we joined the flotilla of marine craft fortunate enough to witness daily the lovely 'lady', I was very sad to relinquish the Burger to another crew, having no idea it would be the last time any of us would ever see her.

My musing had stirred Russ's memory also. "I'd forgotten so much of that itinerary; must be the storm blew out some of my brain cells along with portions of my house. I think retelling those events you'll have Eddie anxious for another new trip. And we both know it's in his blood."

"I really hope so, Russ, and if nothing else, we'll have all the outrageous situations we seem to get ourselves into; more than enough stories to tell into our old age.

Chapter Eleven

Absence is another word profoundly familiar to our vocabulary now. Absence of good friends, of fine boats and many beloved things that lost their battle with a ferocious wind, and soon to be, the absence of sharing an entire island we've happily called home. And sometimes when I least expect it, it nastily makes room too for the tangle of concerns that can easily find a home in the void that any absence leaves behind.

And now once again our patience was being challenged, someone's thrown a wrench into the carefully planned project. Those often laughed about stamps are hard to come by when the clock is ticking. And even with our combined knowledge forged from many years, these delays that could occur often and from many quarters still aggravated, causing us on more than one occasion to wonder why. Why not just give it up, surrender to the situation? Why a project like this one to be completed most always at the whim of the mechanics of tropical life. And still we waited.

Then, finally, in late spring when we thought we could wait no longer, the paperwork that had gone missing from some government office mysteriously found its way into the proper hands, sailing conditions were good, and the boat was ready. Fortunately, Eddie had always been a stickler for details and safety precautions, so before heading out of St. Margeaux for the last time, he had replaced the navigational gear, flares, batteries, even purchased a new Emergency Position Indicating Radiobeacon, an EPIRB, things hit the hardest by the storm. He bought a new life raft too, though not as sophisticated as the one that went flying during the night, but certainly adequate.

A simple plan had been put forth. Russ would fly back to accompany Natasha and me and lend a hand with our belongings in order for us to join them as soon as possible. Mick planned to stay, help Eddie, and make last minute upgrades to the small rooms that he and Natasha would soon occupy. The living quarters consisted of two bedrooms, one bath, and a small communal area where they could relax as well as share time with us when our usual gatherings were in order and work set aside.

Mick said he'd already stocked plenty of rum and he was putting in a few bookshelves to house Tasha's desired collection of cookbooks. And, he was dressing up the bathroom for her feminine tastes at least as best he could without her being there. Russ had a separate one near his small store, so she could do pretty much what she liked to theirs. And Mick had found a couple of small display cases Russ could use to show off some of the new merchandise they'd sent for from the states. I also had an inkling that some of that space might work for Nessa's latest hobby, jewelry making. This new project had come about after the hurricane left her with so much time on her hands, and she'd already found a small market for them.

According to our primary plan, we would then bid goodbye to the fabulous *Artemesia* and her crew, along with an island that had provided us all with community, passion, excitement and determination. It wouldn't be easy, nothing ever was but we'd be together in the ways that made us happy. That's all that really mattered.

Before leaving, Eddie and Mick had taken some time to see those they'd felt closest to and say their farewells, but not being very good at that, their goodbyes probably meant no more than a few beers and a pat on the back. And probably held an invitation to join us whenever possible to whomever they encountered. That was the way they solved most things and that's why we knew to plan for lots of guests.

We would soon be taking up our new residency as small business owners on a spit of land that looked out without interference toward Africa. Honestly, thinking of sitting on that flat stretch of white sand and be able to literally watch the next hurricane coming toward us on another search and destroy mission caused a chilling spine tingle, and I tried to ignore the feeling. This was after all going to be just another adventure and the 'if' and 'when' type of worries about another killer storm had to be taken out of the equation. The odds were in our favor.

One thing that was extremely important to all of this timing for our move was the ability to stay in touch. So before leaving us, Eddie set up a schedule for radio calls between the yachts not only while they were en route, but also after their arrival on the island. We had to be able to assess their timing with that of the departure of the *Artemesia*.

"Don't worry, Lil, Josiah and I have this all worked out so you'll always know what's happening. We'll be in touch every day, promise."

For a moment, I had no idea who Eddie was talking about. From Russ's first introduction, the captain was known as Cap as if that were his given name.

Inching close to him, pointing thumb and forefinger, "Well then, Captain Josiah and I will be all ears my love, because we're this close to our new dreams."

And then they were gone, as excited as if this were their first sail. But I wasn't kidding myself; I knew I was still nervous about everything and quite contrarily I was also impatient to be settled. I hated feeling like a vagabond without a place to call my own, even a boat that I had willingly accepted for our future. And even the storytelling was becoming an ineffectual way to pass the time without our entire cast of characters, those times where a new version could grow out of the exchange replacing a forgotten memory. And it was at long last becoming tiring to try and relive what no longer existed except in our minds. Perhaps Eddie knew best—this change would be healthy and refreshing on so many levels.

Natasha was the only one of us not bothered by any of the waiting. She busied herself with not only writing recipes but also testing them out in the beautifully modern galley and helped the crew serve up some of her latest culinary creations. Her innate shyness, always very endearing in new circumstances, started taking a back seat to a more confident personality. She had found her niche.

And as always, her timing was spot on after she got to know you and an opening appeared in a story just big enough for her dry accented words to plow through. When we had been a full complement of friends, part of the fun of having experienced so many noteworthy happenings was the ability to adjust the events, expanding the joys or shrinking the fears accordingly sort of like a fish tale, everything with time gets bigger and better. But now all of that had noticeably begun to change.

Once again, I found that it helped to pass the time awaiting the daily calls in my favorite way, putting pen to paper. But instead of my usual journaling, I decided to try out a new concept, writing more as an outline for our intended chartering. I had been doing quite a bit of querying among those in the business and still had much to learn. And while it was easier just to jot down some forward-thinking scribbles, mostly suggestions for the intended operation, thinking of all Eddie's admonitions regarding my ideas and the time and space available to fulfill them, I was still keenly aware that if I lingered too long, my words could turn against me. And then I'd flounder, on the brink of changing my mind again, and have to force myself to remember the new goal.

When I wasn't coming undone, I knew that at least some of my notes could be useful in sorting out the customary needs of the tourists we certainly hoped to lure and how best to accommodate them in their quest for leisurely vacations. I had to consider everything since our new guests would have to quite quickly acclimate to the interior spaces aboard the *Wanderer*. And even as I wrote logically and with thoughtfulness, tossing in ideas that would successfully highlight that guest's first time with us, my heart knew only too well that the *Wanderer* would always rightfully reverberate with the voices of the friends of St. Margeaux.

It was a given that the charters would most certainly showcase many of the magical places Eddie and I had discovered together. But these charters would probably be fairly fast turnovers so it would be important to pack in as much fun or quiet time as the new visitor might require. I had a lot of reading to catch up on and guidebooks to memorize, much of it borrowed from a friend on a neighboring island. I had ordered more but they were slow in arriving. Thankfully, I had less to worry about regarding menus. I knew Natasha would gladly provide me with readymade provisions to augment what I would be able to do in the galley, making that part a lot less stressful regarding the time factors.

Wanting to formulate my ideas into some kind of context that I could follow without much difficulty, I placed many on 3 x 5 index cards that I could tuck into a handy spot easily retrievable as needed. So from my perspective, it appeared that my part in this charter business was taking shape rather nicely, at least on paper. My greatest desire was to become engaged in an active life once more and when I looked at the daily writings, it seemed that was about to happen.

Eddie was good to his word, and the calls came in every day even after their arrival. We began to visualize our new home, taking some of the edge off waiting. During his last call, Eddie had mentioned that there was room for an outdoor terrace on the existing property that could allow the restaurant more open space for special events. This would be useful not only for island functions, but could be adapted for our charter schedule as well, and what did I think of naming the new bar 'Last Stop', Mick's first choice? It won out over the few others: 'The Deep End', 'Salty Dog's Pub', and 'The Angler's Retreat'. 'Last Stop' seemed apropos since there was nothing beyond view but the wide expanse of ocean as far as the eye could see.

I couldn't believe it. At long last, nearly everything was finalized for our move, and even I knew the tide was turning and the project as a whole beginning to feel more important once again. There came a renewed excitement with everyone both here and on Anegada bustling about with a stronger sense of purpose, whether over the charter menus or color schemes, and drink choices sans tiny umbrellas. Whatever, it was forming the framework for a new adventure in the making. But ever realistic in my awareness of the personality and habits of the man I'd fallen in love with, there would always be the eventuality that even this new placement of ourselves might not quell the need for him and his stalwart friends to take on another needy client for another long distance cruise when the time was right. And after so many conversations with Russ, I wanted that to be the case.

Over time I had come to fully recognize these men grown from boys with their never ending thirst for adventure, hoping to fulfill many of those childhood fantasies discovered between the exciting pages spilling out from the likes of *Treasure Island*. These novels more than likely read by flashlight under covers into the wee hours, leaving behind a bit of wanderlust to linger always; the type that would more than likely sprout up again in the not too distant future. I had learned to be prepared. And because I'd followed my own dream, I'd learned to love it all.

The daily calls reinforced and kept us constantly buoyed. Plans to reinvent our personas as entrepreneurs now stood side by side with everything else. And after so many hours and days and for me nights talking with the stars, we would soon face the unpredictability of another outpost, the waiting almost over.

Soon after making landfall on Anegada, Russ had flown back as planned. Eddie and Mick had quickly taken on the tasks of cleaning and sorting out the restaurant facility, and stocking the bar, so there would be a different sort of work waiting for us when we arrived, more aligned with decorating and prettying things up.

With each new call, I could sense their growing enthusiasm about what they now called the settlement, and realized how far their own imaginations had gone. There was a quick reference to the weather picking up but that was brushed over just as quickly; we were still weeks away from the start of another hurricane season. And as years of pattern stated, the earlier summer weeks held little threat. Natasha and I were packed up and ready but Eddie suggested we wait a few more days until we booked our flight just in case it got a little stormy. He knew my feelings about flying in bad weather.

After nearly two months aboard this creampuff yacht, eight months after the devastation, I knew we were at last ready to sail into what clearly for us were uncharted waters—business owners with big responsibilities that had taken pretty much the last of all our savings. Power had finally been restored to St. Margeaux, but phone problems continued to exist, making us grateful still at being able to count on the two radios.

Luckier still for us, the owner of the *Artemesia* canceled their plans for a major transatlantic crossing, choosing instead to have the yacht delivered back to Fort Lauderdale for interior changes in early summer, thus allowing our departure to match that timing. The owner's wife apparently had ideas for new fabrics and colors and insisted upon its return for that scheduling. So for these last days we helped out the crew of our floating hotel as much as possible to ready her for their trip back.

Natasha's meals had made a big hit by then and the chef had been taking notes of his own so she cooked up more than enough meals which he in turn placed in containers in the freezer compartment. I hoped the owners wouldn't mind the hint of tomato sauce that seemed to linger throughout the galley and lower deck areas. Somehow she was always making something requiring it. Cap promised a visit to Anegada when they could and I knew she would be ready to show off more than tomato-based dishes by then. She had been hinting recently about a few unusual seafood platters.

Russ was now the one getting anxious. All we needed was the go-ahead from Eddie, and I remember waiting for that last call, mostly because it was a Tuesday morning and Russ had been complaining about a last minute appointment in town and was fretting about the time. He had rushed back to catch Eddie's radio transmit, but none came.

"Damn, now I have to go back to that miserable secretary and apologize for rushing off. I wouldn't let her talk me into waiting for a couple of documents that weren't quite ready."

"Oh, Russ, please don't have a meltdown; he probably got busy and forgot the time."

Russ's personality had never adapted to pressure; he was straining now. After calming down, he once again jumped into *Artemesia's* dinghy with its high-powered motor, an apology forming mentally for the secretary, to finalize the sale documents on his property. But when he returned from that second trip the call still hadn't come in.

"Maybe they've had some mechanical problems or just forgot the time. You know how Mick can talk. Eddie's probably gotten distracted," he said, obviously having used the dinghy time to work things through.

"You're sure? You don't think something's gone wrong." This time I was readying for that little meltdown.

"No, Lil, my guess is they've gone to pick something up from the ferry and just lost track."

It was obvious we were both concerned and not quite willing to admit it, but by the next day I couldn't find more excuses not to be worried. I knew Eddie too well and he knew me.

"Something's wrong Russ, isn't it? Tell me the truth, don't you feel it?"

"Eddie and Mick are both competent. I can read it all over your face, but I think we should give them a bit more time before you charge down there. They might have sailed over to the neighboring island to get supplies or possibly the radio is acting up. I'm sure he'll call any minute now."

I noticed a slight pulse in the side of his cheek as he said all this, and knew he was trying to keep his composure for my sake.

I don't remember a lot of what happened next but before the day was over that call did come in. Only it was from Mick. A lot is foggy after that, but Russ, together with the captain, came out of the salon to tell me that there had been an accident. My heart nearly stopped and if Russ hadn't been there to catch me, I would have landed hard on the after deck surface with the voice bearing the news that our boat had hit the reef, still echoing in my head.

Russ's voice grew stronger as I pulled myself through that dark space; explaining it all as he watched my face, "Mick said Eddie had been alone trying out some new gear that just came in. Remember, Lily, he was sending for that before he left here? It was for chartering.

"Mick went out to the tender to call him on the VHF and from Eddie's response he could tell he'd become preoccupied with the equipment. While they talked, he said Eddie noticed the squall bearing down on him, coming out of nowhere. He thought Eddie sounded really agitated, but then he told Mick not to worry, he was going to tighten up the sails and outrun it.

"Then Mick said he heard metal in all the wind noise and while he's telling me this, my first thought was it was probably the halyard clanging against the mast. Eddie told Mick that the squall was close and he was hustling to bring her back in. After that there was no response, just static.

"Mick also wanted you to know he's doing everything he can. I could tell, Lily, that he was trying not to panic but he's really upset. When it all first happened, he'd gone out to look for him, unable to see anything because of the heavy rain and he knew Eddie might be way too close to the reef. And without radio contact, the only thing he could do was call in a mayday to the Coast Guard."

I wasn't digesting the words; they made no sense, but Russ continued with the worst of it.

"By the time the patrol boat got there, *Wanderer* looked pretty bad. They told Mick there was a gaping hole in her hull. Also, the life raft was still on board but there was a large jagged piece of orange fabric stuck to the back stay that makes it safe to say, he had his life jacket on at least." Russ's shaky voice was again talking through a long tunnel.

Natasha was suddenly by my side, holding something for me to drink and I nearly choked trying to swallow through tears caught up in my throat. I didn't know how to react, but I desperately wanted to throw something or scream at everyone but all I could do was gasp and retch overboard until I was dry and spent. A nightmare, I must be in a nightmare. This wouldn't happen to Eddie, he's too careful and too accomplished a sailor. There must be a mistake; someone will call back and say it had all been a huge mistake. He was just out of radio contact; it was another boat on the reef!

We all sat there, sometimes not talking at all; there was nothing left now but the waiting. Nessa stayed with me spelling Natasha with more kind words and soothing tea. And all I could do when I moved at all was walk, slowly and quietly covering every square inch of *Artemesia*. I roamed the deck, through the wheelhouse, then the salon, on through the interior to the companionway, down to the galley, into the engine room and back up the corridor to the staterooms and crew cabins and started all over again. I refused food and knew very quickly that if this habitual roaming continued, someone would try to medicate me. I needed to feel the pain if I was going to believe that Eddie was still out there, to sense him alive with all my being.

An important sounding voice from Sector San Juan finally made contact with me directly the day after Mick's call though I have little recollection of time, so numbed by shock. They offered no concrete information, polite but short in their answers, but said they'd sent out a helicopter on a search and rescue mission feeling that Eddie may have been knocked out and fallen overboard. Hopefully, with the piece of material from his jacket, it would mean that there was at least the strong possibility he could survive in the warm waters for a little while longer.

I knew Mick was already out there in that little powerboat they'd been so joyful about, such a boon for fishing and ferrying of customers coming soon. But for now, it would be churning up the coastal waters in search of his dear friend while the helicopter blades spun purposefully above.

The wait went on. Four more excruciatingly long days and nights went by and then another call from San Juan to say they were suspending the search due to a lack of any tangible evidence of survival. Tangible evidence! What does that even mean? They couldn't find any signs of Eddie?

Mick had already told them Eddie had a new EPIRB, but what if it was a manually activated one and he'd been knocked out before he could do even that? I was too conflicted to remember which type even though I remembered seeing him take it out of the box. But that didn't mean Eddie was dead. How could they give up? What if he was still out there, helplessly treading water without a lifejacket; how could they NOT keep searching? Maybe the EPIRB malfunctioned and Eddie is floating out there thinking the signal was received and help is on the way. Their assurance that many miles had been covered thoroughly by helicopter didn't convince me. I was that crazy woman reincarnated after the betrayal by my sister Carrie, screaming and railing at the gods.

Was I making too much of our closeness? Would I really sense internally if he were gone? Somehow I thought this was so, and yet I had all those practical people telling me they had done everything possible and I'm supposed to live with that.

Mick, also refusing to give up hope, urged Russ to fly down immediately and join him in the search. Then they would take the tender with its shallower draught able to get close to the reef and the *Wanderer* and go through what would be left of her for any obvious clues as to what may have happened. That could now be accomplished since the brief spate of stormy weather had abated and softened the surf.

Natasha, Nessa and I sat for hours working through every scenario we could think of that would have caused something like this to happen. They did most of the talking, I was useless, and they stood by my every mood swing, giving me courage to hang on to any thread of hope no matter how small. We all knew Eddie was a highly qualified sailor and even in a squall he wouldn't have lost control.

I had sailed alone with him for years and could remember similar scenarios in Drake's Channel. Squalls happened, and we too had once outrun a similar block of very black sky bearing down, a huge squall line that seemed to rise out of nowhere. Back then it was more difficult than it would have been for Eddie nearing that reef because we changed those ridiculous 'tea cup' winches for the bigger more powerful Lewmars soon after. He never lost his cool then or at any other time like that; it had to be something else.

But I also knew how accidents could happen, and that coming about on a sailboat if things went terribly wrong could send someone into the sea, especially if caught off guard by the boom. My instincts kept telling me there was more to it; something else must have happened as he neared that still unfamiliar stretch of reef, but will I ever find out the truth?

Chapter Twelve

There was a recurring theme to the many nightmares awakening me during the nearly five months that passed painfully by after Eddie disappeared off the reef at Anegada. It would cause me to scream in terror, the entire scene leaping out at me resembling a Vermeer painting, its edges all brownish black and beginning to crack like aging varnish. The light would circle the top portion of the sail and then the edges would curl as though burning in the blackness of the squall, and the sound of my voice would wake me.

I slept little in those months, afraid of my own thoughts. I wouldn't allow myself to give up hope completely, but there was never any offered by the Coast Guard or island authorities. Only my closest friends tried to maintain a semblance of it in order to sustain me, but I knew they were failing in their attempts and feeling inadequate in that failure. I was alone for the first time in many years and totally unable to adjust.

His accident had occurred on the twenty-third of June at the beginning of what turned out to be a remarkably quiet hurricane season. For that we've all been grateful, but his disappearance prompted many changes and pointed out that there would be nothing to keep me from leaving ahead of a major storm anymore. It didn't seem to matter. But leaving meant that I would truly lose more than just the hope. There was the awful possibility that I'd lose the image of Eddie I kept tucked inside my heart, keeping him alive out there somewhere.

The attorney for the LaBelle Reef Corporation was able, without huge difficulty, to redo the licensing, removing not only Eddie's name, but mine as well. And some of the insurance on the *Wanderer* helped defray part of the cost forced upon the remaining three.

Soon after, Mick reluctantly returned to St. Margeaux to pick up a few stored items still feeling that it put a stamp of finality on such a horrific episode that he had been all but helpless in. The island finally has full services restored making it easier for everyone. Then he and Russ and Natasha began to put the pieces of their dreams into action much as we had all planned. I was happy for them; not wanting them to sacrifice because there was nothing more they could do for me on St. Margeaux.

Before leaving, however, a gathering was held at Long Point Cay for one last time. It seemed fitting with all the many glorious hours we had spent there before anything really bad had ever happened to us and even then became a shelter when the island was forced into its prolonged darkness. I felt Eddie would have so appreciated that particular gesture and that of all the many toasts in his honor. He after all, loved a good story, so in his memory each of his closest friends told a shortened version of their favorites.

After learning of Eddie's disappearance, Maxine and Reno came back for a brief stay not only to console but to help and I was grateful to let her take over the planning, however modest under the circumstances. So characteristic of her concern for details, she had picked the date when her friends, a colorful couple from Aberdeen could be here. They had remained in one of the safer ports of Venezuela after tiring of all the worries of a hurricane season many years ago. She remembered that they had sailed with Eddie in their early years here, before I arrived.

Marly and Maggie, the perfect pair to rejoin their old friends and allow me another glimpse into the character of the man I loved. Marly had brought along his bagpipes, famously turned out in his kilt bearing the Scottish tartan of his clan, exposing bony knees that invited many a hoot and holler from a crowd that while sad, couldn't help but be a little irreverent too. Eddie I knew would have been party to the same, trying to get him to reveal what everyone always wanted to know about kilts.

And like that day, the sheepishly coy answer was, "You'll have to ask Maggie".

It felt good to laugh again; Eddie would have done so and everyone knew it. But when a diminutive Maggie without warning chose to sing Amazing Grace in her sweet alto voice she left not a dry eye among us. I have been comforted by all their friendships, and in that gathering also felt Eddie's presence more strongly than ever since the chaos surrounding his disappearance.

Well before the plans for the ceremony, Mick and Russ had tried to fill in the empty gaps for me even knowing full well it would never be enough. They discovered once the boat was finally salvaged that something had happened to the steering mechanism, a sheered pin in the rudder housing; they couldn't be sure it was the only thing. In a high wind and without forewarning of anything amiss, it would easily have prevented his retreat from the overbearing squall. Logic indicates that the boom was more than likely the ultimate culprit since without steering, the sails in that kind of wind would cause it to careen back and forth wildly, but we'll still never be certain of what took place.

The beautiful *Artemesia*, sparkling from the constant upkeep right down to her highly polished hull, left our tropical port as scheduled for the Fort Lauderdale marina where her owners awaited her homecoming with lush fabric rolls and blueprints for changes to be made to her already beautiful interior, instead of the many Mediterranean ports of my imaginary travels.

And now that the yacht has gone, I have returned to land, a major adjustment for me, staying at the remodeled apartment of my dear friend Nessa, at least temporarily until I figure out my next move, or she gives in and permanently moves to Anegada to be with Russ. She has had a few extensive visits with him leaving me to my thoughts, pitching in where she could within their newly organized operation, and I'm inclined to think she might now be ready to actually concede to setting up a real housekeeping situation with him. All that has happened has increased their sensitivity to one another. And while the group may

never do any chartering, the rest of the business offers plenty to keep
them happily occupied and earning again.

I'm happy for them all. They have so easily fit into their new home,
meeting the many fishing and boating aficionados who pass through
their portal, just as I believed they would and so far they've not been
threatened by deadly hurricanes. But in the many quiet hours I spend
alone I still torment myself with the '*what ifs*' and '*how could this
happen*' sentences running amuck in my brain.

Occasionally, I even allow myself a little pity party, crying at
length over the untimely loss of the man who'd given me an opening
into a world that beckoned me in like a long lost lover. A place well
seasoned by its many natural gifts and offered up on the strong currents
of an ocean that has begun to feel flat and lusterless with only his
memory. A place I wasn't certain I could still function within, or
without.

Nessa, with her dark compassionate eyes offers no false bromides
and will not allow this wallowing in self pity that occasionally rears its
ugly head, no matter how many times I try to sneak those moments past
her. She's feisty and outspoken and exactly the friend I need. However,
she is in total agreement with me regarding our placement on this
earthly mound of rock and sand, even more poignantly now that a flat
coral island accommodates their needs.

We have spoken often about the meaning, having been through so
much together and have come to a mutual understanding. We
wholeheartedly agree that we have both been more fully awakened here
in this inconceivable way of life, and also cognizant that it will never
look quite the same to us again.

It will, of course, regain all its natural beauty that had lain disguised
and bruised for a long time under the rubble. But whatever comes forth
now or later, I also believe our footprints will forever be buried deeply
here in this place where it all began and our friendships took root.

And darling Essie, along with a rapidly growing Georgia no longer
clinging to her mother, have been such an integral part of it all for me.
They visit often and always with a tasty offering, usually carried in a

pretty basket that shows Moses' trademark weave. Essie now has a sales corner for her baked goods set up in a new specialty market that grew up out of a newer need, featuring island goods. The only thing that's changed is the prices and that was something we had always encouraged her to do. Her products are superb!

She generally picks Georgia up from the sitter, bringing her in to delight my eyes with her bright hair ornaments, nearly ready to join the plaid-skirted children, so reminiscent yet again of my first taste of genips and our strolls through town. We both wish that Eddie could be witness to the changes in that once shy little person. For some unknown reason, Georgia always made a grab for Eddie's hair, wrapping her small fingers around a patch, pulling for dear life until Eddie would yelp loudly, forcing great giggles to erupt from her tiny mouth. No matter how often Essie said no, she continued as though they had a pact to defy; it was their game and theirs alone.

Before leaving for Anegada this last time, Nessa and I drove out to the house where Eddie and I had survived the hurricane, each and everything these days creating a new touchstone for our memories, but now there was a new For Sale sign displayed in front. I was proud that the owners could return from Europe to find their island home damaged only slightly in the grand scheme of things, and grateful for their good fortune. The house withstood the onslaught far better than we ever expected, making repairs and clean up more easily accomplished than for many others less fortunate.

I knew from their recent letter, that they moved back abroad permanently, leaving the property in the hands of a local realtor. The scrawled lines exuded their happiness and total thrall with Italy and its gardens in particular, exclaiming over the Boboli and Villa Gamberaia of Florence as well as Villa Carlotta in Lake Como. Then adding as a footnote, an invitation to visit when they completely settled. I sense it is a more natural place to position newfound treasures without perhaps quite as much worry as experienced here in the tropics and can only imagine their desire to compete with those glorious foreign gardens.

I've assured them that I would love to explore those far away ports one day.

But I often mark time now by the wind changes knowing with prescient clarity that I will soon come face to face with that storm anniversary, terrifying still, as if one can smell the fear a hurricane spews ahead of itself. My heart beats a little faster at even the thought of it, sensing a maelstrom of emotions will appear out of the blue and take over.

The corporation, now without the lead of Tim Brownell since his home was also destroyed, goes about rebuilding the resort. And I know my time there is marked as well because my heart is no longer in it. But at least I am able to wander about more easily now that life has picked up a bit here, although still without its usual flow and always in my somewhat lackluster ennui, the one I've become so comfortable with it is like a second skin.

When I can, I walk alone out on my favorite curvature of pebble and rock along the north shore much the same as when I first arrived in my bewildered state, wondering aloud once more as I seek answers. Due to the previous year and a slower tourism business, the turf is still pretty much my own. But something else seems to have occurred there as a result of that huge hurricane. There is more sea glass than I remember, scattered everywhere—in cobalt, magenta, shades of green and yellow, some bright and shiny and others dulled by force. I feel I should gather them so that Nessa can make more of the type of jewelry she sells on Anegada. She had already found an opportune supply and they've made quite a hit featured in a special display case in Russ's shop. But even with the feeling that I might be letting her down, I refuse to concentrate on collecting.

Instead, as I finger them like worry beads, they do make me think of the lambent moon that more than once spread its reflection brightly across the water, dominating our shores. The sea at that time appearing to give up its struggle under the huge beam in order to lie quietly and as flat as plate glass, retiring under its care for the night. Its color that of so many shades thrown together to be non-existent on the color chart;

the thing that would happen if all these glass pieces were ground to powdery pigment and mixed together. Something a painter wouldn't do, but the 'man in the moon' is the artist in control on those unusual evenings.

And when this full moon phenomenon occurs and seems larger than possible, enticing me to witness from the rim of a high hill, all the time knowing the lack of wind to ruffle the dark surface is not a sailor's delight, but bears witness to another strange occurrence. That is when in total fascination, I see small boats with big motors flitting across the calm, obvious from this height only because the reflection is so widespread. I feel as though they are actually rushing toward the amazing ball of light as if it is the trophy.

Moments such as those are silly miniscule things to keep in one's mind, but I enjoy the feeling as if we alone on this island had claim to it. And it is lovely to take pleasure in any that cause a curiosity and bring a smile, even if it is just bits of glass.

Blessedly, I learned in the aftermath of the hurricane, only a few lives were lost to that warring wind, remarkable in itself given the high probability. Moses is gone. He died in his sleep days before we lost Eddie. We would never have known by his stamina and vigor that he was 92.

And adding to all the changes predicted, there've come others who now fill the practiced shoes of the many who have departed. Someone recently told me, remembering how many hours wiled away there, that a string of new musicians have passed through the doors of the rebuilt Top Deck bar trying for a new tone. I have yet to attend, but who could fill Matteo's seat after all?

Lew has replaced his chair and pole, but had to set up shop temporarily in the little wooden shack near the square. That was one of those miraculous situations where everything around it blew down and the tiny structure long ago abandoned survived with only its windows blown out and its door rocked from the hinges. The little tin roof held, though rusty, and some new trim paint appears in an odd shade of pink, but he stands proudly in the doorway each and every day to welcome customers not only for clips, but that small bit of neighborly gossip that seems indicative of the profession.

When I pass by there now on the way to Essie's, I can see his bright white smile from behind shiny new windows, far more modern than the building called for but giving Lew a grand view of everything while he works.

My favorite terrace is clean once again, but the faces around the tables are now mostly strangers and the new furnishings cannot replace the imprint of our presence from the hours and hours of experiences shared there. But I am also positive that new memories will be created by the many who now enjoy the space. It is only natural, and years from now I hope they will look back and be grateful for the open-air conditions from which to toss their own secrets aloft. It is obvious the island will once again catch its stride.

While I reflect on all that has come about in this renewal, at least here in my peaceful place near the water, things are nearly the same. The small hermit and sand crabs still return to 'our' spot and seem to pay attention when I arrive. They continue to move among the remains of the day, noticing if possible that I'm less interested in picking it all up again. They obviously see that I've barely begun to pick up my own broken pieces, since most times I prefer to just simply sit with them quietly and talk aloud. Could they know that it helps me after all this time to continue my writing especially now with all that's happened, of the more exciting exploits of the past; all those occurring at different points in time on the many bodies of water?

Or are they just a convenient audience for me to try out a new voice, one that is trying hard to heal? They watch me with a wariness that doesn't offend, but I wish they could respond; so many questions are yet unanswered. And they do appear to pay careful attention as I sigh aloud or fling my arms in exasperation when the images take hold and the pen is impotent. They do this as if they've had years of practice at rebuilding.

I've already told them of the recorded words begun such a long time ago. And knowing I will never run out of stories I've begun anew, this time using a beautiful deep burgundy leather booklet that just arrived, filling its virginal pages in testament to the life I've had here.

Eddie's accident shocked and angered and nearly depleted my spirit, but it couldn't obliterate the long and wonderful time together. That in turn has triggered many wonderful remembrances for others because of his powerful impact on them. That intrepid hardworking sailor who opened the door to my heart and the tropical world around me has bequeathed me a mountain of memories to dig through. It is easier to do that here feeling watched over, even if only in my imagination. And maybe one day I will find a way to put them into a story about the 'mates' who would stop at nothing for the ultimate gift of laughter.

Penned in this morning, however, is a notation ringing familiar because I find once again I cannot make up my mind to go or stay. Sound familiar? And I know while I'm here on the beach pondering it all, a stranger named Eddie Tremain will not show up to save the day. The thought of his never showing up again hits me hard, again, knocking some of the breath out of me. If I leave St. Margeaux, which has now taken on a new and different significance because of that large circular spot that blew onto the map with strength to kill, what will I find elsewhere? Is there anyplace I can again call home, or was my home destined to always be on that moveable feast like the *Wanderer*? Can I be content to once again be landlocked?

Carrie, for a long time, represented home after we lost our parents and had watched out for each other during those late college and early career years. But she destroyed even that opportunity for me with her betrayal even though she didn't end up with Rob. It has been many years since, and I think they tried to make it work after I left. Gussie filled me in a little when I reached out to her for help after Carlos disappeared, but in the years since she and Dee visited St. Margeaux, they always represented more of a family than Carrie. I would not be able to place my fragile thoughts in her hands after all that went before.

The Chamberlains still talk about their first-time sail aboard the *Wanderer* during the one and only visit to the islands. It had taken much to pry Dee out of New York, but the dangle of a long Caribbean sail finally did the trick, even for a man who broke a sweat carrying groceries for Gussie.

Eddie had surprised them during that lovely day, with a stop especially designed for those blessed with great curiosity, when after a magnificent morning out, he sailed up to a mooring showing off skills that allowed me to capture the line to the weighted ball planted there for those like us wanting to stay and have lunch. The restaurant was not on the culinary maps, nor any other type, but should have been. Its only invitation to enter was a small dock leading to the steep stairway up to the balcony where we would dine while looking out tenderheartedly at the island of Puerto Rico.

It had been another of the balmy tropical days as advertised to snowbound communities everywhere, captivating them from the beginning. The few tables were laid with charming batik cloths and good silver and the seafood was as fresh as the breeze. We had toasted heartily with champagne that day, brought along and consumed before lunch sitting in the cockpit of the once beautiful *Wanderer*, admiring it all, committing it to memory for their return to the city. Then during a superb lunch, finished off with a vibrant Pinot Gris from the restaurant owner's special stash, recounted the day's rewards. The owners didn't get many visitors except those of us with a marine radio, since it was mostly word of mouth attendance and they shared the best with those of us who took the extra time to stop and savor.

I can still see Dee, his enormous frame leaning over toward the love of his life as though he truly and finally understood the word paradise, which is of course what we had all bought into from the very beginning. But now even the kindness of my New York friends wishing my return to their beautiful living quarters until I get my bearings holds little appeal. They have tried to console me in their own dear way, but I'm not quite ready to be so cosseted. I see instead, by my new notes, my need to walk this mental path of places touched and times gone in order to move forward. That's the only way I know how.

In addition to their wonderful visit, the Chamberlains solemnly delivered the answers we had long awaited to fill the void in the mysterious way we lost Carlos. It was easier hearing it all in person. I had called upon them for help and they brought the satisfying report that James Warington, the man sought after as a material witness, fled the country and was eventually picked up by Interpol at the Madrid airport. He had become careless in a botched smuggling operation.

Authorities were at last able to tie him conclusively to the body discovered on Copper Island; forensic science had evolved importantly, forcing him to confess to murdering Carlos to prevent him from testifying. He had used a slow acting poison undetected in the difficult autopsy, giving him time to escape; knowing that a substance of that nature would have left Carlos, an innocent man, flying alone with no hope of ever reaching San Juan. The explanation offered so much and gave Rosa her much needed peace of mind.

The murdered stranger, the form in the Whaler that Carlos had seen from the air, had been hired as a front for Warington who was trying to establish himself as a legitimate collector. He then admitted to using the .38 to smash the man's skull before tossing it into the sea. The case was closed at last.

But even though grateful to the Chamberlain's for all their efforts and their tender caring expressed weekly through their loving phone calls, I cannot go back permanently to the noise and rush of the crowds anymore. I no longer have the stuff of a city dweller. I wouldn't know where to begin there anew, and more importantly I don't think I want to. And here on St. Margeaux with each new visit to sit among my tiny friends of the sand, the question remains, how will I go it all alone without my comrades, my cohorts, my glorious friends with big smiles and bigger hearts? Will I work near the water in that new home or on boats if possible, being content to paint and varnish like the old days, to earn extra money? Where do I begin to find the answers?

Perhaps that is why I'm again having this conversation with one of these little beings flirtatiously flitting to and fro, just like the first time I walked this very beach as if time has stood still. Logically, it is not the same tiny creature; however were it to be, would it better suit the situation? They seem so unnerved by anything, tenacious in their right to be here traipsing across their granulated surfaces almost expecting me to feel the same and yet undisturbed by my inability to do so.

Putting the pen down for a while, replacing it with the binoculars, that so cherished object, I'm made curious by a boat, a very large boat, a power yacht perhaps eighty or ninety feet long. It is a long way off on the horizon and difficult to tell. The atmosphere blurs the edges, slowing the speed of the powerful engines, moving soundlessly.

This time the tears stay put inside the warmth of my eyelids as a new thought occurs. Maybe I could sign on as crew for a yacht like that, perhaps like the *Artemesia*; for all I know, that might even be her. How would it feel to make major crossings with strangers after life on this island and the security of those who always cared? Her crew had been wonderful to us, but Russ had been a lifelong friend of her captain after all, and it takes time to build the kind of trust that we all once shared.

It is very enticing, even stimulating to watch the vague crawl of power so far away. It also brings a stirring of more than a little interest to imagine crewing on her, remembering the embrace I once had for everything related. Time, for quite a while now has become diluted by nothing but memories, more than I ever thought possible, so many it has caused me to write them categorically in order to keep them separated from each other.

And thankfully, not all are sad enough to feel crushed by them. Recently I've even let a few of these sneak by, the ones that can make my very cells remember how joy once felt. Like now, watching that familiar looking boat, they are fully diligent ready to haul me back to a time lovingly referred to by Eddie as my maiden voyage. Those hundreds of nautical miles embarked upon during our second year together will forever be the standard by which to measure them all. And the *Brisa Marina* was the perfect yacht to provide that setting. It is by now firmly established, however, that this particular time with Eddie adding up to many journeys in the subsequent years, was like our first kiss, not easy to forget.

Looking down at my little guest, the one that had nerve enough to get close, "I must always remember that I've been blessed to have many incredible times, all beautifully enriched by others who felt the same, and I know them to be rare. I also know you've made my days better with your presence."

The sand crab skitters away as my gratitude falls over him, diving into his small cave away from my voice. He'll be back, especially when he hears me talking with the sea, reflecting on Mariah's words, waiting for a whispered response. I'll never forget that my friends had teased me often about those visits to her, decrying her credentials and abilities, but I continued. It was hard to explain why really, but up until then I had thought my choices when leaving New York were completely accidental, but what if she had been right? What if none of this was an accident, but fate predestined in some way? Stories like that abound everywhere, why not for me? Would it make it easier to bear the losses—Eddie, and island community, and a man named Carlos who had meant so much?

I'd often reassured and comforted myself with the fact that this has all been the stuff of dreams—when a sad, disheartened *girl* from the city became an island *girl* who was gradually transformed into a *woman* with a lust for the sea. This rarified connection never once imagined while walking those long concrete streets, innocently offered up by nature for anyone willing to examine it. A tie that even through the indeterminate times of pure fear could not deplete the genuine love for it all. And Eddie's presence while that love grew makes it all the more bittersweet.

Chapter Thirteen

The present day legend of the *Brisa Marina*, far and away unlike those legends that held my attention through books for so long, had begun for me steeped in high anticipation. She was a 58' Hattaras motor yacht that had been romantically christened two beautiful words meaning sea breeze, and my emotions regarding that journey were an impressive mixture of excitement and pure fear.

Daily, I made a point of acknowledging her regal appearance because of her owner's choice of a forest green fiberglass hull, though no matter how much buffing to the paint, it had a tendency to show flaws. It was an unusual choice advocated by those new owners and, I already knew, difficult to maintain. And I especially remember casting not only a loving glance but also a soft stroke over her each time I strode up the boarding ladder with provisions. Back then that touch was trying to steal a little confidence from her too; hoping to cast away some jitters over what I'd been told could often be a difficult crossing from Miami to Puerto Rico before culminating in St. Margeaux.

We had been forced into alternating crew because of work schedules but that would also allow each of our closest friends to be part of the adventure even if only for a short period of time. Taking turns as time permitted, were Russ, Mick, Reno, Sam and Boomer. I had just met Sam, but he and Eddie had become friends through business dealings at his insurance agency and he'd expressed an interest in that trip.

And gratefully, Maxine was able to join us for a short leg as well, very unusual in her busy schedule, but making it the best of times for me especially since Natasha wanted nothing to do with that sort of hazardous voyage. Eddie had planned it out carefully for a safe crossing with as much fun in between as time and weather allowed.

What noisy and electrifying activity we encountered after the final provisioning, awaiting our exit out of Governor's Cut with just the weather holding us up! Quite literally overnight the dynamics of our timing was made very clear when we discovered it coincided inadvertently with a major national event, the Mariel Boatlift. Any boat in our midst on the Little River over fifteen feet was for sale or rent as the news spread about the mass of refugees leaving Cuba for the tip of Florida.

Eddie had been afraid to move from the dock in case we became mired in the water traffic, possibly causing us to delay our departure any further. It really wasn't until we were safely in San Juan that we were able to comprehend all that actually had happened as we caught up on newspaper and radio accounts. The "Freedom Flotilla" in the spring of 1980 turned out to be a horrific story of fast boats, blue water and 100,000 refugees ending up on the Florida shores, but to us on board a craft we had barely become acquainted with, it was a riveting social experiment and a frightening time.

As if that weren't enough, we had other issues to be mindful of. After we finally left Governor's Cut for the open waters, we began to sense there might be mechanical troubles. Thinking everything had been completed in the surveys and repairs already done, Reno, in fact a master mechanic, felt certain it wouldn't be anything too serious and he could take care of anything that came up while at sea. At least we had extra parts for everything tucked tightly away on board.

What came up, unfortunately, were very big seas. But before that and even before we were able to have some good old-fashioned fun with stops throughout the Bahamas, we had our first challenge with law enforcement. Eddie was as always quietly alert to our surroundings and the equipment in front of him. I knew from his friends that he rarely spoke when he was at a new helm outside our usual boundaries. It made him seem stern, but it made him a captain much sought after. I think he always struggled between his own love for the sea and that of the earth from which his many design creations could grow, making him unusually contemplative in the isolating moments of navigation.

As we entered Nassau Harbor, Eddie pulled back on the throttle to lower the wake for nearby boaters, mindful always of the well-placed signs, while the rest of us searched the inner harbor for the marina where we would tie up for the night. As always, this first major stop would give us a little time to go over what Eddie always referred to as the 'shake down' miles for this or any new boat in our care. And having Sam and Boomer on board, it would be a chance to give them more of a crash course on what to expect when we hit that open ocean for a longer period of time.

I thought Sam an unlikely candidate for this cruise, but he was certainly affable, happy to do whatever was asked of him. He, like Boomer, also loved cigars and between them we were always surrounded by their heavy smoke rings and puffy clouds as they seemed to constantly be in competition. Sam had hair like Boomer's too, though without the saltwater distinction and it fell almost romantically over his forehead, like an old movie idol.

His indoctrination to this world of cruising turned out to be a shocker.

"What the hell is that?" he croaked, over a newly lit cigar from Boomer's stash.

"From the look of that wake, they're on some sort of mission. We're in for a roll," Russ said, hating that motion.

Instead, the fast gray boat marked by prominent black lettering on the hull slowed very slightly as it neared, gave us a wide berth and then slowed further as it closed in on us, softening what would have been a huge wake. Once by our side and with no forewarning, four men completely dressed in black right down to their tire-kicking boots and wielding automatic weapons, very agilely jumped aboard the *Brisa*. We were all too shocked to say anything as they faced Eddie, still at the helm, and demanded to search the boat.

They were in fact the Bahamian Marine Patrol and had every right to do so, but it was beginning to take on the appearance of a very bad movie, only far more frightening. Then using their weapons to point out their directions, they demanded that I show them the below deck area and that nearly did me in. I'd never had a gun pointed anywhere near my person nor been alone in small quarters with men who looked more like villains than the law, but I didn't argue, just shakily went below and followed their orders. I didn't realize that Russ had taken over the helm so that Eddie and Sam could discretely follow. Boomer was trying to communicate with the captain of the patrol boat but was getting nowhere.

I caught a glimpse of Sam over my shoulder as I went about opening all the cabinetry, and the way he was biting down on the cigar said volumes about how worried he was. That of course, made me more frightened. Was I in danger? They began to intensify their search with more speed, without words like they knew exactly what they were looking for, and standing me aside, proceeded to go through every nook and cranny including the refrigeration compartments. I was totally baffled and ready to yell at someone for putting me in this position, though I couldn't figure out who that would be. Eddie would probably get the brunt of it, but no one was off the hook.

In what seemed like a long time but in fact took less than half an hour, the large patrol boat caught the signal from the search leader and moved back in to allow them to again jump across to their own boat just as easily as they had arrived. I silently wished for at least one of them to fall into the murky water they'd churned up, weighed down by those black lug soles that had done a nice job of marring the deck.

"Good thing we're not into hauling contraband; that could have been very dicey. Even though she's documented, I'd still like to look up her provenance and see if there's a sister ship we've been mistaken for. There have been a few reports of pleasure craft used to fake out the patrols right under their noses, in plain view. Scary business," Eddie said, reining in his emotions.

"Well, Eddie, if they had done a body search, I might not be making the trip at all as planned," Sam said, looking very chagrinned and holding up a joint he'd had in his pocket.

"What the fu....?" Mick yelled out, about to land a punch as Russ propelled his slim body forward to grab his wrist, stopping the connection, silencing him.

"It's only because I get seasick and I didn't want to let you guys down if things got rough out there and I couldn't pull my weight, especially since I knew how much you needed an extra hand on this one." Shaking his head, "I know, I know, it was stupid...I'm sorry I really screwed up, but it seemed harmless at the time. Honest, this is it; there aren't any others."

Eddie remained calm, his knowledge of Sam's inexperience in foreign waters taken into consideration, but the look on his face said enough, especially with the responsibility of someone else's boat in his hands. Sam sheepishly threw it overboard still insisting that was the only one and that proved itself out during the voyage. It was a risky thing to do and he knew it.

Relieved and feeling pounds lighter having shed the worry of being locked up in a Bahamian jail, refreshing ourselves with sleep and good food, and the timing of Max's flight, we took off a few days later for new harbors. We made for Bimini and, impossibly, the water became even more beautiful. We toasted ourselves in the barroom of the Compleat Angler, a must for our own motley crew, holding up a glass to Hemingway's photos, feeling strangely as though we were a part of something larger, realizing his niche there and that touched us in a strangely personal way. As did the need to go fishing but alas, there was no gear. That, of course, didn't stop the stories once again of the 'one that got away'.

As we continued checking off the coordinates toward home port, we found along the way the smallest most prized beach of pure white sand sprinkled with minute flecks of pink coral on a little isle hardly noted on the chart, which boasted a tiny airstrip and a large pool table. You could lose yourself and all your troubles by first dipping into the lightest turquoise water I believed existed on the planet, then dining in the long informal room filled with memorabilia of bygone sailors and pilots hanging from every available source, followed up by a lazy game of billiards and falling asleep like a baby under the stars on the deck of your boat.

But of course, after chaos, comes fun, and in some cases, more chaos. That is if you happen to have someone like Andy aboard your boat. He was a last minute arrival, supposedly coming on in Nassau with Max, but missed a flight forcing him to catch up with us in Clarence Town. Knowing his reputation, I think Max was actually grateful. He had always been great fun, very smart, witty, charming but with little boating experience…and extremely accident-prone.

Andy, dark haired and very youthful looking, intrigued me and everyone else. He was the epitome of Murphy's Law; anything that could go wrong did. But old Murphy would have exhausted all his reason had he known Andy. I don't say this lightly or with malice since it would be very difficult not to be charmed by him. He was almost boyish in his demeanor and certainly smart enough. It was more as if he had a particular type of aura following him that changed everything around him, and he was the least athletic of any of us, which may have accounted for a lot during the trip.

Poor Andy—he got lost going about as a tourist instead of waiting at the airport for his outbound flight to Clarence Town, nearly costing us an extra day. Then he tripped and sprained his ankle handing off a line to the dock attendant at the next stop, the beautiful island of Providencialis, while standing awkwardly in the stern ending up entangled in the rope. It had already been a difficult entry requiring a guide boat to bring us safely through the shallow cut and I could see Eddie's brow in a constant furrow as he realized what we might be in for if there were any more accidents. I knew this was a payback trip for Andy since he had helped Eddie out with some complicated accounting records the year before, but the wisdom of that was already being tested mightily.

But a few days later Andy, now feeling spryer with a freshly taped ankle, proceeded to leave a body print wherever his butt made contact and I mean everywhere because he had used a suntan lotion that had an ingredient strong enough to stain anything. Sadly, he burned badly in spite of the foul lotion, requiring medical attention as soon as we arrived in Caicos. And his only saving grace was that he rarely seemed to notice his own bad luck.

He became ill overeating the South Caicos 'goat', the islanders' name for the biggest, sweetest overabundance of lobster in the Caribbean. And was nearly shot for trespassing when he noticed the enormous quantity of conch shells lining the shore and followed the trail to the conch meat hanging to dry. They were as irresistible to him as a kite to a child, noticing their resemblance to bats with wide wingspans. They'd been strung side by side with wooden pins on long clotheslines secured between tiny wooden buildings nearby. And he had become completely fascinated by the fishermen who loosened the meat from their protective shells and almost smashed his finger in two attempting it himself.

There were so many small incidences that each of us stood our watch not only at the helm, but of Andy, to guard against any real mishap before we made it back home. I don't know to this day how he survived but he did and arrived back to a waiting, ever-doubtful wife, a bit of a superhero for doing so.

The events in Puerto Plata, however, still remain a mystery to me and I'll never know exactly what happened while tied up there. There was a hint about a broken salon window on a neighboring yacht caused by an errant boat hook, and that a little expensive scotch went a long way with the local *comandante* but at least he and Sam made it back to the *Brisa* in one piece just in time for our scheduled departure. Some things were just better left to the imagination.

As I look back on that time, the jumping off point for so many travels, I recall that much as I hated to admit it, I nearly quit the cruise when we reached that port on the Dominican Republic because the seas prior to arriving reached epic proportions way before the deadly Mona Passage. I didn't think I could handle more of the same.

Unfortunately, it was immediately understood that no matter her history, prior to this, the *Brisa* had stayed in her comfy slip at the marina in Florida. We knew she had been recently outfitted with beauty and grace befitting her name, but without a stitch of practical clothing. Tables should have been secured to the floor with removable hardware and larger pieces fastened or built in some way to prevent extreme roll in high seas, but instead only items resting atop the tables were fastened, which misrepresented her interior seaworthiness and had to be quickly dealt with as incidents happened. All of this was discovered during the nineteen-foot swells we'd just crossed.

There was a particular piece, a lovely porcelain dolphin matching the one on a lamp base that I found myself coveting, even knowing that nothing of this preciousness would have been seen aboard the *Wanderer*. Unfortunately, when the tables fell over, those pieces never stood a chance. The end result had me cursing the stupidity of the interior decorator having gone to the trouble of making it only worthy of a fine dockside cocktail party.

I shall never forget even though this same span of water was crossed again at a later date without quite the same difficulties, the continually discussed and much dreaded Mona Passage. It would be debated and rehashed often, as was its right; that often-turbulent section of water that led to the Puerto Rico Trench could never be taken for granted. To do so could mean disaster.

Maxine, tired of worrying constantly about Andy and having gotten the tan she was looking for, departed with Sam who was still nursing his bruised ego. They'd opted out before the dangerous approach, tired of lengthy discourse regarding safety and fearing possible delays that would leave them in a difficult situation. Their departure by then was inevitable though unintentional on our part.

There had been horror stories summarized often by many sailors who'd tackled the turmoil of confused seas and the long shipping lane where huge tankers crossed the region many a night on autopilot. We had already been advised to pay particular attention, especially to Andy short of tying him down, with everyone on watch to avoid being run down by these unknowing forces traversing that section in darkness. We knew that the giant ships set on course without human eyes awake and watchful, might easily and without fuss plow us under with no one the wiser. Even with all necessary lights on illuminating our black surroundings, if the notoriety were true, ours would be no match for a freighter as we slogged through the deep troughs and high swells.

The forewarned monster sea had no difficulty living up to its reputation and we quickly found out that it is no small thing to feel insignificant in a vessel that was not undersized by any standard. We were being tossed about like crayons in a schoolroom all the while trying to settle into some semblance of a comfortable groove. In the middle of it all we were forced to watch as if on schedule one of the feared freighters looming off in the distance set on a course that could overtake us should we falter our vigilance in any way.

At one point, when the alarm signaled engine trouble, I went to a cabin below, pulled a mattress off a bunk to protect myself from those hard surfaces, and prayed. Fortunately for all of us, Reno went to the engine room, balanced himself between the engines and fixed the leaking hose and became my hero forever. I knew Maxine would be especially proud and couldn't wait to tell her, but we still had miles to go.

Many hours later, totally bruised and battered, we exited the chaotic sea half expecting a welcoming parade or at least a bit of fanfare for the many tumultuous hours given over to the cause. While extremely grateful for being unharmed, there was an anxiousness to get home and share the many (embellished) stories. Why else would one put themselves through such craziness if not for that small reward?

And in the sunlit early morning hours, nearly exhausted from the hyper-vigilance and with quiet celebration, we found ourselves crossing through the fringes of the wide Sargasso Sea. I was reminded of the fascinating book of the same name, one of the many taken on the advice of my friendly librarian. I lacked the knowledge of this odd hiding place for plants, microbes and other remarkable species residing unidentified and couldn't wait to call on her for help. Then someone remembered the imaginary line and we all raised an imaginary glass while crossing the Tropic of Cancer. It was way too early in the morning to break out the rum even for us, and we still had a few obstacles ahead.

As we moved on it was becoming evident that in certain spots appearing surprisingly shallow considering where we were the coloring changed, lightening in shade, becoming more transparent and ethereal. Notably it also seemed to be the area for another private celebration. What at first appeared to be a giant log visible in the distance turned out with closer scrutiny to be a pair of mating loggerhead turtles just lolling and rolling in their own dance of union, sharing in our enjoyment of calmer water.

The remarkable entries in the captain's log were overflowing and so were mine, documenting all the locations and inhabitants whether on water or on land. The entries mounted up quickly and as the days flew by, no matter the earlier concerns, it would be difficult to see the voyage come to an end and also to say goodbye to Boomer who would fly out from San Juan. He too would have many stories to share with his friends in that other locale and probably raise the bar a tad while telling them and who could blame him? I had grown very fond of him; his quiet honesty came out at every turn and his knowledge of the sea invaluable. I'd hoped he would be joining us for another trip when the time came.

Because we knew how, we certainly did make up for any minor unhappiness over finished business, by a nearly all night celebration beginning as soon as we tied up in San Juan. We were more than glad to shake out our stiff, sore bodies that had been all but pounded and pummeled against every hard surface imaginable. After that even Andy was able to celebrate, unscathed any further yet as bruised as the conch he tore after with such abandon. The rest of the way to St. Margeaux would seem almost boring by comparison.

It became obvious as the trip was toted up event by event that we would all gladly do it all over again given the opportunity. After all, the seas never moved the same way twice. The next time it might be as flat as a mill pond, and wouldn't *that make us want to cruise around the world?*

Once back home, there was one last thing to do, and that was to make the yacht presentable for her owners. *Brisa's* would be flying down in a few days to take possession and I wanted her to be welcoming. The men took care of the topsides, removing salt and polishing up the chrome and varnish, but I was better left to myself below.

That's when it happened. While cleaning up one of the smaller heads I noticed the cabinet looked strangely askew. There had been massive movement throughout the passage and more than likely something had come loose. I carefully pried open the mirrored door in case anything inside was broken and spied a blunt-topped metal hinge not quite flush and yet not out far enough to grasp. This so-called 'medicine' cabinet was built into the wall just like in a house but they normally don't move. As I felt around to make sure nothing was broken, the hinge moved again, this time enough to get a grip, revealing a two-part door as the entire shelving area in its frame swung toward me. Now I can look directly into a secret compartment that looked like a small deep well behind the wall—a safe for valuables, or perhaps drugs?

I yelled for Eddie and he came down followed by Russ who then yelled for Mick by then displacing me since the room was small. They in turn moved out to let Reno in—Andy had been dismissed after slipping on the foredeck—and though the compartment was deep, clean and entirely empty, we knew why the Bahamian patrol had wanted to do a thorough search. The idea was ingenious. Obviously, it had not been used for smuggling by any recent owners but once it was shown to the present ones, they expressed their gratitude along with a nice tip and their plans for redecorating which included immediately sealing up the hidden compartment.

The many other voyages during our years together, while great fun and always interesting, never quite captured my heart like that first one. Eddie had gladly accepted more opportunities for deliveries, jobs he secretly craved like an addiction, eliciting the help of our many friends. The only exception was that Sam decided he was better at selling insurance so we saw him only in a business capacity after that. And Andy thankfully retired his deck shoes for tools, trying his hand at even more dangerous home repair projects. Before leaving the island, he was already showing the signs of near mutilation from his power drill.

Chapter Fourteen

The extended visits to the cove had by now forced the regurgitation of so many separate instances of lives entwined on an island. Whether long dissertations said aloud or just plain ordinary nonsensical musings, I found that they all tied easily and compatibly into the yarns, tales or narratives that by this time seemed inbred. But whichever, they still have such a powerful hold over me that I feel both forever blessed and somewhat haunted.

While I still commune with the rocks and the moving currents, more often than not I'm now able to experience a smile, and I sense a small healing has been taking place. I believe I worried that if that happened it would break some internal tie to Eddie and perhaps even displace him in my heart. I'm getting better at understanding that by feeling alive again, however long it may take, it won't diminish him in any way.

And it was after a more uplifting visit like that, stopping as I often did to quiet myself after another unfulfilling day at work that is nearing the end of my term there, something most unusual happened. I returned home, which is still Nessa's apartment, empty now without her, to find a letter waiting for me from a distant relative in of all places, Maine. I say that because it seems a world away from this island, although I know it is filled with waterways and its long shoreline leans against a wide breadth of the Atlantic. I only had a holiday mailing list of a few family members remaining and they were in the northeast.

It was a long and lovely letter, sent from an uncle I barely knew while he had been married to my father's late sister, and spoke of wanting to reach out to the remaining members of my clan since he was in retirement and with more time on his hands feeling the need to connect.

My "clan", as he called it, was now down to two and I did not know whether Carrie received a similar letter, but my feeling was that as the eldest, mine took precedence. He of course knew we were on our own, but apparently, there were, as he called them, 'shirt-tail' relatives in that part of the country. The letter was a bit old fashioned in tone, but it achieved the goal I believe he was striving for, to raise my curiosity.

I studied his handwriting that curled interestingly in such a way as though he might be left-handed. It was more than just a lengthy letter. It created a small, colorful album filling in bits and pieces of a family I'd never really known. The letter brought me back to long forgotten childhood notions and silly perceptions of adult conversations of the past.

Enclosed within the stationery, a pretty shade of blue that may have been purchased by his wife solely for this purpose, were a few photos of him with another man fishing on a river called the Kennebec. It was definitely taken in his younger days and the other man, according to the writing on the back was my great uncle "Spider". There was even a tiny, yellowed clipping referring to his prowess as a champion log roller in his time.

What else, I thought as I re-read it, could be in that part of the country that I didn't know about? I stopped myself just short of calling Nessa, wanting to digest more of the letter before I pulled her in.

Uncle Eben, I noted, had remarried and the words were obvious that he was very happy. He also hoped that life was treating me well, handing over another one of those homey expressions with such ease. And how strange, before reading this long accounting of his northern life, I'd forgotten so completely about that part of the country. After I moved to New York and married Rob who was a native Floridian, it slipped away like a thief in the night.

I kept the letter on my table near my precious shell hoping it would invite me in, give me reasons to be more curious about it. Instead it seemed to conjure a very old, completely familiar stirring, one I half recognized. I couldn't put my finger on it, but the more I retraced the words, the more I found I was reading between the lines, picking up on something very akin to a similar feeling remembered from a long time ago. Something I've learned to trust and let propel me forward.

I laid the photos out side-by-side like a deck of cards, and paid particular attention to the geographical area where they'd been taken. The more I looked, the less untenable the situation seemed, almost against my will. After all, they had ships and rocks and blue skies too. But it was cold, so cold; a cold I no longer related to and didn't know if I could survive.

Would this drastic change be the answer for me, at least for a little while, something so opposite life on St. Margeaux? A change to at least blur the stain on the map that still exists? I know I'm less tearful these days, but still in need of repair, some type of bandage yet that might eradicate some of the emptiness, a new purpose at least.

A long year has passed and another anniversary is on the doorstep, along with a hurricane season able once again to bring about reminders of old horrors. My body, like so many others having experienced the disaster, still harbors the emotional DNA that we now realize is inevitable. It takes very little to set those fears in motion all over again. It's something hard to explain to those never having gone through such a thing, and whether it is simply caused by the mind's re-enactment or by pressure changes that naturally occur at this time of year, it is a definite agitation.

I at last gave in and called Nessa, and found her suffering those same twinges from that same bad storm memory.

"What do you think, Nessa? Would I be remiss if I didn't investigate, uncover that New England family? It kind of overwhelms me to think about it. And if I do decide to, will you promise to join me in New York for a little while and help me sort through some of this jumble I've got going about everything to do with Maine? This seems like a lot more trouble and effort than I think I'm prepared for, but surprisingly, it also seems a little exciting too."

"Maybe it has more than a little to do with that underlying feeling of place and belonging. We've talked ad infinitum on that topic, as you well know!"

I'd kept fingering the photos while we talked. I'd already re-read the letter half a dozen times at least, but now I needed her common sense approach. She of all people understood I might act more on impulse and I liked to have her weigh in on the extremes in any situation. It was just her nature; she kept things calm and grounded.

I could hear the wheels turning as she thought through my proposal. "I'd love that Lily. I've never been to New York other than to pass through airports—it could really be fun. And they can spare me for a week right now. Things are beginning to slow down with the beginning of summer. It's so great to hear you excited like this."

"Let me pull it all together then, and I'll call you when I have the date nailed down. I know we can stay with Gussie and Dee; they've been after me for a while now and I know it would make them happy."

While talking with Nessa, I'd been fondling the small treasure resting by the phone. Russ and Mick had done so much to make the *Wanderer's* salvage easier for me and I never wanted to learn more about those details, feeling it would leave me too raw and exposed, very much like the open hull. But I'm glad they were so thoughtful about these small items. Wherever I go I will have the conch shell with its now broken tip caused when it was thrown harshly from the shelf, along with a laminated chart found floating in some shallow water on the galley floor. I can now gaze all I want at reminders of treasures and sailing ships and unfulfilled destinations. All at one time had had a better purpose of place, but they are still valued.

Most importantly, I have Eddie's binoculars. They survived in their waterproof case tucked into that same shelf that had held the conch shell. They may have many uses; to clarify and define tangible objects, or in my mind's need for solutions, magnify the opening into the future choices I must make. But they would surely be with me as a gentle reminder of good and wondrous things, and I know will bring about the occasional laugh at myself for my inability to adjust their complicated settings correctly.

Uncle Eben's letter had certainly presented me with an enormous challenge, particularly if a real change were to come of it, as well as an attitude adjustment, to say the least. It presented an unexpected invitation and has been left to settle in my bones, an expression I'd learned from Mariah, and is gaining a stronger foothold daily.

There is something, however, that still bothers me, a particular detail to confront. Life here in the island is slower, which I believe is not only due to the heat, but also there is no unnecessary rush to get things done in their season, as there is very little change month to month. The only exception being of course hurricane season and that is beyond anyone's control. Whereas my sense about the four-season climate and particularly that far north is that everything has its own season in which to accomplish. Time itself does not have the same cause and effect.

These minute details nag at me, but I know I'm making much of nothing and I realize it is only my way of stalling, a tactic that doesn't have a lot of merit right now. I'm simply not sure I'm prepared for any of it—leaving the tropics after so many years, adapting to the newness. I'm spoiled by habit too. Even in my sadness, I know where to go for comfort. I'll have to leave behind the silent friendship of the cove and its inhabitants.

Before Nessa could have a go at all my worries, using her highly skilled rebuttals, or before I could change my mind about at least a chance to meet Eben and his family, I made a flight reservation with, quite naturally, the first stop San Juan. I could see Rosa and tell her of my plans and knew she would try and guide me smartly as before. She was still running the inn but now with the help of her niece and Jorge, who had finished his schooling and had become the night manager. Then it would be on to New York with Nessa.

It was June 10th, the first month of the official hurricane season and I felt many emotions as the nose dropped down through the clouds over San Juan. This time Rosa was waiting for me at the gate, leaving the posada in the capable hands of her niece for a few hours. At least by now we could laugh more about my 'coming to life' adventures with Carlos.

"Lily, you have changed so much since I last saw you; you're thinner even. So much unhappiness—this is not good for a young woman. I think your friend Nessa is right, this visit north could be very good for you."

"I know, Rosa, and I feel as though I'm acting like a child. I'm always torn between my love for the islands and my own common sense. I know I'm stagnating, accomplishing nothing important except cataloging old memories. I don't even know what I'll do after that."

"Try and remember how you met my Carlos. You didn't think you would be happy again when you arrived here either. And look what happened, so much happiness and excitement. I wish I were younger!"

Rosa's words stuck with me all day, reminding me of the trajectory of my life and the woman I'd become back then; the woman with spirit and spunk. I didn't dare lose her now; she and Nessa were both right.

Returning from lunch, I let her guide me through the various changes to the inn with great flourish. She was filled with pride over the augmentations her niece, Jovana, had put into place and took me on a grand tour before dinner. The major changes were in the modernized kitchen, its freshly scrubbed appliances glistening and the air highly scented with wild rosemary as it used to be after Carlos and I would pick the rampantly growing sprigs for her in the hills. I knew this was more for its aroma than its use, because she favored the ones in her small kitchen garden, the herbs used in creating pulses for the basic cuisine she shared with her guests. There was green coriander, mint, oregano and bay leaf always at the ready and today was no different.

I noted that Jovana had also changed the fabrics on the cozy seating arrangement that welcomed when first coming through the door, this time to solids in earth tones, not my personal preference, though still inviting. Additionally, there was an expensive looking antique furniture set placed near the entrance to act as a formal front desk in welcoming the arriving guests.

Then I took a small break before dinner to sit by the pool, as lovely as ever, the air still filled with the sound of pounding surf. The previous landscaping had been altered only slightly by the addition of glamorous patio tiles and furnishings with more flare, but I wanted to take it all in at least once more before leaving.

By the time I heard the small bell ring, that familiar clinking graciously announcing dinner, the short rest had done much to restore my appetite and I rushed in eagerly to join Rosa and finally meet Jovana. Hours later, having reminisced until the last bite of dessert, a now more sophisticated crème brûlée replacing Rosa's popular flan, and all washed down with dark richly brewed café, I retired to my old room painted now in taupe, and slept without bad dreams of any kind.

The next day, true to her word and with more energy than I would have thought possible, Rosa drove me to a nearby town in another district to see the orphanage that Carlos had insisted on helping. After just a brief look around the grounds, we each touched our fingers to the small plaque in the vestibule bearing his name, in gratitude for that generosity, bidding him farewell.

I'd done what I set out to, paid my respects, received Rosa's maternal blessings and bolstered some fortitude. There was nothing left now but to await my departure time. It had been a very short stay and wonderful to be on San Juan soil again where a small piece of my heart will forever remain. And we both knew it would be much harder to leave it this time.

How strange it feels now to pass through familiar airports with destinations in reverse but emotions still in turmoil. I was no longer that angry woman without a plan, but I am still without a plan and in a confused state of mind. Sitting in the waiting area nearest the gate, watching the many passengers come and go, I tried to wrestle with everything sifting through that core matter of my brain, then found it simply easier to observe in order to pass the time as I waited for Nessa.

Many of the men were wearing white guayabera shirts, a fashion I'd nearly forgotten about, and something I always thought a charming replacement for the jacket and tie look. They were hurrying through the terminal, most carrying briefcases, more than likely the lawyers and businessmen attending to affairs on nearby islands. I knew that only because I had met a few of them while dating Carlos.

A few women stood with fussy children as they waited for visiting relatives or a returning husband, managing to keep their tempers in check or simply passing them on to a handy grandparent. Others flitting past on high heels clicking musically on the tile floor looked either tanned and relaxed from their time here or frazzled and anxious to begin their stay. I remembered being one of those and almost wished I could stay longer to filter among their crowd as if before.

But even the crowd roaming the airport environs near the northern seeking gates seemed to move differently, as if they'd already absorbed the endemic flow, causing me to wonder more about my ability to change my own pace to suit the stateside standards. Had everything been hastened up while I had slowed down in that other place?

But before that thought could fester too long, Nessa came flying through the gateway door, arriving in perfect time for our late flight out to New York. I was up and out of my seat before she noticed me, worried she'd missed the connection, hugging her with far more intensity than necessary.

She already guessed that I had sprouted a new burgeoning desire to tap into that bedrock of the past since Eben's letter. She had once more accompanied me to the little second story room to have my chart read. That time she wasn't as skeptical. Mariah had made her case convincingly. And in truth, it was the main reason that was propelling me northward, curiously important enough to leave my home.

Trying to keep her voice below the engine noise so as not to disturb other passengers, Nessa whispered, "Where do you plan to start looking?"

"I'm not sure. First I need to feel out Eben as to what knowledge he has, if any, of relatives who may have had any major connection with seafaring, shipbuilding or anything possibly related. Then I guess I'll have to go to the capital where there may be archives I can study or at least go through town records if they exist. He's probably thinking I'm just going to look at pictures and maybe drive around visiting those other relatives, but I've got much more in mind."

"I think it's healthy that you have even that small goal. It's about time you looked forward to more than just walking around that cove of yours, no matter what you say."

I sure knew she would be up front with her feelings, but I hadn't realized she was so concerned about me. I hated making anyone worry.

"Well, one thing's for sure, a small immediate goal will be to show you 'my' New York, at least what I can remember of it. It'll be a great girls getaway!"

And as expected, the Chamberlains were waiting with open arms, offering a hand with luggage and anxious to include Nessa in the retinue. They were also anxious to nurture and coddle with home-cooked meals and ones in restaurants I'd nearly forgotten about.

Leaping right into the fray since time was tight, we excitedly explored the theatre district and shared fun gatherings with their close friends. This usually ended at Elaine's on Second Avenue, as always, whose devotees included many notable personalities, something I knew Nessa would enjoy telling about back on Anegada.

We listened to great jazz at an out-of-the-way club that while much enjoyed, was the only time that the familiar pervasive sadness reached through my fragile barrier. Eddie and I had so loved the prominent strains of a smoky sax and fluid notes of the many renowned musicians heard on the radio while reclining in the cockpit of our long gone home or seen in person during our few off island jaunts buying equipment for the boat.

Nessa and I were like kids at Christmas, shopping along prominent avenues spending the bulk of that time at Saks and Bloomingdale's while Gussie worked. I made her ride the subway route that I occasionally used. And just for old time's sake, stopping for the hot pretzels that I always had to have from the street-smart vendors with thick accents.

And a stop in Chinatown was necessary and anticipated to visit an old acquaintance. Pumpkin and her husband owned a very small

teashop and apothecary of herbal medicines, although she alone ran it. I
knew Nessa would love Pumpkin with her beautiful open face helmeted
by thick glossy black hair, and she would most certainly be wearing
something in her favorite orange color. It was her husband who
nicknamed her when they met at UC Berkeley where he was in the
college of engineering and she studying nutritional science. And I knew
that Gussie and Dee would enjoy a special gift basket artfully put
together as a thank you for allowing us to share their home.

Nessa was shocked at the miles covered on foot. That's how I met
Dee the first time. Leaving my apartment on Second Avenue allowing
for the time, I would meander the many unfamiliar streets ending up at
59th, enjoying my own game as I walked their length, discovering
something new each time.

There was an out-of-the-way flower shop, an antique jewelry store
with a few trinkets to tease set outside on small tables, watched over
carefully by a myopic owner. Or sometimes I would end up in front of
an embassy building, importantly fronted, gated and attended by people
spilling out of limousines. I never knew from day to day, where these
turns would take me and it never failed to amuse me.

With our last remaining free evening, giving Gussie and Dee a
quieter night together for cards, we chose a small neighborhood deli
that beckoned with a bold flashing neon sign and signature sandwich
done up in color on a laminated menu posted to the window. I'd almost
forgotten about the crowded interiors of the local delis and how much I
used to count on them, especially if I worked late and didn't feel like
cooking.

Decidedly the sandwich was large enough to share and she'd never
had an authentic vanilla cream soda. And if God is in the details, as the
waitress   stated,   this   well-touted   sandwich   was   His   own
accomplishment. Large thick slices of freshly baked pumpernickel
instead of rye to please Nessa, slathered heavily with their homemade
dressing, and heaped with thinly sliced corned beef and pastrami, still
steaming slightly from the kitchen. And, as always, accompanied by a
huge dill pickle.

We had come armed with not only our appetites but also two small yellow pads and sharp pencils. These rested in full view while we ate, the blank pages prompting our on-going discussion between bites. I was trying to strike a balance somewhere between those pros and cons facing off against a very pragmatic Nessa. It's an easy game we played.

This time I took the converse side of the list and was surprised to see the opposite one on her pad filling in so rapidly—impressive. There would be much to chew on besides the sandwich before the night was out. She had me outnumbered eighteen to twelve by the time we left and stated emphatically, "I rest my case!"

We kept a lot about those lists from the Chamberlains since we had only one more night with them, and I did not want to upset them over my consternation and have them tiring themselves with answers for my dilemma. But in their need to keep us entertained and happy, they'd already insisted on treating us on our last night in the City to a gourmet dinner at the Russian Tea Room. It was an especially generous offer knowing my penchant for its style and glamour. I also now hungered for their borscht, vodka martinis and little Russian pancakes called sirniki, and was thrilled to be able to savor it all once again. I could tell Nessa was beginning to fall in love with all the richness too, filling up on it as one starved by time and distance would do. Without realizing it, the trip was nearly as advantageous for her and would stay with her for a long while.

The entire room sparkled with a gaiety that had been missing in our lives for so long. Now it was embracing us as we sat in happy reflection, flushed pink in that happiness, beaming back from the many surrounding mirrored walls. Change could be good after all.

~~~

Dee looked a bit bedraggled from our long, spirited evening and pulled his old navy sedan out of the parking garage, the layer of dust quite evident from lack of use. Gussy had declined the ride-along to the airport, hating long goodbyes, but adding for his sake that Nessa would be leaving from the gate marked for all Caribbean Islands, with necessary ID, and I would be heading to Portland, via American like an alien in need of a passport. That was her 'morning after' assessment of our previous evening's conversation, said with verbal frugality. Her head hurt.

Chapter Fifteen

Shakily, I picked up my rental at the Portland airport and even though it was June, I was already chilled to the bone from the dry wind, or perhaps it was simply nerves. There were new highway patterns, more speed and great concentration needed if I was going to manage. Whatever it was, cold air or nerves, I kept hearing Nessa's logical words in my head..."just put on another sweater"...I did. The added bonus to being in New York was the even more logical purchase of warmer clothing even if only a couple of new sweaters and some jeans. After all, it was only 61 degrees out there.

Most importantly, I had packed the binoculars...for indeed, I would be 'looking' for answers. It would be a talisman on those days when thoughts of Eddie still overwhelmed, something tangible to push away dreary notions should they begin to get the best of me.

Crossing a portion of the Kennebec River, I was reminded of the term, "land of the pointed trees" that one of my friends had thrown out to me when hearing of my new plan, and she was right. Trees as far as one could see, standing tall, pointing up the landscape with the same pride as my beloved mahoganies. There were long wisps of striated clouds like mares' tails veering off in differing directions against an amazing color of blue. And then the tightened seatbelt began impressing itself on the beginnings of hunger, forcing me to stop for lunch. The large highway was not as heavily trafficked as I'd feared, and it was easy to catch the sign advertising seafood style lunches and since it was nearly halfway to my destination, a good place to take a break.

I found myself surprisingly charmed by what I'd already seen quite a lot of, that New England style. Here, it is in the spare and tidy use of the shingled, white trimmed restaurant building and bungalows resting slightly apart. There was a compact pool set slightly away from the outdoor dining deck that looked the perfect place to untie the knots in my shoulders from gripping the wheel so tightly. It had taken all my effort to keep the car in the correct lane, especially when turning and passing, and the high-pitched squeals rising above the happy children was a wonderful diversion. The pool was already a hub for their activity.

I had passed the signs for a beach called Popham, enjoying the rounded sounding name, but still could not imagine swimming, especially this early in the season. And finally the sun started to warm my skin. Everything felt new—the air, the look and scent of the different trees replacing my statuesque palms and especially the predominant browns, reds and grays of the buildings. I would now have to look beyond the pastel colors that had made the days brighter still. And just beyond the terrace was a short wooden dock—the only thing even remotely familiar to me, with a small fleet of tiny sailboats and kayaks bobbing unevenly in dark water.

"Can I interest you in lessons this afternoon?" asked a handsome blond wearing the insignia of the resort as well as an ear-to-ear grin with flirt stamped all over it; he'd managed to sidle right up next to me while I was concentrating on the boats.

"Not unless you can heat the ocean up to at least 68 degrees," I replied having the strangest déjà vu feeling of a strange voice invading thoughts and my non-existent flirting skills, again like that other time and other place.

"But thank you anyway," I said, trying for a more polite tone. "Do you suppose there are more resorts like this one farther up the coast? I think I'd enjoy sailing one of those smaller boats."

"Where are you headed?"

"Near a place called Pershing Point, but I left my notes in the car with the exact spot. I'm meeting someone there."

"I'll jot down some names for you and get them back before you finish your lunch," he said, still polite even though his flirtation fell flat.

Lunch was better than expected. My first lobster roll, accompanied by perfect fries and a small brewery beer. Good to his word, the blond dropped off a couple of names with easy directions. It wouldn't be long now.

It took most of the afternoon to get to Trescott Cove, a small picturesque town where I planned to stay the night. Eben would join me there and then he hoped I'd follow him inland. Apparently, there is an archival seat where most of the family records would be, much as I'd hoped. He told me when I called from New York that he felt it important that I get acquainted as soon as possible. I guess I really was expected to get to know the deceased as well as the living and the idea made me smile. Mariah would have been a willing party to it all. Too bad I couldn't have brought her with me.

The picture postcard day was filled with small surprises—a sharpness in the air that kissed my skin, revitalizing, filled with a variety of aromas I didn't recognize, much of it from the sea and far stronger than any I'd known. All of it continued to follow at each stop.

Eben was waiting at the small bed and breakfast where we'd arranged to meet and it automatically brought the word *quaint* to my lips. Buff colored with deep green trim, tall windows, wide steps leading to the Victorian doorway and already bursting with colors from newly planted boxes. A season was beginning.

"Oh, Lily, it is so good to meet you at last. Your aunt told me so much about your family, and I've tried to remain close to those few still living up here, but you are the missing link." Eben said, with unadulterated joy.

"And you look so much like your aunt, it's uncanny, except of course, for your height," he added, turning a bit red.

I knew my height always surprised those familiar with my family. "All I can say is it must be a throwback to an old great aunt on the other side of the family, the one who lived in Florida.

"I really want to thank you for writing; the timing couldn't have been better, and I'm really glad I made this trip after all. You've been very kind, and you'll be happy to know that all the while driving along the coast, I sensed something special here. I want to know more, and I'm anxious to tell you all about the islands too.

"But on top of that, I don't believe I've ever seen a sky this clear a blue as today. Is it like this all summer?"

"Can be, just nevah know. As we're fond of saying round here, 'if you don't like the weathah, wait ten minutes', he said, enjoying his own joke, putting on an affected broader stretch to his normal Maine accent.

"I want you to come stay with me and Lucy for a while. She's anxious to get to know you too, and maybe we can fill that curiosity of yours. It's very like your great grandma Becca's, ya know. Things would've been a lot different for her if she'd been able to follow her heart like you have. And there are still lots of photos for you to go through; we saved all we could find.

"I know it's been hard on you and Carrie, especially because of your grandparents' generation and all their divisiveness, but it would be my pleasure to help sort things out for you. Let's just see what unfolds."

I don't think Eben meant it so literally as we stood there in the front parlor of the guesthouse, but later taking a walk around the grounds toward the water another kind of unfolding was taking place. An unexpected tiny welling up of joy from somewhere beneath my breastbone, insignificant at first and then rising as if to break free from bony constriction, almost as if the clear air was responsible for the call. But it was, I knew, the simplicity of hearing my similarity to my Maine relative, someone I never knew or knew of.

My head was filling as fast as the tide pool in front of me, though momentarily focused on all the colors. I'd seen as many shades of blue as my mind could process in so short a time. My vocabulary was being expanded here with all the newer ones, but most surprising was the seamless way the water met the sky in shades I couldn't as yet name.

The importance of being here began striking louder still and after meeting Eben and sensing his genuine concerns for my family, I was at last comfortable that I'd made the right decision. Any worries I may have discussed earlier with Nessa regarding what the trip represented, had already taken a back seat, and I was anxious to call her.

The evening was about to take on a lovely softness and it brought with it a surprise—that mysterious tug of my heart, the one that still yearns to be near the water, so reminiscent of my indoctrination to the islands. Although I had much to discover inland and was anxious to get started, I was determined I would be back before long to this spot and many more that ran the length of the state. It was hard to keep up with myself; I hadn't expected so much.

Everything around me was responding to the late afternoon light. The early summer sky had slipped into its natural saturation, starting with ribbons of pinks and violets deepening in and out of focus while I watched, blurring edges and sharpening lines, until it was at its sunset peak; all of it affecting the stark white lighthouse and heavy granite spread below. Then the measureless rich color of the sea became infused with all that new light, and while beautiful beyond words, it still brought with it that singular awareness that had drawn me in so tightly to those islands, especially as it touched the edges of newly curled waves.

The dramatic effect worked its wonders. It beckoned my spirit toward it, making me long once more for full participation in a rich landscape, maybe less innocent, but with the ability to be newly excited by my surroundings; something so long overdue.

As the sky darkened and emboldened the softer shades with new unnamed tones, I was reminded of my last conversation with Nessa. She'd tried to make an analogy about the need for deep roots to hold against the heaviest storm winds. Maybe it was time I witnessed the roots of my own tree that kept certain of my family strong throughout their history. Maybe that's what I'm meant to find here in a place quite unknown, even if only by me.

I took in a full breath of clear, northern air carrying the very heady well-memorized and well-loved brine scent, sending minute shockwaves through my system. It was chilling as it hit my lungs, prickling my skin with little bumps. It had all but reached out from the deepest recesses of the ocean and I watched in salutation as the faraway waves tipped their golden bonnets in response.

And once again I felt I was not alone. As before, I seemed to be accompanied by a whispering, probably just the waves, or so I thought, as it was becoming habit now to think that. I could almost hear Eddie's voice, "Better grab your pen, looks like this could be another big adventure!" But of course, it was only the wind rustling the trees.

Sensing my need to absorb so much in this short time, Eben had waited before coming to sit beside me, and now he stretched his legs out comfortably, anxious to talk some more. "Lily, there was something you mentioned before about connections and the sea and especially your love for it. Lucy found something in all those papers that made her curious too. This big landmark here just reminded me of that but I don't know whether it was a seaman or maybe even a lighthouse keeper, but I know it had something to do with the water and some kind of accident. She's been a big help going through the photos and all.

"But I have to tell you, I don't believe in that stuff you women go on about with mysterious things, but you may have a willing partner in her, especially when you tell her about that woman you mentioned, that Mariah. I wish I'd paid more attention when Lucy was talking; I'll hear about it now!"

I felt my heart leap. Eben had no way of knowing the impact of his comment; it was a place to start. This shoreline offers up a new breed of ocean for my discovery, but perhaps there is some piercing, undeniable reason I'm sensing such a strong draw here too, not unlike that other precious sea? I had to at least try to find out; I had nothing to lose now.

"Uncle Eben, you've given me a wonderful gift today, and yes I would love to stay with you and Lucy. I thought I was a little crazy thinking that someone somewhere in my own family might actually have had some connection like that. Don't laugh, I know it sounds weird but I'm serious. I hate to think of tragedies that may have occurred but I know I won't rest until I find out as much as possible.

"And, something you might not understand, but I like the feeling that Eddie is watching out for me somehow. I know this sounds crazy, but sometimes I think I can still hear him."

"I think this is really something you better take up with Lucy; it's all right up her alley. She's going to just love you."

He was so engaging, and I knew I would love her too and I could see why she made him so happy. He lit up like a young man just talking about her.

"I can't wait to get started and I bet I have trouble sleeping tonight. I look forward to so much, I'm near to bursting."

Eben chuckled at my phrase, understanding what I was doing and I think a little charmed by it. He had already called Lucy to be waiting for us sometime before noon. He had a favorite diner to visit in the morning to introduce me to a very local breakfast. Said I'd better start now 'chunking' up for the coming winter, 'cause if I planned to stay, it would be part of my survival kit against the cold. I hadn't a clue what he meant and wasn't quite sure I wanted to do anything sounding that drastic just to keep warm. Since he'd already commented on my height, I guess this was referencing my new thinness as well. Then he added for good measure, "Won't be wearing any bikinis up there."

I suppose Lucy had already forewarned him of the more common costume of the younger set, especially where I lived, and since they didn't live near a beach, I imagine he thought I might be apt to wear one anyway, just because it was summer. This obviously was his polite way of letting me know the boundaries. I didn't bother to tell him I didn't think it would ever be warm enough for me to even consider it!

Not wanting him to get sidetracked on my real mission, I said, "I can't wait to begin searching through everything with Lucy. And I won't be a burden, I promise and I'll not overstay my welcome."

Just then a sense of folly pulled at the corners of his eyes as if he'd thought of his own joke. This made his square face become almost impish, wiping away his actual age, "From the sounds of it, you two will be leaving me to my own devices for a while. A man could get used to that right quick, don'tcha know?"

Everything would be all right. I was once again 'coming home', against all odds that I would want to, or that it would touch me so deeply, but it had. I didn't know what would come next but I knew it would lead to more discoveries and they would be powerful.

And I knew I would always carry Eddie close, not only inside the little locket I purchased before coming here, but silently beside me the rest of my days, taking up no more space than was necessary to smile. That would be his legacy and now, with their help, I would set out to find my own.

EPILOGUE

The old country house had once been a strong marker on this land. It still had a smart presence even in its run-down state. Uncle Eben had made good on his promise to help but it was Lucy who loaded the pick-up she liked to borrow from him occasionally to trek all over the county townships to find the markers for those passed on and lost in the wars.

I have the beginnings of a 'tree' with many leaves to still be filled in, but I've decided not to rush. I'll not plunge forward to the mysterious man of the sea as I first thought was absolute, not yet. Instead, I will take my time, branch by branch to place him properly. I'm still reading everything I can get my hands on, looking for the answers that ring more true in this part of the world.

I'm committed now and have decided to stay for as long as necessary. When the yearnings for St. Margeaux take over, I pick up the phone and call Nessa and have already enlisted a promise that she and Russ will visit next summer when the season slows again and they can be released from Anegada without qualms.

I've begun telling her of the roots beginning with my great grandmother Rebecca and her hard struggle here in Maine. Becca, as she was fondly known, had been forced into marriage by her unyielding father and became the bride of Jarvis Steele. Old Walter Hale wouldn't cotton to Becca learning things that would pull her off the farm, so she had no choice for her own well being and future security, but to cave to the marriage.

I'm not so crazy about learning more of this Walter Hale, but he is of course, part of that essential tree. For a while I will roam in the other direction and place the names of Becca's twin boys onto their branch, my great-uncles Jasper and Louis. The visit to the farm still haunts my thoughts with the footsteps of this family that began their own journey there in 1868.

My story will begin there too for now and when it becomes too much, I'll return to the small rental cottage near Trescott Cove that has given me so much pleasure. It is walking distance to the water and occasionally I hear the very roar of her might with the type of weather I'm learning to handle here.

The foghorn has become a new norm for me, replacing memories of quieter nights, but it is not an unwelcome sound. On the other hand, I've quite come to love all the newer sea-related noises there in that new place. Now the big fat herring gulls compete with the crows big as cats, for scraps left behind, and the steady purr of heartier engines come and go through the morning mist in search of lobsters, bulkier in form and a tad meaner because of their aggressive pincers than their Caribbean cousins. Fortunately, the taste is still compelling.

And when I'm particularly homesick for St. Margeaux, a beautiful schooner with lusty sales filling in with the offshore wind will pass by with the bounty of tourists who flock here too.

So Nessa was right, roots can make a difference to the strength of the tree. And while I'm finding my roots and my strength, I've made a pact with the whisperer's call that I'll always be near the water, awaiting her answers.

CHERYL BLAYDON is the author of *The Memory Keepers*, a fictional memoir that begins with her childhood in a small town in upstate New York. She has traveled throughout the Caribbean, and explored the cities of Europe, always finding memories to put on canvas. She now divides her time between painting and writing in her home studio in East Boothbay, Maine.

To learn more, visit www.mainelyseascapes.com